EVERYTHING
IS
MINE

ALSO BY RUTH LILLEGRAVEN

Sickle

EVERYTHING

IS

MINE

A NOVEL

RUTH
LILLEGRAVEN

TRANSLATED BY DIANE OATLEY

Text copyright © 2018 by Ruth Lillegraven
Translation copyright © 2021 by Diane Oatley
All rights reserved.

Excerpt from "It Is the Most Beautiful at Dusk" ("Det är vackrast när det skymmer"), by Pär Lagerkvist. English translation by Hélène Lindqvist at www.theartsongproject. com/gunnar-de-frumerie-det-ar-vackrast-nar-det-skymmer-its-the-most-beautiful-at-dusk/

Previously published as *Alt er mitt* by Kagge Forlag AS in Norway in 2019. Translated from Norwegian by Diane Oatley. First published in English by Amazon Crossing in 2021.

Published by Amazon Crossing, Seattle

www.apub.com

Amazon, the Amazon logo, and Amazon Crossing are trademarks of Amazon.com, Inc., or its affiliates.

ISBN-13: 9781542020831
ISBN-10: 1542020832

Cover design by Damon Freeman

Printed in the United States of America

First edition

All is close, all is far away.
All is given man on loan.

All is mine, and all shall be taken from me,
Soon all shall be taken from me.
The trees, the clouds, the ground where I'm walking.

—Pär Lagerkvist

PROLOGUE

CLARA

1988

"The car hit the water with such a horrible bang that when I opened my eyes, I was surprised we were still alive. I've never been on an airplane, but I bet it's like that when a plane crashes. For a second or two after we hit the water, everything was completely silent and I thought it would be fine, that we would just float away in the car like it was a boat until somebody rescued us. But then water started trickling in through the air vents and everywhere, and I knew there wouldn't be time for anyone to save us.

"Oh, sorry, I was supposed to start at the beginning . . . Well, it was a Wednesday and our home economics teacher was sick, so school let out earlier than usual. I could have gone home to Daddy—since that's where I live. But Magne, my stepfather, had said we could drive to the hospital and visit Mom one day if I wanted. She'd had an operation for some kind of lady thing. Since I didn't have school, I thought it seemed like a good time. So, I walked up to the farm where Magne and Mom live.

"Magne seemed happy to see me. We got into the car and drove down the steep gravel road from the farm. We got to the main road and turned right, toward the hospital. The sun was so bright when we approached Storagjelet, it blinded us.

"It's kind of hard to remember this, because it happened so fast. But one minute we were driving into the turn and the next we were barreling over the drop on my side. We must have made the turn too wide, too fast. I only had time to scream, really, before we hit the water. Magne undid my seat belt and shouted that I should roll down the window so I could get out. I thought he was going to do the same thing, but when I turned to look, he was still just sitting all straight and stiff in his seat. I didn't understand why. I tried to open my door from the outside, but it wouldn't budge, like it was locked. So, I tried swimming around the car. That took a while. The car was starting to sink, and I yanked and tugged at Magne's door, but it was completely stuck. I banged on the window, trying to make him see me but he just sat there, and the car kept sinking deeper and deeper into the water. Finally, I had to start swimming toward land.

"It was much colder in the water than you'd think. I was frozen stiff. I barely made it to shore. Then I sat there on a rock, shaking and crying. I don't really believe in God, but you can't really know for sure, right, so I even prayed a little. But Magne didn't come and finally I understood that he wasn't coming, ever, that I would never see him again. Oh, sorry, I wasn't going to cry, but it's awful thinking about how he helped me, and I just let him disappear down there. Poor Mom. Poor Magne."

"Thank you, Clara," the policeman says. He nods at the orange soda and sweet custard bun on the table, encouraging me to help myself, but the mere sight of the trembling, yellow custard makes me sick to my stomach. The policeman is nice enough, but I wonder if he's the kind of officer who doesn't understand, doesn't want to understand.

Through the window I can see people parking their cars to go to their doctor's appointments at the clinic right next door to the municipal building where we're sitting. Across the road I can see the store.

The school. And the old folks' home. There are mountains all around, watching over us or shutting us in. Behind all of it is the fjord.

"I know the rest of the story," he says. "Don't feel guilty. Getting out of the car the way you did, trying to save Magne—that was smart of you. What's important now is that you're alive and that you'll be all right."

PART 1

CHAPTER 1

HENRIK

Whatever you do, don't get divorced.

Axel, a lifelong buddy of mine, who is divorced, had given me this warning the evening before, over a beer and with the sound of the Premier League soccer game in the background. "Divorce is fucking expensive," he said. "You'll be taken to the cleaners. Take a financial worst-case scenario and multiply it by two. No, by three! That's how much a divorce costs."

So, I hang in there, do the best I can.

The door to the balcony slams hard, Clara's passive-aggressive way of waking me up. Through the fluttering white curtains I can just make out her tall, slender silhouette on the balcony outside the bedroom.

Clara is a creature of habit. She loves standing out there for a minute or two in the morning, striking the same Titanic pose she always assumes whether we're on vacation in Western Norway or at our home in Oslo.

The past few days the heat has hung quivering in the air with an almost violence. It's unusual after a long, hard winter and a spring that came and went in a flash. At the boys' school, on the street, in the store, everywhere, people are talking about the winter that was just here, about the spring that didn't happen, about how unseasonal this premature African heat is.

Personally, I'm enjoying it. If Clara can lock in the support she needs for her bill, maybe we can take a trip to Kilsund. My parents are not getting any younger, and the cottage needs to be opened for the summer.

"You have to get up," she says when she comes inside again. "Or you won't get them to school on time."

It's our turn to drive the car pool this week, and I promised to take care of it.

I notice a sickening aftertaste of IPA in my throat. I had one beer too many; apparently, I can't drink at all anymore.

I keep my eyes shut, pretending I'm still asleep. It has always irritated Clara that I'm not as bright-eyed and bushy-tailed as she is in the morning. But that doesn't mean I won't manage to get up and get the children to school. I am usually the one who does.

"Henrik?" She knees me in the thigh. It actually hurts.

"What the hell are you doing? Abusing me?"

She sighs. "I have an important meeting at eight o'clock and have to leave in a few minutes."

"I'm working the night shift tonight," I mumble.

"You're not the only one saving lives."

I sit up, swing my legs out of bed, and yawn. "Have the children had breakfast?"

"They're eating now."

She starts moving toward what she considers her own private bathroom to put on her ministry face. On an impulse, I jump out of bed and dash past her. Without closing the door behind me, I raise the toilet seat and start peeing with such force that it gushes in the toilet bowl.

Clara doesn't say a word.

Why does she have to trudge around the house long after she should have left, nagging me about how late she is and how I need to get a move on? Why does she need to control me and breathe down my neck, as if I'm not used to being alone with the children, when she's the one who's hardly ever home?

Since she started working on the new bill and draft resolution, she's been calling to tell me that she'll be home for dinner, rather than to let me know she won't make it.

I walk out of the bathroom whistling.

Without looking at me, she marches into the bathroom, locking the door.

I get dressed and go downstairs.

The boys are sitting at the table. I always find their pajama-clad bodies disarming. A feeling of tenderness fills me at the sight of their slender necks, Nikolai's sleep-mussed hair standing straight up and the curls on the back of Andreas's neck.

But then I notice they're eating Cocoa Puffs. And dammit, they're both staring at their iPads as well.

"You're only allowed to eat that on the weekends," I say, and point at the box of Cocoa Puffs. "You know that. The cardboard box they come in is more nutritious than that crap."

"Mom said we could," they shout in unison.

In the cupboard I find an aspirin and swallow it down with a gulp of milk straight from the carton.

"And what does Grandmother say about iPads?"

Again the boys shout in unison: "Stupid!"

"No. She says they'll make your eyes square-shaped."

The boys slurp down Cocoa Puffs drenched in milk, which is now light brown, while they argue about some Fortnite game that strictly speaking they're too young for.

Clara comes downstairs to join us.

"Cocoa Puffs?" I raise my eyebrows. "Seriously?"

"They refused to eat anything else. And you weren't here. Somebody had to get some food into them."

"Oh my God," I mumble. The boys suddenly leave the table, and still in their pajamas, they run out the kitchen door. "Hey!" I shout. "What are you doing? Get back in here! Now."

They come back almost immediately, each of them holding a lilac sprig in his hand. I'm about to yell at them for going outdoors and picking lilacs but bite my tongue. They're so cute and proud.

"One for Mommy and one for Daddy," Nikolai says. Andreas gives a toothless grin. "Don't argue anymore."

"We won't," I say. "And thank you, how nice of you." I dig one of the scalpels from work out of the junk drawer to clean the stems. But on the second branch somehow the tiny blade slips, cutting into my fingertip. "Fuck!" I shout.

"How many times have I told you not to leave those scalpels lying around all over the place?" Clara says.

"Thanks," I hiss. I'm bleeding profusely.

"Daddy, what happened?" Nikolai asks.

"Damn it all," I say, distracted. "It seems I cut my finger."

"Does it hurt?" Nikolai persists.

"A little. Luckily, I'm a doctor so I can do my own stitches." I try to sound reassuring. They don't look convinced.

"Surely, it's possible to exercise a bit of caution," Clara says, always empathetic. She seems disappointed if one of us hurts ourselves. I think she views it as a sign of weakness.

I inspect the finger, tear off a piece of paper towel, and wrap it around, trying again to be the tough daddy.

"Swearing isn't allowed, Daddy," Andreas says.

"But are you OK?" Nikolai asks.

"See you," Clara says, and walks with quick steps through the kitchen and down the hallway. It's only after the door slams shut behind her that I relax my shoulders and smile properly at the children.

This is us. This is what we've become.

CHAPTER 2

CLARA

A cabinet minister will seldom, if ever, call personally. Usually, it's Minister of Justice Anton Munch's secretary, Vigdis, who calls and asks if I would mind stopping by. Her tone is polite, but it's a rhetorical question. You have been summoned and must appear. Pronto.

"I'll be right there," I say now. I get to my feet, adjust my suit, and save the document I'm working on. My third child. The proposal for an amendment of the laws of Norway. Bill and Draft Resolution No. 220. Seventy-eight pages of text. Eleven chapters. Background, objective, current legislation, assessments, and proposals. At the end, comments. And then the proposed wording of the act.

And at the very end, the absurd standard phrasing: "We Harald, King of Norway . . ."

The bill is intended to ensure that employees of all public institutions—hospitals, child welfare authorities, kindergartens, and public health clinics—feel a stronger sense of responsibility for sounding the alarm in the event of any suspicion of violence or abuse.

The duty to issue such alerts has been vague, and professional secrecy has been emphasized in all contexts.

Things will be different now.

The bill is almost done. I'm tightening and adjusting, polishing the text, as if it were a marble sculpture, trying to make every word shine.

I've always taken pride in avoiding the vague ramblings that characterize many of the texts we legal practitioners produce, with comma upon comma, condition after condition, until whatever we write becomes an illegible, tangled pulp that causes communications people to tear out their hair when they're trying to write press releases. Year after year they hire a series of consultants to come and hold courses for us on so-called clear language.

Clear language is what they will get.

I click my way through the hallways. This building houses the offices of the governmental departments, all staffed by civil servants like me, and is also home to elected and appointed politicians. I am heading to the political section. Hard black stilettos against brown wood floorboards. In the departments the floors are linoleum, while here, in the most sacred of interiors, the flooring is teak with black stripes between the floorboards.

The first thing to greet me here is the ridiculous stuffed polar bear standing on his hind legs, said to have been shot on the stairs of a church in Svalbard. His back is straight and his gaze frozen. The top of my head only comes up to his elbow.

I have been working directly with Munch, the cabinet minister, for an extended period, without following the usual official channels. During the past few months I've come closer and closer to him and thereby ever closer to my objective.

All my superiors' objections and questions have been resolved in the past few days. Although the bill must be circulated for comment before it can be submitted to the Norwegian Parliament, once the cabinet minister gives the green light, a large part of the job is done.

A ministry will notice immediately whether the appointed cabinet minister is a leader. Munch has been here for a year now, long enough for people to understand that he's something of a show-off, but due to the bill, my personal judgment is less harsh.

The turning point came a week ago when we were sitting in his office and he leaned back in his chair, put his arms behind his neck, and said, "OK, Clara. Let's do this." He was seated behind the huge brown desk in front of matching shelves, as he is now.

He threw out the artwork that was hanging in the office the day after he received the keys. In its place he has installed an enormous flat-screen television and decorated his office with hundreds of miniature helicopters and emergency rescue vehicles, which, of course, all the journalists make a big deal about in their articles.

The shiny teak conference table, the fruit, the white coffee cups, the screen, the blue ring binders behind him, the stacks of documents—none of it is particularly remarkable. But the man behind the desk holds one of the most powerful positions in the country.

"Come in," Munch says, without looking up from his cell phone.

"Hello, Clara," a voice says, and it is only then that I notice Ernst Woll sitting on the other side of the conference table, almost in the corner.

All the top political staff members are men. Woll is the sharpest and the only one with legal expertise. He has been given the biggest office and is the highest-ranking member.

Previously, there was always just one cabinet minister and one state secretary. This has now expanded into an entire team of state secretaries plus political advisers, all of whom are vying for the minister of Justice's favor, and for recognition as the most hardworking, the most tenacious.

When you hold a political position, you must at all times demonstrate that you're there for a reason, and that's difficult to accomplish without meddling in all sorts of things. That's why state secretaries always create process delays and take up the time of executive officers who should be doing other things.

And while the cabinet minister is busy being a figurehead and a spokesperson for the important political issues in the media and on

Facebook, the state secretaries attend meetings, stay close to the executive officers, and make many of the political decisions.

Nonetheless, I have succeeded in getting Munch to become passionate about my bill. And I have avoided Woll. Until now.

"We won't keep you long," Woll says.

"I'm fine."

"Well, Clara." Munch finally looks up from his cell phone. "Our bill has been a topic of discussion at the cabinet meeting."

Silence.

"Yes?" I say, and understand that this is not the kind of meeting I'd anticipated. The two of them exchange glances. Munch looks uncomfortable. Woll shrugs his shoulders and seems ready to be done with this.

"And yes . . . we have to put it on the back burner," Munch says finally.

I can feel the skin on my arms crawling under my white silk blouse.

"What do you mean?" I say, my voice husky. "The cabinet ministers have read and approved all the government memos I've written."

"This kind of thing happens all the time, you know that. A controversial bill. Coalition government. The others think it's too radical. And there are many other more pressing matters that I need to push through right now."

"But this will be the most important thing you'll achieve during your time here," I say. "Do they understand the significance it will have for the most vulnerable group among us?"

Behind my back, I hear a short, little laugh from Woll.

"You win some, you lose some. The decision has been made," he interrupts me. I can detect a trace of malicious pleasure in his voice, something crackling underneath his words.

That's how they are. It's all about power.

Everything is up for negotiation. A political squeeze can always be brought to bear.

"The prime minister has communicated her decision. But thank you for coming," he adds, getting to his feet. A ministerial dismissal.

Munch is looking at his cell phone again and doesn't meet my gaze.

I turn around, almost surprised that my body is still functioning. I walk out the door, past the desk of Munch's secretary, past the gigantic fruit bowl, twice the size of those in the other departments, out of the political section, and through the hallways.

Finally, I'm inside my own office, where I close the door behind me and slide down, leaning my back against it until I'm seated on the floor, my knees pulled up in front of me.

Henrik likes to call me the ice queen. He cries at the drop of a hat.

I haven't cried since that day thirty years ago and I don't plan on starting now. But I have to put my hands over my face, press my fingertips against my eyes. I try taking deep breaths, but now it doesn't work.

When I was around thirteen, the year after the accident, I started spending the night at the summer farm by myself, sometimes for three or four days at a time. I prepared my own meals, lit the stove, read, and went for walks.

Once I came up with the idea of hiking up Trollskavlen Peak. It was a long and rugged climb, but Daddy had explained the route he used to take when he was young, and I had seen it on the map. I knew I could manage it. I would have, too, if the glimmer of sunlight that was there when I started hadn't turned into a thick layer of clouds.

When only a few hundred yards remained until the summit, a heavy fog crept in.

At first, I could no longer see the top. Soon, I couldn't see a thing.

Everywhere I looked, it was white.

I took out my compass and started walking in what I believed had to be the right direction. Finally, I reached a steep rock face that I thought I remembered having climbed on my way up. I turned around and started making my way down it, facing inward, until suddenly I was stuck, splayed out like Spider-Man, in the middle of the rock face, unable to move up or down.

I had landed on a ledge, like Daddy told me the sheep did from time to time. Then they just waited there, on a narrow green shelf, smack in the middle of a huge rock face, bleating and bleating.

Sometimes, if they were discovered in time, it was possible to bring them up. Other times they simply had to be shot.

Now I was the one trapped there. There was a drop of many yards down to the ground below and nowhere to place my feet.

After a while I began carefully worming my way down, little by little. One foothold here, another there.

This worked for a yard or two. Then I was catapulted outward.

When I hit the ground, I lay there stunned for several minutes, gasping for breath, before I was able to get a sense of whether anything was broken.

And that's the same feeling I have now, sitting here on the floor of the Ministry of Justice, thirty years later.

I have invested so much in this bill; it has meant more to me than anything.

Now the two of them in there have taken it away from me, destroyed it, without any idea of what they're doing.

CHAPTER 3

Henrik

As soon as I've pulled on the white top of my scrubs and stepped through the doors of the unit, I understand that this is going to be a marathon shift. The entire city has run outdoors to make the most of the beautiful weather. The results of this come to us in the form of injuries and illnesses. There's a steady stream of patients:

> 3:35 p.m.: A little girl in a diabetic coma.
> 4:21 p.m.: A boy with asthma suffering from allergic shock.
> 4:53 p.m.: Two siblings from a car pileup.
> 5:20 p.m.: A seriously dehydrated six-year-old.

And then, at 6:53 p.m., another family comes in.

The man is in his midthirties and is carrying a little boy who's about four years old. Probably Pakistani Norwegian, or possibly Afghan. The boy is wearing blue shorts and a red sweater. There's a Star Wars Band-Aid around his right index finger. Grime under his fingernails. A bracelet made of small beads bearing letters. Bluish-black hair on his tiny head.

He appears to be unconscious.

"Let me speak to the doctor," the father shouts. He is wearing a blue Chelsea jersey and cap. The skin on his cheeks is pockmarked with old acne scars.

And Roger follows right behind him, protesting, accompanied by the scent of aftershave. The smell is sweet, outdated, maybe Jean Paul Gaultier, the kind that comes in one of those bottles that look like a male torso or a sailor suit or God knows what.

I have of course nothing against homosexuals or male nurses. And Roger is a brilliant professional, competent, experienced, warm, and caring. A man with many fine qualities. But his perfume is a bit too much.

"I tried to tell him that I'll admit them," he says. "They should have gone to the emergency room. But he just came here directly with the child . . . And we're not going to send them over there now, are we?"

"No," I agree.

The best trauma team in Norway is here at Ullevål Hospital. The worst cases are redirected here from other hospitals, usually by ambulance to the main entrance for admission. But from time to time people bring in their children themselves. If they know where the pediatrics unit is, they'll often just come straight here.

"I'm the attending physician on duty," I say to the father, as diplomatically as possible. "What's happened to the boy?"

"Are you blind, doctor?" the man says, positioning himself directly in front of me, his eyes full of fear and rage at the same time. He reminds me of the troublemakers who used to hang around the schoolyards in Vinderen when I was growing up. "Don't you see that he's unconscious? He won't wake up!"

The mother is wearing a hijab on her head and sweatpants beneath her traditional *kamiz*. She is talking and gesticulating. The father says something to her, speaking a language I don't understand, and she falls silent.

The child is tiny and thin, with narrow hips and a bird's neck, the same blue-and-orange sneakers that Andreas has, but these are worn-out, dirty, with a hole in the fabric just below the big toe.

"How old is he?" I ask, lifting the boy out of his father's arms and laying him down on the examination table.

The father holds up four fingers. The mother looks at me pleadingly, hands folded under her chin, knuckles white.

"What happened?" I ask.

"He fell," the father says. "From a tree. But then he just fell asleep. And now he won't wake up again. Do something, doctor!"

I give Roger a sign indicating that he must summon more staff. "He has to go straight to CT," I say discreetly.

The mother starts crying, the father shouts something at her. I stop walking, pausing in the middle of the room to catch my breath. I need a moment to collect myself, one second, two, three. The boy is unconscious. Outside the window the birds are singing, making me yearn to be outdoors.

Because now I can feel that ticking sensation, the one you get when you understand that the headache is in fact a brain tumor, that the rashes are leukemia, that quite soon you will be obliged to give somebody news they don't want to receive.

The feeling clings to me like a chill.

I bend over the boy. He smells of sour vomit. But of dust and sunlight, too, and something else—chewing gum, toothpaste, shampoo, and a faint whiff of ginger, garlic, and curry.

"Why don't you go for a little walk," I say to the parents. "I'll take good care of your son."

They seem skeptical but leave the room. A few minutes later Sabiya comes in.

"What's happening?" she says breathlessly.

Sabiya is barely five foot one, and her light, soundless gait makes it seem like she flies across the floor. Her hair is shoulder-length, always shiny and put up with a barrette. Her hands are without rings or nail polish, in keeping with the regulations. She moves efficiently but gracefully. Slender hips, a regal curve to her neck.

19

"Don't know," I reply. "A serious concussion, at best. He fell out of a tree."

She stands motionless, inspecting the boy with a strange expression on her face.

"I see," she says finally and starts to undress him, while giving orders to Roger and Bente, one of the other nurses.

Behind Sabiya's back, I wink at Bente, who blushes as usual.

This business of undressing and checking children is one of Sabiya's pet obsessions. A few weeks ago, she gave a talk about it at a morning meeting, going through a PowerPoint presentation peppered with images of backs scarred from whippings, mouths full of lesions, X-rays of broken bones. We learn about this as part of our training. But when you start working, you're busy all the time and it's easy to overlook the signs. So, we must be on the alert, take those extra few seconds, even check those patients who seemingly are there for something else altogether, she said, and then people nodded, a bit guilt-ridden.

Now she leans forward, rolls up the red sleeve of his sweater.

"Damn," I say when I see the marks on the inside of his arm where there absolutely should not be any marks. Clothes can be eerily deceptive; they make everything appear normal. Sabiya retrieves a pair of scissors, starts cutting away his garments.

More bruises are revealed, on his shoulders and thighs.

I draw a breath. "What the hell," I say.

"Yes, there's no doubt here," Sabiya says, maintaining her impressive professionalism. With the help of the nurses we move the boy onto a gurney and jog through the hallways toward the emergency unit where the CT will be done. In these situations, Roger is invaluable. Nobody has more frontline experience than he does, nobody has lifted more injured and sick patients in and out of ambulances.

The CT is done at 7:40 p.m. Sabiya and I stand around, waiting for the images. Radiologists and anesthesiologists arrive.

Then we hear footsteps behind us. The boy's father bursts in; he must have followed us here.

I walk toward him. "This area is off limits," I say firmly.

He stands in the doorway without budging.

"What did you say, doctor?"

"You have to wait outside."

"Fucking racist," he says.

"These rules apply to everyone," Roger says bluntly.

The man moves reluctantly away from the doorway, but stomps around outside like a raging bull.

When I turn around, Sabiya is standing there looking at me with an odd expression on her face.

"Do you know him?" I ask.

She nods but says nothing more, and then the CT scans arrive. It has to be the first time I've heard Sabiya swear. I lean over her shoulder and look at the huge shadow on the image.

An ominous inkblot.

"Traumatic cerebral hemorrhage. He needs surgery as soon as possible."

Sabiya nods almost imperceptibly. Her eyes are dull, and she looks unwell.

We wheel the boy back to the unit with the father on our heels.

When we get to his room, the anesthesiologists check his blood pressure, pulse, blood oxygen saturation level, and heart rate on the monitor. They prepare the general anesthesia and intubation, set up the respirator.

The parents enter the room and the mother is crying. The father is roaring something or other about how we must get it together, do our job. Somebody pushes him out again. Roger goes out into the hallway and tries calming him down.

Sabiya goes over to the boy and starts gently stroking his cheek, where there are traces of dried tears on his dusty skin. She takes the little hand with its Star Wars Band-Aid in her own and starts speaking calmly and softly to him in Punjabi. The boy is tiny, pale, and incapable of explaining or giving an account of anything. But it has to be all right; soon, he will open his eyes, slowly come around. In the coming days I'll drop by, take my time, talk and joke with him, observe how he perks up and becomes happier, more secure.

At the exact moment I am having that thought, his pulse and blood oxygen saturation levels start to drop.

Shit, I think. Shit, shit, shit. Desperation overwhelms me. We mustn't lose him now.

The anesthesiologist immediately inserts an intravenous catheter into the boy's arm for an adrenaline infusion.

"Requisition an emergency blood transfusion," I say to Roger.

We give him a second injection, this one containing medication to keep his blood pressure from dropping. The boy is wheeled to the operating room. Sabiya and I jog behind him. Outside the operating room the anesthesiologist takes over and we are obliged to step out.

The time is 9:10 p.m. Nobody says a word. Sabiya wanders about restlessly. I walk over to the window. The streetcar rumbles past. Cars stop for a red light as they drive down Kirkeveien Street. While people toast the summer at outdoor restaurants in Majorstuen in one direction and Torshov in the other, while the world goes on about its business as usual, the little boy is wheeled out of the operating room again.

The neurosurgeon, one of the most experienced, is shaking his head.

"An enormous amount of bleeding, not compatible with life."

What I most feel like doing is sitting down on the floor and crying.

Four years the boy got. Four years of bruises.

The boy is wheeled back to the unit.

"We have to notify the next of kin," I say. "And the mother doesn't speak Norwegian."

The moment I speak the words, I realize how cowardly and pathetic I sound, that this is a way of making the task Sabiya's responsibility.

Without replying she takes the parents aside.

The father pounds his fist against the wall. The mother breaks down. Sabiya strokes her back. The rest of us stand by silently, helplessly. Later another CT of the boy must be done, to establish that the blood circulation to the brain has ceased, and he will be declared dead. All this takes time. It probably won't be done until tomorrow. Then we must ask the parents about organ donation. We try to give the next of kin some time before asking, but we can't wait for too long.

There's a warmth among our group that is out of the ordinary. The experience has united us. It's painful. But we also have other patients, children lying in bed and waiting, children we haven't had the chance to attend to while this has been going on. The state of emergency cannot continue for much longer.

Then the father comes running toward us. Bente tries to put one hand on his shoulder, but he shoves her away.

"I'm sorry for your loss," I say.

"Where's the prayer room?"

I don't say what I'm thinking: a father who has beaten his son to death has no business visiting a prayer room. There's no forgiveness for what he's done. I just turn away.

"Bente," I mumble. "Will you show him where the room is?"

As his back disappears through the glass doors, I place the palms of my hands against the wall and bow my head between my arms, breathing deeply.

Once, twice, three times.

CHAPTER 4

Clara

Today I don't feel like talking to anyone, not even my father. But I usually call Dad every single evening, year-round. He'll be worried if he doesn't hear from me. So, once the boys are in bed, I give him a call.

"Hello, how are you?" I say when he answers the phone.

I can picture him; he is probably standing by the window looking out across the fjord while he's talking. Dad likes to gaze at the view, stand there gaping, as my mother used to say. I probably get that from him.

"I don't know . . . ," he says meekly.

"What is it?"

"Well, I wasn't feeling quite up to snuff, so I went to see the doctor."

"Yes?" I say, noticing how the skin of my scalp is prickling again. He mumbles something so softly that I am unable to hear him properly.

"Daddy, can you speak up?"

"Yes, then they sent me here in an ambulance," he says.

"What?" I say, sliding down onto the floor for the second time today. "Where is *here*?"

"The hospital. They think I might have had a minor stroke or something . . . . Are you there?"

"Yes," I say, clearing my throat, feeling dizzy.

"I'm sure I'll be fine," he continues in a tone of voice that belies his words. "But I'll have to stay here tonight, maybe a little longer. And listen, now they've come to take some tests. We'll talk again later."

As I'm hanging up the phone, I feel it.

Something wet trickling out of my eyes, something impossible to stop.

And then Henrik calls.

CHAPTER 5

HENRIK

"Yes," Clara says. Her voice sounds thick. She has probably been nodding off over her Mac, as she often does. "Henrik?"

It's 9:40 p.m. The unpleasant mood of this morning should be forgotten by now, even though she tends to bear a grudge.

"Can you go check on the boys, make sure they're safe and sound?" I say.

"What do you mean?" She doesn't sound angry. Just tired and sad.

"Just a little peek. To make sure they're fine . . ."

"But seriously, I've been in the living room since I put them to bed. They're sound sleepers, like you. They wouldn't wake up if a fighter plane broke the sound barrier over the house. What's really going on?"

I swallow.

"Has something happened?"

I'm alone in a washroom in the unit with the lights off.

And then I break down.

"There's a damn gangster in a Chelsea jersey, cranked up on anabolic steroids . . ."

"I don't understand."

"He came in with his four-year-old son. Claimed that he'd fallen out of a tree. We examined the boy and discovered that his body is covered with bruises, scratches, and burn marks . . . The CT shows a massive cerebral hemorrhage. Now he's lying there, brain dead, and we're just waiting to turn off the life support."

"Good Lord," Clara whispers into the phone.

"And as if that weren't enough, the father has gone around raising hell in the unit ever since he got here, as if it's our fault. Now he just came and demanded access to the prayer room. To pray! After beating up his son! What a fucking horrible world. You should have seen the boy, Clara, he reminded me so much of our boys at that age. He was even wearing the same sneakers that Andreas has."

There's silence on the line for a few seconds; I can hear only soft sounds, as if she's moving around. Then I hear her whispering—she must be in the doorway of the boys' bedroom.

"The boys are asleep," she says.

"Thank you," I whisper back, and I really mean it.

At ten o'clock I go outside. I must have a break if I'm going to make it through the rest of my shift. I remind myself that when I go inside again, I must call the police—standard procedure for cases like this.

In the lobby there's a huge pirate ship flying a black flag with a white skull on it. As I pass it on my way out the door it strikes me as inappropriate.

I walk around outside for a bit and am about to go back in when I notice somebody standing doubled over and retching beside a bush.

"Sabiya . . . ," I say. "Are you OK?"

"No," she says, placing her fingers against her eyes and wiping them angrily. She hits her hand against the brick wall, wincing as she does so, and then strikes her forehead with her hand several times instead, as if to punish herself.

Sabiya is the most professional, the calmest of everyone, but now she seems to be falling completely apart.

"I understand . . . ," I begin.

"You don't understand," she says, and there's something wild in her eyes. "Mukhtar Ahmad used to live not far from me. On Sverdrups Street, at the far end of Løkka. He's two years younger than me. My father knew his father; they worked for the urban transit company together."

"Mukhtar who?"

"The child abuser. Even back then we were afraid of him. I played with his little brother when we were the same age as his son. You don't understand . . ." Her face crumples into a grimace, and her eyes are full of tears again. "I'm sorry," she says as I lift my hand and stroke her cheek.

"Don't say that," I say, and take her into my arms, patting her hair the way I usually do with the boys. "It doesn't matter. Just cry."

She leans against my chest for a second or two. Then she stiffens, straightens up, raises a clenched fist, and hits my shoulder with her knuckles several times.

"Good Lord, Henrik. We're just standing here."

"Yes," I say, and look into her eyes.

She looks straight at me, her gaze unwavering.

"That damn well won't do. We have to do something."

CHAPTER 6

ROGER

I see them when I come out.

Henrik and Sabiya.

They're standing under some trees talking or arguing. She is waving her arms, gesticulating; he shakes his head, embraces her.

What are two attending physicians on duty doing out here now? I stand there watching them for a few seconds, and then I walk away.

It's 10:05 p.m. There's almost a half hour left on my shift, but I must find Ahmad. I must tell him what he's done, make him understand it.

The last thing he deserves is to lie on a prayer mat feeling holy.

Sabiya and Henrik and the others are fluttering around like chickens with their heads cut off, like flustered old women, while a child killer walks around on the loose.

When they were busy working on the boy earlier this evening, I knew right away that he didn't stand a chance. I've spent many more hours beside vital signs monitors than any of the doctors, but they scarcely notice us nurses. Can you get this, and can you get that, can you fix this, can you fix that. Otherwise, they don't talk to me if they don't have to, don't ask my advice, even though I've worked at all the units here, delivered thousands of babies, taken care of newborns in the maternity unit, watched over premature babies at neonatal intensive care, consoled parents, and held mothers by the hand.

The only thing they see is a nurse, somebody whose rank is lower than their own.

Askildsen, the chief physician, told me that there have been complaints about my aftershave being too strong. Imagine! Don't think for a second that the complaints came from patients or next of kin. No, it had to be one of the doctors. Four children—they won't settle for less—along with a Volvo and a dog and a cottage in the mountains, vacations in Italy, and family photographs on Facebook . . . but behind the facade it's completely rotten.

Henrik was standing there patting Sabiya, like she's a puppy or something. The man is attractive in his slapdash, posh-side-of-Oslo way, but I don't like him. He's too nonchalant, always cruising around on the surface, as if he doesn't really care about anything at all, the way people do when they've grown up in huge houses with huge gardens. Good natured and on the up and up, yes, but still an upper-class prick from Vinderen.

And Sabiya?

It's possible that nice-girl look of hers with the pearl earrings and subtle lip gloss fools everyone else. But I grew up on her side of the tracks. And even though you can take the girl out of the ghetto . . .

Ahmad and Sabiya are cut from the same cloth. The difference is that she's learned how to behave.

I live in the Rosenhoff neighborhood. People think that sounds dismal, a part of town on the east side of Oslo. But I have a view of the fjord, I have my music, I have my television series and my friends and my mom. I visit her every day, sit there holding her hand and talking to her. I don't have a partner or children, but I try to lavish all my love and caring on the children who come into the unit.

That boy, he was one of the most beautiful creatures I've ever seen. How innocent he looked, resting in his father's arms. How is it possible to do such a thing to your own children?

I'm hot and sticky after running around the unit all evening. Sweat is dripping from my armpits. When I get home, I'll take a long, cold shower, and go to bed on fresh, clean sheets.

The evening air helps a little bit, soothing the agitated heat of my skin like a cooling embrace.

But at that exact moment I see him, the man who stole the future from his own son. Suddenly, he's walking right in front of me.

I follow him with as much silence and stealth as I can muster and grow hot all over again. He walks in the direction of a more deserted part of the hospital grounds.

Nobody else is outside, and it seems as if the guy in front of me is wandering around aimlessly. Was the whole praying business just a smoke screen? Or hasn't he understood where the prayer room is?

I'm walking just ten yards behind him, but—hard to believe—he's wearing earbuds, so he doesn't notice me.

Finally, he stops, walks up a metal stairway, and opens the steel, blue door. This is where they go to pray, those hypocritical Muslims. The same individuals responsible for shut-ins being assigned home health aides who refuse to buy them the food they want. They are the reason ethnic Norwegian children are bullied at school and innocent gay people are clobbered in immigrant ghettos like Grønland for walking hand in hand with their partners.

Everything about this prick infuriates me, the thickset neck, the close-cropped hair, his cap, the blue Chelsea jersey—the old kind, with a Samsung logo on the chest.

I feel a demented desire to pulverize his face, smash his head against a wall, do something . . .

CHAPTER 7

Henrik

A little before midnight I'm standing in the middle of the corridor, examining the tip of the middle finger of my left hand. Band-Aids don't mix with handwashing, so I removed it, but I've made sure to wear gloves when I've been in contact with patients. Luckily, the cut stopped bleeding quite quickly and it seems like it's healing nicely, but I must try to cut away the little flap of loose skin the first chance I get.

Two uniformed police officers walk through the glass doors of the unit.

The man looks like he's close to retirement age, but he is also slim and fit. Appropriately suntanned, short hair, and a hawklike gaze. The kind of guy who has been working on murder cases forever and, despite his impressive physique, is headed for a heart attack after many years of not enough sleep and too much work.

The woman is younger, around forty, girlish with freckles, discreetly manicured nails, and a long ponytail that is blonder toward the end than at the top.

They introduce themselves. They're from the violent crimes task force. I catch only their first names. Elin and Morten.

"Are you willing to make a witness statement? You have the right to refuse."

"It's fine," I say. I've been through this before on other occasions when we've had to call them.

"Would you like to have an attorney present?"

"No, no . . ." These stiff, formal phrases almost make me giggle.

"Then we'll get started. Do you have a patient here named Faisal Ahmad?" Elin asks, and it's only then that it hits me, what I've forgotten to do.

Call the police.

As an attending physician on duty it was my job. But the fact that the police have shown up must mean that Sabiya has taken responsibility and called.

"Have you had any form of contact with Faisal Ahmad's father, Mukhtar Ahmad?" the policewoman asks.

"Yes, of course," I say. "He was here for most of the evening."

"When did you see him last?"

"Well, around 9:40 p.m. He left to go find the prayer room. Maybe we should have tried to keep him here, but given the situation he was in, it was difficult to tell him no."

They glance at one another. I can see they're a practiced team, that they like each other and work well together.

"You're here because of a notification, right?" I add.

Now the woman shakes her head.

"We're here because an unidentified body was discovered on the hospital grounds. Mukhtar Ahmad's ID card was found on the dead man. At admissions we were informed that one Faisal Ahmad is supposed to be here in this unit. Is that correct?"

"Yes, in a manner of speaking," I say.

I am bound by professional secrecy, even in relation to the police.

But a dead man, found on hospital grounds.

It takes a couple of seconds for my brain to process what they have said.

"Excuse me, but did you say that Mukhtar Ahmad is dead?" I stare at them with my mouth open.

"That's what we're trying to establish," Morten says.

"But back to Faisal Ahmad," the policewoman says.

I try to collect myself.

"The boy had a cerebral hemorrhage," I say finally. "Earlier this evening, he was operated on, but the bleeding was too extensive, incompatible with life. His father left immediately afterward. Faisal is still breathing but not on his own. Life support will be turned off. He had a cranial fracture. His father claimed he'd fallen out of a tree, but we also found old bone fractures and other signs of abuse—fresh bruises in the wrong places in addition to the serious cerebral hemorrhage. There is no doubt that it's a case of domestic violence."

"What time did you come to work today?" Morten asks.

"I punched in just before three. Around five minutes before three."

"Did you leave the building during your shift?"

I hesitate for a few seconds. "No."

"What was your impression of Ahmad?"

"Not the best," I say, relieved that they've changed the subject. "A bully. Aggressive. Easily offended and threatening. He shouted and carried on."

"His wife, is she still here?"

"No, as far as I know, she went home to be with her other children."

Elin glances at her pink running watch.

"Can you come with us and make a preliminary identification? We want to be sure before we contact next of kin."

"Who found the body?" I ask as we walk through the hospital area.

"A security guard who happened to be nearby. He heard something that sounded like a gunshot and decided to inspect the area. He notified the emergency room here, and they notified us. Now we're trying to map out all the activity in the area during the period in question."

"So, he was shot?" I ask.

Without replying, Elin shepherds me in the direction of the crime scene and I don't ask any more questions.

The hospital grounds have been transformed into a fairground, with police cars and blinking yellow lights. Journalists are lined up and waiting behind the police tape that encircles the crime scene.

We climb the five steps of the steel stairway and walk through a blue door that's ajar: the multi-faith prayer room.

The area of the room is perhaps sixty square feet. A man wearing a blue Chelsea jersey is lying on the floor in the middle of the room, on his stomach.

"Walk on the plastic here," Elin instructs.

I want to ask if it's really all right, my waltzing in here now, but stop myself. They're the ones who have asked me to do this.

Two crime scene investigators wearing the same kind of white protective suit that I had to put on are on their knees, taking photographs from different angles. One of them takes a close-up of a dark, singed area on the Chelsea jersey.

I bend down and inspect the face that is turned toward the door.

His eyes are glazed and his skin has already acquired a rubbery quality, and his natural skin color makes him less yellowish than a Caucasian would be.

He must have come in here, washed, prepared for prayer, all those things.

Had he been grieving? Did he feel remorse? Or had he simply fumed and cursed the world in general, angry with everything and everybody, as he'd behaved with us? Who was he really? Was he a devout believer or had that merely been pretense, so he could leave the unit?

Had he felt ashamed? Had he loved his child?

Regardless, I'm unable to feel anything but a sense of relief over his being gone. The policewoman clears her throat behind me. I stand up, nod at her.

"Yes," I say when we are outside the room again. "That's him, the man who came in with his son."

"Good. Thanks for your help. We'll be in touch," she says, and surprises me by putting a tiny pouch of snus in her cheek, General Portion, extra strong.

I get out of there as fast as I can without breaking into a run.

On the way back to the unit I see police with search dogs. Others are walking around with metal detectors. There are people everywhere.

In pediatrics the night shift is calm, but the chief physician, Askildsen, has arrived. Someone must have called him.

"Quite a story," he says, and shakes his head after I've given him a quick briefing. "I'll be staying here tonight."

Askildsen is a medical nerd who is single and lives and breathes for his job. He enjoys Scotch and watching Liverpool soccer matches on television. Apart from that, the unit is his life. The day he retires he will probably crumble into dust.

"It seems calm here now," he adds.

"Yes, finally."

"You can go home, Henrik." I'm about to refuse, but then I notice how done in I am. The shift for physicians with specializations is from three o'clock in the afternoon until ten o'clock the next morning. This is grueling enough on an ordinary day. Today it feels unendurable.

"Thanks—I might just take you up on that."

I go into the office, sit down, and take out my phone.

The murder at Ullevål Hospital is already the lead story on *VG Nett*, the national daily's online news site. The video they've posted shows a blonde journalist standing outside the main entrance, waving her arm to indicate the building behind her.

I put the phone down and sit staring out the window at the velvety-blue summer darkness, at the moon, at the rooftops, at the lights in the windows. I reach for the scalpel that has been lying in the corner nook where my desk and Sabiya's meet. I want to cut away the loose flap of skin on my fingertip. But the scalpel is gone. Sabiya must have moved it.

There's a photograph of Sabiya with her husband and three children on her desk. Happy people dressed in summer clothing. Attractive, all of them. But the eyes of her husband are piercing, disturbing.

The stars glitter above the rooftops. Inside these buildings thousands of people are lying in bed asleep. But the hospital never sleeps.

In the old days I sometimes heard my father sitting in his workroom talking to himself when he was faced with a difficult problem.

Now I try doing the same thing.

Overall this shift had been disagreeable, but all the same, it was just one shift among many others, I tell myself.

Sometimes kids come in that we can't save. And sometimes people are shot and killed in Oslo, just like in other big cities. Things that shouldn't happen, happen.

But the pep talk doesn't help. It's impossible to erase the image of little Faisal's body or the glazed-over eyes of his father on the floor of the prayer room from my mind.

I have a feeling of estrangement in my body, the sensation that everything has changed. It accompanies me down the stairs, into the garage, on my bicycle through the streets.

The night is sumptuously beautiful. The moon is luminous; there is nobody out, just me, in the middle of the summer night, in the middle of Oslo, moving through the scent of buckthorns and lilacs about to bloom.

Everything is blooming early this year. Blooming and dying.

CHAPTER 8

CLARA

When I woke up, Henrik was lying in bed asleep. He was supposed to have been at work until ten o'clock this morning, but for some reason he must have come home during the night. I'd left without waking him to take the boys and the rest of the kids in our car pool to school as planned.

I've now been at work for a few hours.

"What a shame your bill was killed," the political adviser says, smiling. He came into my office as I was packing up my things to leave for a meeting. He entered without asking permission, without knocking, just walked straight in.

The man's face is full of pimples, even though he must be almost twenty-five years old and has found the time to produce three children in Southern Norway. His hair is glistening with hair wax, and the smell is nauseating. It reminds me of the boys back home in the 1990s.

While the state secretaries often have work experience from the nongovernmental sector, the political advisers are brats from the youth party who've never been a part of the real world.

They keep track of calendars and appointments, coordinate political meetings, are the point of contact for the communications people in the ministry, run the Facebook account, and believe they are irreplaceable.

The truth is that nobody is easier to replace than a political adviser.

"Listen, I'm in a bit of a rush," I say, and glance at my watch. "I have an important meeting in half an hour at—"

"Fine, I just wanted to give you this," he says, and tosses a folder onto my desk. "From the office of the cabinet minister's secretary. A few tasks for you to enjoy now that you have some time on your hands."

I open the folder. Good God. Letters from the public.

He could just as well have asked me to make coffee.

Most of the people who write to us are completely nuts. We're still obliged to reply. The folder contains a thick stack of letters.

The adviser doesn't have the authority to assign me this. It's supposed to be passed on administratively, down the line. I know that he knows this. But I can't be bothered to sink to his level or spend time on this now.

"Thanks" is all I say.

Somebody clears their throat behind him.

"What's going on here?" Secretary-General Mona Falkum asks. She's standing straight as a poker behind him, dressed in one of her classic, charcoal-gray suits.

The adviser snaps to attention.

"Nothing," he says. "I just dropped in for a little chat."

"Well, Clara doesn't have time for small talk now. She and I have an important meeting to attend. Are you ready?" Mona asks, as the adviser backs out the door.

"Yes," I say, slipping on my shoes. "More than ready."

Mona was my first boss when I started working at the Ministry of Justice and she was deputy director general. Now two years have passed since she assumed the position of secretary-general. She is the queen bee who leads the ministry while the cabinet ministers come and go, the kind of boss who sticks up for us, tries to protect us from Munch and his men.

But in one area she hasn't made any progress.

For a long time, she's tried to get the state secretaries and political advisers to send their requests through the correct channels instead of carpet-bombing the executive officers, but without success. Modern-day state secretaries know that—formally speaking—they're not subordinate to the secretary-general, but on an equal standing. They don't accept being schooled by a top-level bureaucrat.

When I started working here, people's interactions were more formal. Now everyone is on a first-name basis and connected online, everyone uses the same case administration system, and emails and text messages are sent every which way. The time when the leaders had full oversight on the information from a cabinet minister's subordinates has passed.

To say that Mona and I are friends would be going too far. A secretary-general doesn't have friends at work, and I'm not the type to socialize at work or anywhere else. But we like one another and communicate well.

"I can't promise that this will do the trick," she says as we walk to the elevator. "But it's at least one final chance to present the bill properly, even though it's been tabled. And maybe you'll manage to slip it through. The secretaries-general have considerable influence when a government memo is circulated for comment. If you can get them on your side, it could all turn around."

"I hope so," I say. "Thank you for trying."

Once a week the secretaries-general meet for what Munch sarcastically calls the "Yes-Men's Club." This is the lunch Mona has invited me to attend.

"But be aware that you will be meeting the eighteen most boring people in the country," she says, and pushes the button for the first floor. I laugh. I know she's trying to cheer me up, get me to relax.

"And here I thought they were in the government."

"Well, among the thirty-six most boring, then . . ."

We're silent until we pass through the revolving door and step out onto the hot asphalt. "Yes, before the 2011 terrorist attack, these lunches were held in The Highrise," Mona says, and nods toward the building where, in the old days, the prime minister's office occupied the top floors, and where there is now plywood over what previously were windows. The building has stood vacant ever since, year in and year out, waiting for a decision.

We hurry past the Supreme Court building, down Grensen Street, and across the main street, Karl Johans Gate, continuing from there in the direction of Akershus Fortress. I struggle in my stupid stilettos to prevent the heels from getting wedged between the cobblestones.

Finally, we reach the prime minister's office on the street Glacis Gate, a huge redbrick building with a modern glass facade, which belongs to the Ministry of Defense. The reflection of the brick walls opposite can be seen in the glass.

I show my ID once. Then once again.

After that, two security gates, one outside and one inside. Inside the final gate there's a polar bear, a replica of the one in our building.

"Yes, indeed, they *are* twins," Mona says. "The prime minister fell in love with the bears the first time she saw them in the other building, so afterward she had one moved here."

We go up to the third floor, ring the bell, a secretary arrives, and she accompanies us to the meeting room. She tells me to have a seat and wait outside while they go through the day's agenda.

I take out my notes, key phrases in a small font I've pasted on four thick sheets of paper, the way speechwriters usually list talking points for a cabinet minister's speeches. I leaf through them and put them away. It's too late to start cramming now. I stand up and start pacing.

After a few minutes I sit down again, trying to breathe deeply, until I am granted access to the hallowed inner sanctuary.

Around the long polished brown table sit the eighteen secretaries-general and the attorney general. On the right-hand side, in the middle, sits the secretary to the government, who represents the prime minister's office and who is essentially the prime minister of the secretaries-general, and the most powerful of them all. They don't have assigned seats, but today Mona is sitting beside the secretary to the government, presumably because she is responsible for the day's entertainment.

"You have all addressed many government memos on this bill," she says. "We know the bill is extremely controversial. Many people maintain that it represents a violation of privacy and that's the reason it was recently stopped. Nonetheless, I would like you to listen to what Clara Lofthus has to say. She is one of the most proficient executive officers at the Ministry of Justice. She wants to explain why we feel the bill is both important and right."

"Thank you," I say, and move to the front of the room.

During the past few hours, after Mona invited me to this lunch, I'd created a concise and targeted presentation that I've learned by heart so it will seem like I'm speaking without a script, even though I have the main points outlined in key phrases in front of me.

"All changes that are truly necessary, that make a significant difference, must be painful," I begin. "If they aren't, it's very likely because they are too moderate, too cautious, too insignificant. This is a change that is *necessary*. Not for my sake. Not for your sake—but for the sake of the youngest among us, the most vulnerable. If we dare to take this step, it can mean the difference between life and death for them."

I know I must be impressive. And I *am* good. I say neither too much, nor too little. I say the right things, in the right way.

"People think professional secrecy is more important than the duty of notification—and that's been a big problem. The duty of notification has been vague, while professional secrecy, on the other hand, has been emphasized in all contexts. That's why nobody has dared to speak up when something is wrong. This bill represents a paradigm shift, the most important thing to happen in relation to this issue in years. I would venture to claim that this will be the most important bill you will pass as secretaries-general."

They are focused and giving me their full attention.

Then I explain how and why there should be a statutory exemption from judicial review. That wiretapping and hidden camera surveillance can be permitted in day-care centers, institutions, and private homes where there is suspicion of abuse. That simultaneously, personal liability will be introduced for employees who fail to sound the alarm in the event of any suspicion of violence and abuse.

When I finish, they nod in agreement.

Some positive feedback is expressed.

But then the secretary-general from MLG, the Ministry of Local Government, takes the floor. He's like so many men in their sixties, with his eyeglasses, a comb-over, and a wart on his nose, the whole package.

Data protection, he says.

Protection of privacy, he says.

Police brutality, he says.

After this, each of them speaks in turn. And now there's nobody who dares say anything positive. The secretary to the government thanks me for my presentation. Mona gives me a nod as I leave.

On my way back, I picture the arrogant, smug face of the secretary-general from the MLG.

What was his name again? Who is he? And doesn't the guy have children?

When I reach Lille Grensen, the heel of my right shoe gets stuck. I plunge forward and recover my balance just in time, lunging into the same position as a runner at the starting line, remaining momentarily suspended with my fingertips touching the ground for a few seconds before standing up.

One heel remains stuck, broken right off.

"Fucking hell," I mutter. I pick up the remains of the broken shoe and slip off the other. People stop and stare at me. Children laugh. It's clearly not every day they see a woman in a suit without shoes.

I continue walking, barefoot, holding one shoe and the pieces of the other in my hands.

CHAPTER 9

Henrik

This day has just melted away. I slept for a long time, after which I wandered aimlessly around the house without doing anything constructive till it was time to pick up the children.

Clara didn't get home from work until the boys' bedtime, and she went straight upstairs with them.

Now she's sitting on the veranda downstairs with her evening joint in one hand and her phone in the other. I see that again she's on Strava. Every evening she sits studying the fitness activity app and examining her segments, running routes, who's run where and what their time was.

The purpose, as I've understood it, is to hold the record. Always. I guess it appeals to her competitive instincts. Usually, I pester her about her Strava obsession, but today I can't be bothered. I just sink into a chair.

"I called to hear how it went with the boy I told you about," I begin.

This is the first time today that we've been alone, and I actually feel a compelling need to talk to her.

"Yes?" she says, and looks at me expectantly.

"They'd just turned off the respirator."

She sighs.

"So, he's dead?"

"Yes," I say. I swallow. Again, I picture his eyes. "But did you hear what happened to the father?"

She nods.

"I read about the murder online. I thought maybe it was the guy you were talking about."

"I had to accompany the police to the crime scene last night, to confirm whether or not it was him lying there . . ."

"And was it?" Clara asks, directing her piercing gaze at me.

Nobody has eyes as blue as Clara's. Even here in the semidarkness they shine toward me.

At first, I called her Bette Davis, because of "Bette Davis Eyes," the 1981 Kim Carnes song about Bette Davis's clear, blue eyes, which could appear brown in photographs, especially if they were black-and-white. Later, the reference seemed out of place, because nobody can mistake Clara's eyes for being anything but blue, regardless of the light.

Clara was refreshingly different from the girls I grew up with. She knew how to do things I couldn't, like prune fruit trees and put up fences and deliver lambs and drive a tractor.

A kind of androgynous child of nature, a raw fragment of the landscape from Western Norway.

"Yes," I say. "Everyone is beside themselves. Management is stressed because it doesn't make us look good. Nobody knows who did it. The police eventually managed to block all the exits, but by then a lot of time had passed. Whoever killed him would have had time to travel quite a distance."

"Why would anyone want to kill him?" Clara says.

"Nobody knows, but he was aggressive. Maybe he had enemies. He had several strange, bluish-red bulges on his skin, by the way, one on his back and one on his side. I saw them because I had to go with the police to the prayer room to identify him, and they were busy taking photographs of him."

"Good Lord . . ."

"It looked terrible. But I've seen those kinds of bulges a few times before. He must have been shot with expanding bullets."

In the course of the day, I'd read up on this type of ammunition. A few years ago, the police were granted authorization to use expanding bullets, because they don't travel straight through people and hit bystanders on the other side, the way ordinary bullets can. Also, this kind of ammunition is permitted for hunting, to ensure that the animal is in fact killed, not just wounded.

"The guy seemed pretty sketchy," I continued. "Not exactly a mother's pride and joy. Or Allah's . . ."

We sit in silence for a moment.

"How are things going at the ministry?" I ask.

When we do talk, I always try to include a question about Clara's work. After all, it is what she cares about more than anything else in the world.

"Straight to hell," she says, and sighs, her face darkening.

"How so?"

"The bill was shelved. It's dead."

"What?" I say, shocked.

It's true there were many moments when I wanted to send the bill straight to that place where the sun doesn't shine, because of all the time and attention it had demanded from her. But now the precious thing is finally finished, and if the bill doesn't see the light of day, she'll be in a bad mood for a very long time.

"What happened?"

"You tell me," she says, blows a smoke ring, and falls silent.

When we first started dating, I liked Clara's obstinacy, that she's so ambitious, so strong-willed and uncompromising. But I also believed she would mellow eventually. That hasn't happened. On the contrary.

She grasps the thick wool blanket, pulls it off, swings her feet down, and is clearly planning to stand up and leave, as she always does when I try to speak with her.

"Relax," I say, and get up. "I'm leaving. Just stay where you are."

She sits down again.

I go inside, closing the door to the balcony. I don't want the heavy, sweet smell of hash inside. Even after all these years, I can't get used to her smoking a joint every day. I hope she'll give it up soon, before the boys are old enough to understand what it is. But I have my doubts.

I wander into the living room and sit down, take out my cell phone, and access the orange icon.

Strava stalker that I am, I have of course taken care to put the Strava app far to the right on my phone, so it's not visible at any time. I've turned off the push notifications. Clara doesn't look at my cell phone, but should she happen to notice the app, I will say I downloaded it to see what's so fascinating about it.

A red number in the right corner of the icon shows eight notifications.

I open the app, scroll down, and access MRSSPLENDID's profile.

She's run the same route in her neighborhood—into the forest and around a pond—that she runs every Tuesday, Thursday, and Saturday, when she's not working. Today she's had a pretty good day, one of her best times on this route. A high pulse rate for the entire run. And this digital data makes me feel a little closer to her.

Great, MRSSPLENDID! I write underneath.

And then: I think you'll be needing some competition soon!

YES! she writes back.

I enter the frame for MRSSPLENDID from last Tuesday and zoom in on a hill, a volcano-shaped mound with a hollow in the middle, a kind of basin shielding us from prying eyes, in the event somebody happened to pass by on the path below.

I close my eyes and think back.

Our place. Our time.

So infinitely distant from the dreary desert landscape that my marriage has become.

CHAPTER 10

CLARA

The first time I saw Henrik was a Saturday in June many years ago, in old Edith's charming, overgrown garden, just a stone's throw away from where we live now.

I lived there rent-free in exchange for working in the garden and cleaning, carrying wood, and performing other tasks. It was far more agreeable than the cleaning job I'd had up until then, where every day I had to take the metro to Lambertseter and clean two disgusting, run-down beauty parlors where the cockroaches crawled across the kitchen counters and there were tiny hairs everywhere. Thanks to Edith, I could afford to quit the salon job and never go back.

Beneath her snobbish exterior, Edith turned out to be truly entertaining as she sat in her deck chair and smoked and coughed and told stories about Paris in the old days, from the avenues and cafés and parties and feuds.

She was a skinny little creature, as wrinkled as they come, but she wore polka-dot blouses, her hair pulled into a bun on top of her head, and earrings. Her face was always meticulously made up. It was difficult to tell how old she was—presumably somewhere in her mideighties.

I quickly understood that it was first and foremost companionship the old woman was seeking.

"Come now, let's sit down," she would say. And even though I tried to point out that I had work to do, we always ended up doing exactly that, often with a bottle of rosé.

The birds sang and the flies buzzed, and the flowers blossomed.

I felt at home in the huge backyard on the fancy side of Oslo behind the gigantic, higgledy-piggledy villa. It was an old house with a wild, tangled garden, like on the farm, although the similarities ended there.

Edith always used to ask me about my law studies. Without really listening to the answer, she said each time that she could not understand why I wanted to inflict all that pain on myself. She'd tried glancing through her son's books when he'd studied law in his day, but no, she couldn't read something so abominably tedious, she said, and chortled that husky laugh of hers. I tried to tell her that yes, my studies were not very exciting, but I believed they would lead to an interesting job, a profession that would enable me to do something important, make a difference for people. Then I should meet her son, was her opinion. He'd come far in his field.

She refused to believe it when I told her I didn't have a boyfriend, not even a flirtation or a crush. This was when the conversation usually turned to the time she lived up by the church in Montmartre and picked up men in cafés sixty years ago.

I tucked my legs under me in the deck chair, lifted the crystal glass of rosé, and listened.

Pretty soon, I understood that Edith must have been seriously betrayed by her husband, an old Supreme Court judge, a position subsequently filled by her son. It was clearly difficult for her to admit having been deceived in this way, as proud as she was. But once the floodgates were opened, an outpouring of thoughts and memories gushed out of her.

"Such things are genetic. Yes, William, my son, he has many good sides. But I'm afraid he's become just like his father, also in that way. One notices such things, you know. People think you must search for traces of lipstick and foolishness like that. It's not necessary. If your man stops pressing up against you at night and simultaneously seems cheerful and satisfied with life, well, then you know. There will be something that doesn't add up, and you'll notice the scent of perfume and other odors before you know it. You see?"

"Yes, of course," I said, and laughed.

Not only was she entertaining, she was also the only friend I had in the city.

It was on a day when we were sitting like this and giggling that Henrik suddenly appeared before us on the flagstone pathway. I didn't notice him until Edith jumped up and threw her arms around his neck.

"Oh, sweetie," she chuckled proudly and the scene acquired a touch of something comical, because not only was she tiny, but the man she was hugging, ungainly in his dark-blue shorts and a white polo shirt, had to be six foot two. His clothes were slightly soiled, but clearly of good quality. I noticed there was no logo visible on his polo shirt.

On his wrist he wore a lovely watch that had certainly cost him a pretty penny. Dark hair, with bangs that were constantly sliding down over his forehead. He was tanned and looked like he spent a lot of time outdoors, on the water or in the forest or fields. Wise blue eyes. Kind of an eagle nose.

He reminded me of my father, in photographs from before me, before Agnes, before everything. But this guy had a natural authority about him that my father never had. His entire person emanated an air of security. I guess that's how people look when they've grown up in a home where they've wanted for nothing. When they've had stories read to them at bedtime throughout their entire childhood, never in doubt about being loved and that everything would turn out well for them in life.

"Grandmother," Henrik said, and hugged her, and I could see how he took care to do so gently. Edith was like a little bird with wings sticking out from her back. I was always afraid of breaking her when I hugged her.

"So, you're Grandmother's latest darling?" he said, and looked at me inquisitively. "I've heard about you."

"I've heard about you, too," I said, and it was true, even though I'd been more interested in what Edith told me about her son than about her grandson, who'd disappointed his father so.

"I can imagine," he said. "The black sheep, right, Grandmother?"

"Exactly right," Edith giggled, supremely satisfied. "Go find yourself a chair in the shed."

"I have plans, but I can sit for a minute," Henrik said, and then he brought out a chair and I found another glass and another bottle of wine.

He later rescheduled his appointment and Edith fell asleep in her deck chair, but Henrik was awake and I was awake, and he talked, and I talked, and the sun sank steadily lower between the tall trees.

And that's how the whole thing started, once upon a time long ago.

I hadn't planned on finding a boyfriend, particularly not then and there.

But I thought I ought to find somebody to be with at some point. Henrik was smart. He was studying to be a doctor, though he didn't talk about wanting to work for Doctors Without Borders, something I wouldn't have been able to bear. He had a calming effect on me. I liked curling up in his arms in the evening, leaning against him.

He was also good with children. I noticed that eventually when I saw him with the children of his friends. Besides, he was as handsome as a sculpture, but at the same time, his appearance was just tousled enough to save it from being too smooth, with his long bangs and beard stubble.

He was often a little rough when we had sex; nobody had ever behaved in that way with me before. Sometimes I could feel it on my skin the next day, that I was a bit sore, and I liked it. I walked around the reading room with the feeling that I had a secret. I would go into the stall of the lavatory, fold down my trousers or lift my sweater, studying small scrapes and bruises. It was as if I had been given new skin. A new body.

I felt like everyone must be able to see it on me, that I was somebody else. That something had happened.

When I enter the living room, I find Henrik sitting on the couch with his cell phone in his hand, watching the evening news on the TV.

"She's the one," he says, and nods toward the television, where Police Commissioner Cathrine Monrad is being interviewed in full uniform.

The woman is dynamic, visionary, has unmistakable integrity, and doesn't suffer fools. The media loves her. Munch does not.

"Damn sexy in uniform, basically . . . ," Henrik continues.

He says it with that crooked smile he uses to accompany such statements.

"Oh, come on," I say. "What a sexist comment."

But the woman *is* attractive; she looks tight-laced in her blue shirt and tie and jacket with gold insignia on the shoulders. Long blonde hair, stylish makeup.

"It's difficult to see the wisdom of this," she says, looking directly into the camera.

She is commenting on the proposal to combat gangs and violence on the east side by establishing locked institutions for juvenile delinquents. Along with an orphanage in Kabul for unaccompanied refugee minors, this is one of Anton Munch's more radical recent proposals.

Several of the critics have drawn parallels to the latest scandal from the US, where the president has approved the systematic separation of unauthorized immigrants from their own children, provoking outrage from the rest of the world.

Munch himself has no comment on the fact that the director of one of his own governmental agencies is expressing skepticism, the reporter concludes.

"Good thing somebody speaks up. There's no justice," Henrik says.

He still hasn't rid himself of this belief that the world is a just place.

"Justice doesn't exist, Henrik," I say. "You should know that by now. It'll be interesting to see how popular Monrad will be in the ministry now. But of course, it's bad. Institutionalized child abuse."

CHAPTER 11

ROGER

It feels slightly surreal that for the second time I'm sitting here giving a statement about a murder at my place of work.

"We know that Mukhtar Ahmad left the pediatrics unit at 9:35 p.m. to go to the prayer room and pray. It takes five minutes to walk there if you walk at a normal pace," the officer says.

Her voice is cool and professional.

Once more they begin by reading me my rights. I'm then asked to give an account of the events of that evening, which I do, without interruption.

They've clearly moved on to a phase in which they want to explore my statement in greater detail.

"You have previously explained that you were in the unit until your shift was over at 10:30 p.m. But the entrance log indicates that you used your card to enter the unit at 10:23. This makes it probable that you were out between 10 and 10:30?"

"I was out, but only for a little while," I say. My voice trembles, as do my hands. It hadn't occurred to me that they would check the entrance log.

"When did you say you went out?"

I try to remember. "Around 10:05, I think. I looked at my watch and realized I had less than a half hour of my shift to go. So, I felt like it was OK to go outside. I had to get hold of this guy. His son was brain dead and it was his fault. I wanted to do something concrete. Speak to him, get him to come back to the unit, take responsibility for his actions. Besides, sooner or later, he would have to address the question of organ donation. I wanted to prepare him for it, increase the chances of getting his consent. If another child could receive the boy's organs that would be *something* positive amid all the wretchedness."

She takes notes without commenting.

"But I *didn't* go looking for him so I could shoot him," I continue, suddenly desperate. "In fact, I've never held a weapon in my whole life, I swear. And when I saw him go into the prayer room, I turned around and went back to work. I thought I'd have to settle things with this guy later. I don't like Islam, but I still didn't want to confront the man while he was praying."

"And what time was it when Ahmad went into the prayer room and you turned around?"

"I don't know. Around 10:10?"

"But you didn't use your key card to enter the building again until 10:23. If your statements are correct, it took you thirteen minutes to walk from the prayer room back to the hospital, a distance you can cover in about five minutes at a normal walking pace. Unless you *didn't* leave Ahmad outside the prayer room but went into the prayer room behind him. Is that a possibility?"

I need to stay calm.

But something starts itching under my skin.

"What the hell, am I a suspect? Then you should tell me so, to my face. I've answered these questions before. Why do you keep harassing me?"

"We're talking to a lot of witnesses," she says, completely calm.

"But it's me you suspect, right? I've already explained where I was that night in detail; I don't have anything more to say."

"OK, let's change the subject," the older officer says. "Roger, can you tell us a little about your views on immigration from countries with a Muslim majority?"

"I'm against it, like most Norwegians. But when did that become a crime?"

He calmly studies me.

"Have you posted comments on the Rights.no and Document.no websites under the alias miketyson66?"

"Yes, but that really doesn't have anything to do with this."

He looks down at his papers, starts reading aloud.

"Well, let's see what 'miketyson66' writes on November 14, 2015, right after the terrorist attacks in Paris: 'The PC elite and mainstream media have hidden the truth. Muslims and ethnic Europeans will never manage to coexist. If nothing is done, if criminal Muslims and hateful imams are not returned to their countries of origin, the day will come when we ordinary Europeans will have to take matters into our own hands.'"

I feel myself getting agitated. I shake my head. "What kind of nonsense is this?"

"It's interesting that you also have another alias," the policeman continues. "A 'grorudgay66.' And 'grorudgay66' writes the following on the Gaydar.no website to 'babylonqueer': 'Are you from Iraq? I love being dominated by little Arab boys . . .' What do you mean by that?"

"This is way out of line," I say, and get to my feet.

"Please, sit down," the policewoman says.

I sit down but my voice is still shaky.

"Are you aware of what's going on out there? Ethnic Norwegian children are being bullied at school about their packed lunches. Muslim pupils have no respect for Norwegian adults, not even for the police. Ordinary people are terrified of walking hand in hand on the streets in Oslo. People who've drawn innocent cartoons are living in fear for their lives. And you're carrying on and pestering *me*? It's ludicrous. *I* haven't killed anyone! Good Lord, I'm a nurse. I save lives!"

CHAPTER 12

HENRIK

We're summoned to a staff meeting with just a few hours' notice. Everyone here was also working on the night of the murder, except Askildsen, who turned up later.

"I've asked you to come here because I think a briefing might be useful," Askildsen says. He seems uncomfortable. "First, let me explain briefly what is happening from the police's side, at least what I've noted. Right after the murder, a provisional central control room was set up; you've all stopped by there. This has now been moved to the police station. The staff is made up of forensic investigators and a tactical team. They are working against the clock to investigate the circumstances surrounding the victim, searching for witnesses and trying to get an overview of the timeline. The objective is to map out all movement on the hospital grounds that night to determine the whereabouts of everyone involved during the time period in question. They're working to come up with a reconstruction of the events that night. You may be asked for your help."

People nod but don't comment. I glance at the trees outside the big windows of the administration building.

As a child I thought that Ullevål Hospital was a castle.

My mother and father laughed at me, but I was always happy to catch a glimpse of the reddish-brown brick castle when we drove past.

Before long I learned that the tower, the beautiful trees, the plants, and the benches were originally all installed as fortification from infection. In the days around the time of the opening of the hospital in 1887, a diphtheria and scarlet fever epidemic was raging in the city, and after five days the unit was already full of patients; apparently, each doctor had had responsibility for ninety-two beds.

My knowledge about architecture is something I got from my grandmother Edith, who had always dreamed of being an architect and who made me want to create beautiful buildings like Nordan and Schirmer had done at Ullevål.

Throughout my entire childhood, Father hoped and believed that I would follow in his footsteps, ascending all the many paragraph-strewn steps leading to the high seat of the law. But after I had surgery for a ruptured appendix and almost died, my calling became neither the law nor architecture, but medicine. I wanted to do something useful.

Since then my father has made it clear that I disappointed him when I chose another profession. Of course, he doesn't say it in so many words, but it's hard not to pick up on his jabs.

"Questions?" Askildsen says, when he has finished the briefing.

"What if it happens again? What's really going on now? And won't we be receiving any crisis counseling? There's been a murder at our place of work," says Roger, who seems unusually agitated and stressed today.

"I don't know," Askildsen says. "But I'll look into it."

"This just shows how bad things are in this city," Roger continues.

It's all I can do to keep from groaning loudly. Roger is the only person I know who reads the articles on indie media sites and the Human Rights Service website. He's always going on about the kids in Groruddalen who aren't allowed to have salami on their sandwiches.

"Will you give it a rest," Sabiya says, sending Roger an irritated glance. "You wanted to see the guy dead and buried—we all did."

The room fell silent.

"Do you know whether the abuse of Faisal Ahmad will be investigated?" Sabiya continues, trying to gloss over her last remark. She must still be distraught; usually, she wouldn't be so sharp with Roger.

"It appears so," Askildsen says.

"What about the boy's mother, will she be arrested as an accessory?" I ask, mostly just to say something.

"It seems like she's under investigation, yes, based on the questions they're asking. And the family is receiving follow-up care."

"But how are we supposed to feel safe at our workplace after this?" Bente says, echoing Roger's comments. "It can happen again, at any time."

"Well," Askildsen says. "I don't think you need to worry about that."

"You don't *think* so," Bente says, and shakes her head. "That's comforting . . ."

"It seems like an isolated event, presumably connected to the guy's social environment. Still, it's important to think about whether you have anything you can contribute, something you've seen or heard. Anything that *could* be of interest—speak up. It's better to contact the police once too often. Leave the filtering and sorting of information to them. And remember, it's in our best interest that the case be solved."

When the meeting is over, I walk across the hospital grounds.

After wearing out my clogs on the linoleum floor of this hospital for ten years, I've concluded that I was mistaken about what I saw from Kirkeveien Street at the age of five.

Ullevål is no castle.

On the inside, these venerable buildings are run down, ugly.

The interiors of the newer buildings are nice enough, but the exteriors are horrendous, as if someone had scraped together the cheapest materials they could find and assembled them in a haphazard heap. It mostly resembles an airport under construction. Buildings everywhere, big, small, old, new.

And an enormous number of people.

I believe we have close to ten thousand employees. It is the largest hospital in Northern Europe, a tiny society all its own. And there's a pretty tough work environment, a battle for prestige, positions—and for something as mundane as permanent posts.

At least one-third of the doctors are overly ambitious fools, and because of them another third are often out on sick leave, and then you have the rest of us, who are hovering somewhere in between, gritting our teeth, working, and slandering each other only now and then.

On the way to my office, I check the internet on my phone. On the online newspaper *VG Nett*, under the breaking news headline "Gangster Murder," there's a picture of the guy.

> Mukhtar Ahmad, raised in the Oslo neighborhood of Grünerløkka, had apparently been a well-known fig-ure in the city's gang community of the early 2000s. Sources tell *VG* that many people may have had a mo-tive for killing him. Judging from the bullets and cali-ber, it has been established that the murder weapon, which has still not been found, is the kind of firearm that is common in the victim's social environment. Presumably, there was a silencer installed on the gun.

The newspaper also reports that the police are going through the records of all weapons dealers to try to link the weapon to someone.

The expanding bullets are not mentioned. The media must not have picked up on that yet.

A kind of film is still playing on my retina.

Now it stops in a specific place and the image freezes.

Mukhtar Ahmad didn't carry his son to the emergency room. He carried him to us.

He knew where he was going. He'd been at the pediatrics unit before.

I should do some work on my article about child leukemia. There are three of us, all doctors, who are writing it together, and my name will come first. Last week I received some comments on the first draft from the others, and they are expecting to receive a revised draft from me as soon as possible.

But when I sit down at my office desk, I can't even bring myself to open the document.

Instead, I read the boy's file thoroughly. Then I do a search for his name in the database.

Bingo. Four more hits. I open the first one, read. I open the second one, read.

In the third one I see something that causes me to lean forward and squint. I take out the little boy's file again and check.

What the hell.

> Faisal Ahmad (born 2014): 04.09.2017: subdural hematoma over the left hemisphere with blood components of different ages. Comminuted occipital bone fracture (left side). There were also multiple nondisplaced posterior costal fractures, 2nd–5th, right side. Bruises of various ages on the chest and back.

The boy was here before. Just thirteen months ago.

I return to the database. Not only has he been here before, but his sister as well.

I read about this boy and his sister, and about all the other families who return again and again.

I read about a boy who came in full of scratches and stings and skin abrasions, whose father had forced him to ride his bike through a wild rose hedge.

About children with deep, bloody flesh wounds running down their spinal cords where they were scraped with a coin to drive out evil spirits.

About children with cuts behind their ears from having been restrained and forced to perform oral sex or with mouth injuries from being force-fed.

About children with many identical scars from being hit with a baseball bat.

About children with sores on their buttocks because they'd been lowered into scalding hot water.

I read and read until I become ill.

It becomes increasingly clear to me why Clara has been unwavering in her certainty that her bill is a good idea. Up until now I've been skeptical; I felt that her intentions were good, but that the bill goes too far and violates the right to privacy. From my father I've learned to hold the banners of protection of privacy and individual freedom high.

Cases like those I'm reading about are reported to the police and child services, who in turn are supposed to respond quickly. However, everyone knows there are recurring cases, that there must be a flaw in the system, or many flaws. We live with it because we don't think there's anything we can do. But maybe we have a choice. Maybe I owe it to Faisal Ahmad to try.

As I shut down my computer, I understand what I must do, what must be done. I must become a whistleblower.

CHAPTER 13

Clara

I stand on the veranda on the first floor looking at the view.

Far off in the distance I can see Oslo Fjord, which is hazy and grayish blue and almost blends into the huge sky.

A bit closer, like a dark-gray stripe with many small dots on it, is the city.

The view knocked me over the first time I came here, when Henrik's parents still lived in the house. Now I've lived here myself for almost ten years. The best part is that we can see the ocean, a kind of bridge over to my father's farm where I grew up, with a panoramic view of the fjord.

It took me many years to understand that for people like Henrik's family, an untamed garden is a mark of nobility. A well-groomed Hollywood garden is cheesy, period. In that sense we are doing well, because neither of us has time to putter around.

The perennials fortunately take care of themselves. The first lilacs are now in bloom; this year they are earlier than ever before.

In June the peonies come.

Both strains have survived five or six generations. The same holds true for the gnarled old apple trees.

"An extremely attractive and traditional residential district at Vinderen," the listing would read if we were to sell. Centrally located but still secluded on Haakon den Godes Road.

The driveway is hidden by a tall hedge, and the houses are situated in such a way as to ensure privacy. The residents can come and go without having their movements tracked by the neighbors.

I turn around and go inside. The bedroom is my favorite room: square, a high ceiling, with the same stucco finish found in all the rooms. Old windows. A balcony. The floor is painted white. White, diaphanous curtains, a wicker chair, an oak chest of drawers, otherwise extremely spacious.

Airy, clean, neat, just the way I like it.

On the work side of my walk-in closet, I have ten silk blouses. All of these are in muted colors. Four or five black, dark-gray, or dark-blue pairs of trousers. Two or three skirts.

Twice a year I go to a store where I know I will find things to my taste, clothing by designers like Hugo Boss and Donna Karan. Or I go to the stores on the upscale shopping street Hegdehaugsveien. Massimo Dutti. Filippa K. Clothing with understated elegance and quality. Always a single color, classic garments, often in linen, silk, cotton. The minimal amount of visual busyness and distraction.

Keep it simple. Then I'm spared having to spend time and energy on shopping.

I now choose a Filippa K suit, trousers and a jacket in dark-blue linen, and a white silk top underneath.

I blow-dry my hair, put on my makeup, spray myself with the exclusive perfume from my mother-in-law, purchased at a perfume farm in Grasse or something like that.

At my first interview at the ministry fifteen years ago, I'd turned up in an expensive suit in a cut befitting a mature woman that I'd bought at a high-end shopping mall with what remained of my student loan. I was used to going to the reading room wearing jeans and a sweater, and I felt like I was wearing a costume.

Nonetheless, I wore the same suit on my first day on the job.

It turned out that the other young executive officers dressed pretty much the way we had at law school. Jeans, a sweater, maybe a blouse or a skirt, at the most a suit jacket. But otherwise *casual, casual, casual.*

On the second day I was about to follow their lead but changed my mind at the last minute and put on a black skirt and a dark-blue polo sweater with the new suit jacket over it.

Dress sharp, think sharp.

It's a means of gaining authority, which I have maintained. At home I just wear jeans, T-shirts, hoodies.

It's 8:00 a.m. when I walk through the reception area, where a television crew is setting up. At the gate I swipe my card, walk in, wait, walk out, and head for the elevator.

The doors open and out walks Munch and his political adviser. The cabinet minister looks up, smiles at me, and I nod back. He must be the person the television crew is waiting for.

The media coverage has changed completely in the course of my time here.

The people from the press are more aggressive. There's a greater focus on errors. And the pace is much quicker, twenty-four hours a day. Even large-scale press conferences can be organized while racing through the corridors to meet with the media.

I enter the elevator Munch just stepped out of. Up on the ninth floor, I swipe my card once more, go into my office, take my laptop out of my bag, and put it in the docking station. While the computer is booting up, I go get some coffee in the hallway before I sit down, skim the online newspapers, and look through press clippings.

And suddenly, he's standing in the doorway. The cabinet minister *himself.*

"Don't get up," he says as I start to stand. "But do you have a minute?"

"Yes," I say, nodding toward the visitor's chair, and looking at him expectantly. Munch is responsible for many initiatives. Even the tiniest of problems must be solved, and he is highly visible. It gives him a good rating in the newspapers. For the moment. But he lacks the ability to prioritize, and he allows the pressure from the media to set the agenda so he can score cheap points. This kind of thing tends to be spotted at some point. And then you're forgotten. Since he shelved my bill, I hope it will happen to him soon.

"Well, Clara, we haven't had the chance to talk properly about your bill. As you know, I thought I would manage to get it passed," he says, folding his hands and cracking his knuckles, a sound I abhor. A thin wedding ring on his finger. I've never seen his wife, other than in pictures from dinners at the Royal Palace, which he apparently hates to attend. "Even though your bill was *not* very popular here in this corridor. Several of your superiors came by my office to object. But you didn't let that affect you. That's a little unusual, I have to say."

And that's when I understand.

He is here to explain to me that I must leave. Or be transferred. To some dull, out-of-the-way department, so they will be rid of me.

He is of course not responsible for it. It will presumably take place through a covert reorganization that involves only one or two people. But he knows it will happen and indirectly has given his blessing in order to calm down all those who are up in arms over the bill. It's to his credit, as it were, that he's come here to communicate this to me in person. He must really have a guilty conscience.

"It's not very pleasant here these days, is it?" he says, giving me a searching look. "That must mean this is not the right place for you, Clara. You're too qualified to wander around here wasting time."

"I see," I say, squirming in my chair. More than anything I want to ask him to leave; I can't bear to sit here listening to him spin my dismissal into a unique opportunity in a manner befitting a true politician.

"The time has come for you to move on. You understand what I mean."

"I think so, yes," I say, and pick at the blotter on my desk. I will very likely be sent to the administration department, to a dusty planning position.

"Well, what are your thoughts?"

"As if I have anything to say about it," I say while staring out the window at the top stories of The Highrise.

"Ha ha, now I think you're overestimating my power. I'm not forcing you, of course."

"You're not forcing me to do what?" I ask, because now I want the man to get out of my office, cabinet minister or not. He's sitting there with his right foot nonchalantly resting on his left knee, wiggling the brown leather shoe. Munch was apparently a promising soccer player in his day.

"Woll's leaving," he says. His tone says that he enjoys surprising me.

"Wow," I say. I didn't see that coming. "Where's he going?"

"Finance."

"I see."

The best of them often disappear into the Ministry of Finance, if they're not headhunted for director posts in the private sector. At the ministry they are transformed overnight into the minister of Finance's armor-bearers in the fight to keep the purse strings securely knotted. It's equally fascinating every time.

"And yes," Munch says, and sighs. "It's a shame of course. But when I found out, I thought, why not do something else . . . if you know what I mean."

"Not really."

"Well . . . to tell you the truth, I was wondering if you would like to be my new state secretary?"

"Me?" I say. "Are you kidding me?"

"No," he says, chuckling. "You're talented, Clara. Besides, you're a woman . . . But no, *that's* not why," he says disarmingly, no doubt because he notices the expression on my face. "That's just one plus among many. Mostly it's a matter of an undefinable X factor. I'm good at spotting such things. You have all the specialized knowledge and experience a good civil servant should have. But at the same time, you have a will for change and you're tough, you're different. You want something, unlike many others. So, what do you say, would that be of interest?"

He is certain I will accept, I can see that, no matter how unconventional his request may be.

A civil servant promoted to state secretary. It's happened before. But not often.

"Well, maybe you'd like to discuss it with your family? That's fine, of course. But I hope you will give it serious consideration?"

"I'll think about it, yes . . ."

"Great! Just don't think too long. I can't hang on to Woll for much longer."

". . . but I don't think it's of interest," I finish, and his smile fades a bit.

State secretary? For Munch? Not even if hell freezes over.

CHAPTER 14

HENRIK

All these things that I thought I would never do.

Now it feels natural. And right.

When I reach Frognerseteren, I walk down the path running below the metro line. This is part of our regular Strava route. Down and across. There's a fork in the path farther up the hill where we meet. I sit down on a stone beside the path below the hill and take out my cell phone.

Three minutes until her train arrives.

It takes three minutes to walk down here.

A total of six minutes until she's here. And then we'll walk off the main path for about a minute, until we reach a smaller path that nobody knows about.

Strava is a brilliant, watertight mode of communication.

If, against all odds, Clara were to stumble upon DOCTORH, she won't find MRSSPLENDID. Because of course, the two of us don't follow one another. But we do give each other kudos, a thumbs-up, or comment on each other's posts from time to time. Of course, in an apparently innocent code language.

What's brilliant is that Clara doesn't know the identities of MRSSPLENDID or DOCTORH. The two of them never call one another. No text messages from a fake male alias, nothing that can give us away. We're not even Facebook friends, though we've considered it. It almost seems more suspicious not to be.

All these rules, first and foremost to protect *her*, but also for my own sake.

I now peer impatiently up toward the metro stop longing to see her, to hold her, and to finally have the chance to talk about everything that's happened. The brief period when we're lying in each other's arms and talking is usually the nicest part of all.

Almost a year has passed since it began, quietly and discreetly, in contrast to the hookups I've had in recent years, quick fucks after an evening on the town, because I deserved it after putting up with an increasingly frigid wife for all these years.

The problem with quick fucks is that they are seldom particularly successful. It's only in films that people have fantastic sex with complete strangers against the wall of a bathroom. In fact, it's often more bother than it's worth. Most of the women I end up seeing only once.

When I met Clara, she liked sex. She was inexperienced but curious, eager to learn. Those days seem remote now. Had she been another type of woman, I would have assumed she had found a lover or maybe become a lesbian. But I think that she just isn't interested, not in me and not in others, not erotically or in any other way.

I knew the woman I'm waiting for before I met Clara.

We used to sit together in the lecture hall, in the first row, write papers together, hang out together in breaks. I never made a move. Not because I was inhibited with the ladies—at the time I plowed through just about everyone in my path. It was a sport for me. But like most Oslo guys my age, I treated Pakistani girls with a kind of deference.

They were forbidden fruit. Moroccan girls, yes, or Turkish or Indian.

Never Pakistani.

During our final semester she married a guy from Karachi whom her parents had found and promoted as a modern man from the city. She'd hated this, of course.

Ten years after our graduation we met again in the unit at Ullevål and threw our arms around one another in mutual joy over the reunion. By then she at least had permission to work.

We've now been walking down the same hallways for two years.

At first, she was just a sweet, fun colleague. Wise. Quick. And sharp-witted in her comments. I liked her but that was it. Until one day we worked the same shift and were giggling about something an opinionated mother had said. And as we stood there, all tired and grubby, she suddenly stood on tiptoe and kissed me.

"Wow," I said.

Wow. How stupid. As if I were one of my sons and not my father's son.

But she just laughed, and that laughter has lit up my life the past year.

Unlike Clara, she's warm, loving, and interested in me. I deserve someone who understands me, cares about me. But lately I've been wondering whether, against all reason and all my intentions, I'm in the process of falling in love. *That* was never part of the plan.

All the women I've had contact with during the past couple of years have had one thing in common. They've wanted more from me than I've been willing to give. No feelings, only sex, has been my mantra. This is different.

Now, finally, she's walking down the path toward me.

A tiny dot, larger all the time.

It's always a little peculiar, this transition, from colleagues to lovers, but usually the awkwardness lasts only for a minute or two. A good thing, because we don't have a lot of time. We must make our way down to Lake Sognsvann by way of the back roads, take different trains, and return to the hospital separately. But we have time to lie in the heath for a half hour, on a hill where only the sun can find us.

The dot grows larger and larger. And then she's standing in front of me, wearing Adidas running shoes, jeans, and a denim jacket. This is

71

not MRSSPLENDID's evening route. She's far from home and the running shoes are unnecessary. But all the same, we log our weekly meeting as fitness activity on Strava. Should there be any questions, we can say that we were using the allotted exercise time included in our working hours. That was her idea. She's smart. That's also what her name means.

Sabiya. The brilliant one.

"I'm going home for a few days," Clara says the same evening.

"Home? To Western Norway?" I ask, and she nods in response.

Clara always says *home* about Western Norway, even though I've tried to point out that home must be the place where you live and work and have your husband and children.

"Apparently, Dad's not well."

Clara and her father are virtually symbiotic. It's often that way when the mother dies. I like Leif, but he's not as tough as his daughter. You should have met him before, Clara always says. Before Lebanon. But I've always thought that if Leif were as strong as Clara, he would have been able to endure Lebanon as well.

"How so?" I ask.

"I don't know exactly," she says, and disappears out onto the balcony.

"OK," I say to her back. "We'll manage, I guess. Since you're asking so nicely."

She doesn't answer. She never does.

Managing without Clara for a few days isn't a problem. We're used to it. I can call in my mother. And I have things to take care of.

My home office is on the second floor, right next to our bedroom, across the hallway from the boys' room.

The built-in oak bookshelves along two of the walls have been there since this was my father's room and I was just a pip-squeak who lay under the table and tried to be quiet so he wouldn't throw me out.

On the shelves are my heroes: Hamsun, Bjørneboe, and Hemingway, in addition to the guiltier reading pleasures of my youth, such as Forsyth and Follett.

There's a huge desk in the middle of the room. A cabinet, a couch, and an armchair, all from the deceased industrial designer Fredrik Kayser's original production. In his day, Kayser lived here in Vinderen and was hired to build furnishings for the houses in the neighborhood. He made the most sedate, stylish pieces; it was a shame that he died at such a young age. Now several furniture companies have started reproducing his furniture, although he wasn't as mainstream as Wegner, Jacobsen, and other famous designers.

I sit down at my desk, turn on the green lawyer's lamp, and open my work computer. I log on smoothly and adeptly and create a new document.

Everything starts with the little boy, Faisal Ahmad.

To be shot in the head, quickly and painlessly, is a fate better than Mukhtar Ahmad deserved. The guy should have been slowly tortured to death, and the same goes for his buddies in Oslo and throughout the country.

I can't make that happen on my own, of course.

But I can, and will, make my contribution, demonstrate that the system fails.

I will collect evidence showing we see children from the same families over and over again, children we've never sounded the alarm about.

There are many recurring cases. God only knows how many there are. The details must be made more specific. Reported in black and white, with as much documentation as possible.

A paragraph about Faisal Ahmad. A paragraph about his six-year-old sister who was brought in one year ago.

Today I've added a new case, a woman named Susanne Stenersen. Her eldest daughter was brought in with a broken arm and dislocated shoulder and other strange injuries. The youngest boy has been brought in with head injuries and burns that were very likely caused by his being immersed in scalding bathwater. There are suspicions the mother is getting high and leaving the children at home alone.

These children have been through the hospital system four times, yet they still live with their mother. It's incomprehensible.

One of the names on the list I've seen before.

Melika Omid Carter, a nightlife celebrity. I remember her from the Løkka neighborhood in the old days. She's been to the emergency room twice, the first time twelve years ago, with a little baby girl for whom there were suspicions of shaken baby syndrome.

I sit there staring at my father's bookshelves.

When I was about the same age as my boys are now, he'd worked intensively for what felt like years to prove that a man was wrongly convicted in a murder case.

He managed it, against all odds. And I was proud of him, of course.

But what I remember best was the comment he made afterward: "It's a brutal world out there, you know, which you will never understand."

How little and spoiled I felt, then. He has always been large and important. I haven't.

Now I, too, can make a difference, for once.

There's no point in presenting this to Askildsen, or to anyone over his head. They must know this is how it is. They've come to accept it.

No, this must go to the media. That's the most effective way.

People think that journalists come up with all these so-called muckraking articles on their own. I know that isn't true because of Axel's ex-wife, Caroline. They were one of the few couples we used to have regular contact with; Axel and I are lifelong friends from Ivar Aasens Road. Clara isn't very sociable. Since their divorce we see only Axel, but Caro, a journalist, explained to me that when a national daily newspaper writes a story about pedophilia, it's because the police have planted it.

Almost everything comes from somewhere. Because someone wants to spotlight something, draw attention to something.

I will have to run this by Clara. After all she does work on these things. Maybe it can be a joint project. I miss our evening conversations. The evening after the night of the murder was a rare exception, and then it was only partly successful.

I am reasonably certain that Sabiya will appreciate my getting involved.

People's motives for doing what they do are seldom unambiguous. We do the things we do both because we want to do something good, make the world a slightly better place, but also because it's something that benefits us personally.

CHAPTER 15

CLARA

I drive across bridges. Through tunnels. More tunnels. The closer I come to my village, the more frequently I encounter stretches of road where there's room for only one car at a time, where at all times I must be prepared to wait for an oncoming car, or in the worst case, to back up.

I've hooked the car radio up to a playlist of driving music. One classic tune after the next. Nena, Kate Bush, Tanita Tikaram, and Blondie.

Blondie is a favorite.

I'm a little stuck in the music I listened to as a teenager. Since then I haven't really had time to keep up. But it's not just women—I also have Tom Petty, Dire Straits, Bruce Springsteen, old favorites that I share with Dad.

I like listening to music when I'm driving, but seldom otherwise and never when I'm out running.

Now Roxy Music comes on.

I sing along, press the accelerator a tad closer to the floor.

On my left-hand side there's a steep hillside plummeting down into the fjord. And the fjord itself, its greenish color that always makes my stomach drop.

I drive past *that* place and avoid looking to the side as I always do.

Here there's only empty space on the other side of the guardrail that has been installed. But otherwise, the edges of the ditches are colorful.

Wood cranesbill, forget-me-nots, dandelions, and buckthorn. And green, green, green.

Early in the summer, like now, it's possible to drive here. It's worse midsummer, when the long lines of campers are backed up and at a standstill. The number has exploded in the past few decades, while the roads are just as narrow.

There, now I'm almost home, just another six miles to go: the ferry trip.

The jaws opening. The grooves on the floor of the ferry under the tires of my car. The hand brake on.

I go outside to stand in the blasting wind, look over the concrete edge painted white and down into the fjord, take in the feeling of the fresh air and raindrops against my face, and watch the green water foaming around the vessel, swirling in an icy, wet crescendo as the ferry surges forward.

In the background I can hear the loud rumbling of the ferry engines. I can smell the diesel exhaust as I watch the staff wandering around in their coveralls, as they do day in and day out, year in, year out.

I never go down to the café; the smell of coffee, hot dogs, and fried food in the stuffy, little, rocking room makes me queasy. People's nostalgic relationship to ferry cafés and the thick griddle cakes they serve is something I've never understood.

All the same, it's as though something inside me that is always switched off in Oslo is switched on here, between the mountains, along the fjord.

Something opens up, the way the jaws of the ferry open up after twenty minutes of droning passage and release the cars, the way the fjord opens up at its widest point where you turn onto the road leading up to our farm, which is located a short distance up the hill from the fjord—in a valley, but with a view of the fjord.

I'm not going there yet.

Instead, I drive into the parking lot below the hospital in the neighboring village, the hospital they are always threatening to close, and because of which the locals are constantly organizing demonstrations, demanding it be kept open.

I stop the car and wait a second or two before I get out. The car, which had been shiny and clean when I left, is covered with a fine layer of dust from the road.

My father is sitting in a Stressless recliner in his room with the television on. It appears to be a documentary of some kind from the US, but the sound is off. His legs are on a footstool, his feet crossed. He has a book in his lap, and a cup of coffee on the tiny table beside him. His glasses are on the end of his nose and he is wearing a T-shirt and jeans.

He glances up in surprise.

"Clara? Are you here?" he says, and touches my face with his hands.

Are his eyes shiny? A stroke can apparently make people more sensitive. But otherwise, he looks the same. He puts down the remote control and the Clive Cussler book, supports himself on the arms of the chair, and tries to stand.

And then I can see it, see how he's struggling with his balance, how he gets stuck halfway up, his legs trembling beneath him.

I grasp his arm under the elbow, help him up into a standing position, push away the footstool to make more room for him, put my arms around his neck, and take in the lovely scent of my father. Shampoo, Neutrogena, Nivea, or whatever it is he puts on his face, his wool sweater, and the nicotine chewing gum he's tormented himself with since he quit smoking.

"Sit down now," I say, and try to guide him back toward the chair.

Daddy. In room 27. In an adjustable bed, with an alarm on a cord, and a nightstand on wheels. On top of it a bowl of grapes, a newspaper, and a remote control. A wheelchair-accessible lavatory, fluorescent lights, and a linoleum floor.

"Are we going home tonight?" he asks.

"Wait," I say, taking his hands between my own. They are surprisingly cold and smaller than I remember. He's always had powerful working hands, tanned, regardless of the season. Now they feel weak. And they have liver spots on them, as if he were an old man.

"Let me go home alone first, do some shopping, make sure that everything's OK, and then I'll come get you tomorrow. Then it will be less stressful for the staff here as well."

He thinks a little, nods, looks down hesitantly.

"Will you be home for a while?"

"I'll have to see," I say, even though three nights is very likely the most I will manage. Then Henrik will be attending a seminar at Lysebu. I've taken a few days of compassionate leave. I've never done that before, never even had a single sick day.

I should just take my father home now, so I can spend as much time as possible with him, but I need an evening alone—to sit there in the silence, look out across the fjord, think over Munch's wild proposal and what I'm going to do about everything from here on in.

"I saw something on television about a murder at Ullevål Hospital?" he says.

So, he's pretty alert after all.

"Yes, the victim was the father of one of Henrik's patients. He's been a little concerned about it, naturally," I say, and regret it immediately. Henrik has always been a bit lax when it comes to professional secrecy with me, but I've always been careful not to pass on any of the information. "I'm going to go see if I can find someone who works here. Then I'll come back, OK?"

He nods.

"Clara," he says, reaching out his hands toward me. "You shouldn't have come all this way for my sake, even though it's nice to have you here."

I lean down and give him a little kiss.

"You and me, you know, Daddy."

"Yes," he says, and smiles, but then his face darkens. He's still holding my hand, as if to hold me in place. "But, Clara, one thing . . ."

"Yes?" I can hear that something is coming that he dreads telling me.

"I received a phone call from Kleivhøgda the day before this happened . . ."

A cold shiver goes through me.

What does that mean? Is my mother finally dead?

"Agnes," he says, stalling, taking a deep breath, collecting himself. "She's started talking. She's remembering more all the time."

A second passes. Two.

Acute nausea. Hands trembling.

And then I'm there.

The car barrels over the cliff, hits the water with a bang. My head is thrown forward, hard, and then back again. The water gushes in.

Everything starts over. Again and again.

PART 2

PART 2.

CHAPTER 16

LEIF

1975

One day in June, as I waited for a package that was supposed to arrive on the bus from town, she stepped off instead, with that long hair and wearing a full-length skirt.

She looked around her in wonder, as if it were just by chance that she'd gotten off the bus right there. I stood watching her and smoking and thought she was the most beautiful creature I had ever seen and that she was not a person somebody the likes of me could speak to. When *she* spoke to me, it turned out she had in fact gotten off the bus at the wrong stop, scatterbrain that she was. She'd arrived at the exact place where the fjord was so very deep and the hillside so very steep and the road curved up toward the valley where my farm was, at the far end.

It was the kind of shimmering, misty day when the mountain and the fjord are almost the same dark shade of blue, and in between everything is green, so green, and the mountain peaks are white. Yes, everything was showing itself to its very best advantage. And the next bus would not arrive for a long time. So she accompanied me up to the farm and I forgot about everything I'd planned to do that afternoon, the animals that had to be tended to, the fence I was going to put up, the grass I was going to mow.

Agnes didn't take the bus on that day or the next.

She moved in with what she'd had in her bag: a couple of skirts, a couple of blouses, sandals, a hairbrush. My parents were dead; the farm and the house were mine. I didn't have to ask anyone for permission to allow her to stay. We didn't discuss it between us either.

She just stayed.

Her legs proved to be surprisingly long and tan under her skirt. In the evenings she fell asleep on my arm. She would often lie there for so long that my arm was numb and stiff the next day, but I never said anything about it. During the night I often awoke to find her kneeling naked on the bed, sweeping her long blonde hair across my face.

In my recollections of that summer, the birds were always singing and the sun was always shining. *Gentle* was the first thing I thought about her; she was so transparent, so gossamer and nimble. And then there was her sense of wonder. Pretty soon, I discovered there were many layers to her. And a strong will. I liked that as well.

So, one day, just a year after she stepped off the bus down by the fjord, at the hospital in the little town an hour and a half away from us, Agnes and I became a mother and father.

It was a girl. She was delivered by cesarean section, and for that reason I was the one who held her during the first hours of her life. She was so small, her head almost disappeared into my hand.

Klara would be her name, after my mother. I had made up my mind about that. But for some reason or other Agnes insisted on the English spelling, Clara. I tried to object, but it was futile. So, Clara it was, even though I found it foreign and strange. Clara with a *C*, as Agnes always said.

Agnes was so tired at first, it was as if everything had shifted a tiny bit inside her, between us. It was difficult to explain it in any other way.

"I can take her if you want to sleep," I said, nodding at the baby, and she accepted gratefully. She nursed and slept, nursed and slept, but struggled with it. Her nipples were sore, her nipples bled, her breasts leaked, like a cow with an udder infection but worse.

When Clara wasn't being nursed by her mother, either I sat in the rocking chair by the window holding her against my chest and looking out across the fjord below or I would walk around the farm with her. Because the work never went away. The animals still had to be cared for and fed, the roof had to be repaired. There was the harvest and the haying, the clearing work and the sheep shearing, things in need of fixing, sealing, repairs, those kinds of things. And Clara came with me.

I hardly slept at night and not at all during the day. I should have been exhausted but wasn't. I just walked around smiling, couldn't get enough of looking at her as she lay sleeping in her baby carriage.

Just think, they're mine, Clara and her mother. My little flock. I would always look after them.

Still, it did worry me a bit that it was almost as if Agnes didn't see her little girl. Now and then she would get down on her knees and babble with her a bit, make faces at her. Clara's entire little face would light up. But it seemed it was all too much for her mother, who would sort of shut down, withdraw into herself, sit there without moving or saying a word. And Clara would begin to squirm and struggle, waving her arms, emitting small cries.

Usually, in the end I would walk over and pick her up, playing airplane with her, making her gurgle and laugh. And then everything was sheer bliss. But sometimes I wondered how things were when I wasn't around. And eventually, it was more and more seldom that I saw Agnes try to speak with Clara. The child sat in her baby rocker and waved her arms while her mother floated around in her own world, absorbed in her own musings.

I started taking the baby with me everywhere. At first, she sat on my shoulders. But it wasn't long before she was running by herself across the yard, on the hills, in the barn, everywhere. No matter where I went, she was at my heels, wearing overalls and sneakers. On her head she wore a sun hat like my own green hat from the state farming cooperative.

Long before she had learned how to talk, I started talking to her. I explained everything I did and why I did it. Eventually, she started asking. About the trees on the hills, about the water in the brook, about the ants in the anthill, and the stars, and the clouds, and everything that was.

The days went by like this, like an ongoing conversation between us. One day I could tell her that she was going to become a big sister.

A baby was growing inside her mommy's tummy and would get big inside there, until one day he or she would come out and would be a little person, would be one of us, part of our little family.

The baby came, had fingers and toes and earlobes and teeny-tiny eyelashes. He was quieter than Clara, sleeping away most of the day. His mother did, too. I was the one who looked after him, dressed him, and drove down to the village with him in the back seat when I dropped Clara off at day care. We had agreed on that, Agnes and I, that it would be good for Clara to go there, meet other children, even though the two of us, her parents, were home all day long.

She came home with drawings and Play-Doh sculptures and heart ornaments made of beads and an abundance of stories. I had been afraid she would be odd like her mother, but when I saw how open she was, how she absorbed the world, I breathed a sigh of relief.

Agnes often stayed in bed until midday, with her back to me and the duvet between her legs, turning to face me briefly only when I came in holding Lars in my arms.

The days came and went, and Lars got so big that I dropped him off at day care as well in the morning. Then the two of them stood side by side just inside the doorway and waved at me.

Clara with her blonde, curly hair in little pigtails on either side, pigtails I had braided that very morning.

Lars with his hair in a tangle, sticking up every which way.

Agnes started getting out of bed. She took a correspondence course, wanted to get an education, she said. Sometimes she came outside and worked with me.

Life was good.

A lot of the responsibility did fall on my shoulders, but every evening when I finally sat down in my new leather armchair, I thought about how lucky I was to have these small, warm creatures who were mine.

CHAPTER 17

CLARA

I sit down in Daddy's shabby, light-brown leather armchair and look out the window.

The final remnants of winter are clinging in white patches to the sides of the mountain. Sheep and lambs are grazing on the green hills. The lambs are at their sweetest now, energetic, giddy, but still so small. Even in here I can hear them baaing and bleating. They are calling for their mothers. And the mothers respond.

A belt of lush forest land budding spring green lies below the hills.

And then, farther down is the fjord, which from here looks like a gray-blue carpet, but which I know is glittering and sparkling in the early evening sunlight.

The fjord. You can never anticipate how deep it is—it could be thirty feet, three hundred, three thousand, the fjord with its many huge fish and porpoises and old car wrecks and God knows what.

The fjord is its own master. I can't conquer it once it has made up its mind. Now mining sludge is being dumped into all the fjords and plastic floats into every inlet, but I imagine that even so, the fjord remains the most powerful. And the most dangerous.

The fjord is mine. Everything here is mine. Safe. And at the same time, not safe at all.

"Good Lord" was all I could say when Daddy told me about Mom earlier.

It is apparently quite common to suffer memory loss after electric shock therapy, the way she did a long time ago. I read up on it, followed along, and learned that the development of this form of treatment is quite peculiar and surprising.

The number of electric shock treatments administered is on the rise, often without consent. A man suffering a midlife crisis had been given an electric shock treatment after a short period of minor depression and awoke with no memory of the past twenty-five years. He had no memory of his wife and children. Naturally, he was deeply upset about having lost his entire life, his history.

Maybe Mom felt the same way. Maybe she was indifferent. I have no idea; I have never really known her.

For the past thirty years I haven't even seen her.

"The woman who called wanted us to visit Agnes, she thought it would do her good," Daddy had added.

"Good Lord . . ."

"Yeah, it's probably out of the question."

"It is," I said. "Have you been there at all?"

"To the home? No. Have you?"

His face wrinkled into furrows, like an old mountain.

"Never. But do you think you had a stroke because they called about her?"

"No," he said, and smiled wanly. "It would have happened anyway. But Clara . . . Promise me you won't go there, no matter what. OK?"

I had promised.

Now here I sit wondering about whether I should go to visit Agnes tomorrow after all. The fact that she remembers changes everything. But it will still be a big step to take, after all the years when I've felt it was inconceivable.

I put on a wool sweater, scoop up a sheepskin blanket, and go out onto the porch.

Bella, Daddy's fat old cat, follows me, jumps up, and curls into a ball on my lap. Usually, she hates me. But apparently, now I will do.

I light up a joint as twilight slowly descends.

It was Henrik who had offered me the first pipe that summer we met. For him it was a party thing.

For myself I discovered the hash gave me a welcome feeling of numbness. All that darkness, all my feelings are subdued. I escape from myself awhile.

Henrik gave it up a long time ago, of course. Being the happy camper he is, he has no need for such things. Nothing haunts him. He doesn't have my mother and he doesn't have Lars. Life has been easy for him.

I look at Grandmother Klara's big garden. She had an extraordinary interest in plants and shrubs. The garden has gone downhill since her time. When I was a little girl, my mother tended the flowers during her good periods, bending over the beds in her rubber boots and long skirt, like a woman in one of those Nikolai Astrup paintings that were painted not far from here.

She looked like Joni Mitchell back then, only even more beautiful and even more fragile.

I can picture how she looks now. Fat and ugly, wearing a tracksuit covered with food stains, greasy hair, and long whiskers on her chin. Heavy eyelids. A swollen, impossible-to-recognize face.

Her interest in gardening died out. It was like everything else, all talk and little action. And Daddy had too many other things to attend to. Now he cuts the lawn using a scythe; only the hardiest of perennials and shrubs have survived.

The golden rain tree is supposedly the biggest in the village. The lilacs are lavender, dark purple, and white. The jasmine and honeysuckle, both with such bright, delicate, off-white flowers, each with its own distinctive scent. And the spindle tree, my favorite. The beautiful blossoms in the springtime. The red berries in the fall.

Now the garden is getting shadowy and dark. The murmuring of the river, the small birds, the sheep bells, all of this grows fainter as night begins to fall.

As always, I want another joint, but abstain. All things in moderation. I must stay in control, not get carried away. I go inside, lie down on the floor, and do some of my breathing exercises. I did these long before I started smoking, before I had any idea there was something called pranayama. I didn't even know there were breathing techniques.

I invented the exercises myself, experimenting until I came up with a method. Every morning when I woke up, I practiced. When I watched television, I practiced. In the summertime, I lay floating on my back in the swimming hole in the river and practiced.

At first it was a matter of just holding my breath for as long as I could.

When I was a child, the world record was eight minutes for men and six minutes for women. One day, if I practiced and tried hard enough, maybe I would break the record.

I never did. But I still practice every day.

For the exercise that works the best, you pull in your stomach as you exhale and push it out when you inhale, such and such number of times, before taking a deep breath, doing a throat lock and a root lock, and holding your breath for as long as you can. Then you release the locks and exhale calmly.

Usually, I do three rounds of twenty to thirty-five breaths per round.

But if I have time, I will often do the extreme version, ten rounds of one hundred breaths per round.

It makes me feel energetic and clears my head, gives me the drive to accomplish more than I'm usually capable of. I did the exercises a lot when I was working on the bill. Now I'm trying to prepare myself for tomorrow.

I haven't been in the house without Daddy since he was in Lebanon. It doesn't feel good to be alone here now either. But maybe it wouldn't have helped if he'd been here tonight, when all I can do is wonder about whether I should visit Agnes.

I take out my phone and send a message to Henrik: Would it be possible for me to stay here a few more days?

Coming from me, it is an oddly fawning message. But it would be so nice to have a little more time at the farm.

On the second floor the ceilings are low, the log walls painted yellow. The old wooden chests are in their usual places beneath the pitched roof. The floor is green and on it are a couple of rag rugs Grandmother made.

First, I go into Lars's old room. It's the same as it's always been. Daddy and I agreed not to touch it, but I don't think he ever goes inside. When there are others in the house, the door to the room is locked. I sit down on the bed. I pick up Lars's teddy bear, Colargol, and put it on my lap, pull it close, and sing. *Through the window a little bluebird flew, a bluebird flew, a bluebird flew, through the window a little bluebird flew on a day in May.*

I'd sung that song to him every evening at eight o'clock.

His things. The LEGO fire station. The rocking horse. His pencil case on the desk, ready for the first day of school. The bird posters. I pick up the teddy bear and sniff him, hold my nose against the pillow. Everything smells old and dusty. Now I regret having come in here. I put the teddy bear back in its place, walk into my room, and open the window to let in the evening air.

Then I open the top, creaky drawer of my bureau and take out the necklace, a leather cord with a metal splinter on it. I hold it up to my throat and look at myself in the tiny mirror over the bureau. The glass is so old that the reflection of my face is distorted.

My phone vibrates.

Still going to the seminar at Lysebu, have no back-up. Trust you'll come home as agreed.

I put away the phone without replying.

Outside even the sheep have fallen silent. The only sound is the rushing of the river, record high due to the rapid snowmelt on the mountain.

I undress, lift the crocheted bedspread. Beneath it is the light-blue duvet cover with white clouds on it, the one I liked best when I was a child.

Clara in the sky, Daddy used to say when he tucked me in. Sleep well, he said then, and kissed me on the forehead.

I always slept well until I was awakened by his screams.

But tonight, I won't be able to sleep.

CHAPTER 18

HENRIK

I'm sitting outside of Java Espressobar on Ullevålsveien Street, reading the newspaper and drinking a *cortado*. My bicycle is locked to a nearby lamppost. Happy people wearing summer clothes and new sunglasses hurry past. It's like in the old days. During the transitional period from adolescence to adulthood, Clara and I lived just down the road from here for a few years, in one of the English-style stone houses on Geitmyrsveien Road.

It's two o'clock. My meeting downtown ended a half hour ago, and I don't have to pick up the boys for a few hours. But I've taken the rest of the day off and have decided not to go back to the office. I need to clear my head a little, create some strategies for how I will work with my abuse notification system in the future.

In the online newspapers the Mukhtar Ahmad case is no longer the lead story.

The police have found a bullet casing that was hidden between the prayer rugs, they say. Along with the bullets they found in Ahmad's body, the casing gives the detectives a certain indication of the type of ammunition and thereby the firearm that was used.

The time of death is set between 10:15 and 10:20 p.m., in part because of the security guard's statement, and in part because the medical personnel who arrived took the corpse's body temperature.

The fact that somebody followed Ahmad and shot him using a silencer implies premeditation, possibly a perpetrator with ties to the victim's community. At the same time, there was nobody who knew ahead of time that Ahmad would end up in the prayer room that evening. We were the only ones who knew he'd gone there. The location of his murder could indicate that it was less premeditated, maybe a crime of passion. But it's too early to say anything for certain about any of it.

Suddenly, I feel limp and lethargic. I need another coffee. As I'm about to stand up to go inside, I see a familiar face coming out of the door of a café a few yards away.

Sabiya.

She nudges the door open with her elbow, carrying a tray holding two coffees and a paper bag with the name *Pascal* on it.

Why isn't *she* at work, in the middle of the day?

I am about to get to my feet, raise my arm, and shout hello—we are after all close colleagues—when a guy who has been sitting outside waiting for her stands up.

He kisses her. And accepts one of the two paper cups.

The guy is also Pakistani, about my age, or a little younger. He's slim and almost shockingly stylish, wearing a dark suit and white shirt. Sabiya is wearing tight, grayish-black jeans, high heels, and a white suit jacket.

What an attractive couple.

I recognize him from the family photograph on her desk. But his eyes are not hard, false, as I believed. They are warm, full of humor, bright.

It feels like someone has hit me.

Sabiya throws the cardboard tray into a trash bin outside; she hadn't really needed it. Then they start to cross the street, carrying their respective coffee cups. The guy puts his arm around her, she looks up at him, and they laugh.

My stomach turns over. I feel an urge to grab hold of her, ask her what she's up to, why she's portrayed her husband as a horrible monster when they so obviously appear to be perfectly happy?

Instead I just sit there, completely still.

They get into a white Tesla, a huge, shiny atrocity of a car. She's in the driver's seat, while he walks around to the other side, facing the park. And then she turns on the blinker and pulls away from the curb, rolls out onto Ullevålsveien Street, and the car disappears silently up the hill.

I'm left sitting there, thinking about the episode of last winter. Of the gun she had shown me, the one she kept locked up in one of her drawers in our office, and the explanation about her insanely jealous husband. The entire business shook me up so much that I even told Clara about it when I came home.

Of course, I'd insisted that Sabiya remove the Glock from our office. But I hadn't checked to see whether she'd complied.

A seagull flies toward me from farther up the street, where there used to be a kiosk and a taxi stand in front of an artificial pond. The seagull screeches as if possessed, circling above the street before flying over the sidewalk in front of me, where it releases a long stream of shit onto my bicycle seat and flies away again, emitting a few irate shrieks.

Sabiya is hiding something from me. She has a life I have no access to, which doesn't correspond with the image of the terrified, downtrodden wife who is barely allowed to leave the house.

If she lies about this, what else is she lying about?

Still more than two hours to go before it's time to pick up the boys. I may as well go back to work, try to find out why Sabiya isn't there today. But first, I need to find some napkins and clean off my bicycle seat.

The light in the office is off. I turn on the computer, check Sabiya's calendar. All that's written there is *meeting* from 12:30 to 3:00 p.m. I should sit down and work on the article or the abuse notification system, but I am unable to settle down. The workday is almost over. I can start fresh again in the morning.

Outside of Espresso House, I run into a cheerful and energetic Bente. She's about to sit down with a cup of cappuccino capped with a foamy heart.

An idea comes to me. A shameless idea.

"Hey," I say, throwing out my arms. "Bente! Just the person I was looking for."

She blushes.

"Do you already have a date, or do you have time to join me?"

"I can't very well say no," she says, as flirtatious as a young girl.

It's not exactly a romantic location. On the contrary, the hospital's Espresso House is a heartbreaking place where hairless women can sit and enjoy a glimpse of normality.

Coffee. Foam on top. Music. Heat lamps and blankets. Voices chattering, an ambient background buzz. Real life, sort of.

I decide that I can't take any more coffee today and buy myself a green smoothie. Bente takes careful sips of the foam on her cappuccino. Her eyes are hidden behind huge Ray-Ban sunglasses, but her smile is coy, provocative. A former handball player, she has a compact body. She is witty, with freckles and sun-bleached, shoulder-length hair.

She's cute. In a natural way. Refreshing in the way she differs from my other two women. Probably relatively uncomplicated to be with, but she could easily surprise, be a tiger in the bedroom, bringing with her all the roughness of the handball court.

"I can't stay long, unfortunately," Bente says. "I have the children. I can't seem to juggle the pieces. I should have worked at a doctor's office or something, but I wouldn't be able to stand it, so boring . . ."

I nod empathetically.

"Clara's in Western Norway, so I'm alone for a few days, that's more than enough for me. I don't understand how you manage."

Being alone with the children, even for a few days, is something women find attractive in a man.

"Me neither," she says with a little laugh.

"You know what?" I say, taking charge of the conversation. "I was supposed to discuss something with Sabiya, but she wasn't in her office. Have you seen her?"

"Nope. But it's not easy keeping track of that woman's whereabouts, you know," she says, with a crooked smile.

"What do you mean?"

"We both went to Grünerløkka School. Didn't I tell you?"

I shake my head.

"Sabiya didn't either?"

"Don't think so," I say, even though they have both spoken about it. On several occasions.

"OK," Bente says, looking a little disappointed. "Anyway, we didn't live far from each other. But we were never close. My mouth sort of dropped open when she showed up here as a doctor . . ."

"Why?" I ask. "Don't almost all good Pakistani girls become doctors?"

"That's right," she says with a laugh, taking a sip of her coffee and using the teaspoon to capture the foam attached to the rim. "But none of us considered Sabiya to be one of the good girls. Sharp as hell, of course, always smart in school. But she was, like, on the other side, hung out with one of those gangs. You know?"

"Not really," I say, and smile. "There were two foreigners in my class. One was the son of the Portuguese ambassador. The father of the other one was a Brit who headed up Statoil's Oslo office."

"Well, in junior high Sabiya always wore sagger jeans and oversize hoodies so big I thought she'd drown in them. She hung out with the worst people. The other squeaky-clean kids and I were afraid of her."

"Afraid of a girl who was five foot one?" I laugh.

"Sure," Bente says. "They always hung out downtown. At Arkaden Shopping or outside the Oslo City Mall. The usual places. Once a Gambian girlfriend of mine made the mistake of necking with a Moroccan guy Sabiya had dated. The Gambian girl, her name was Jeannette, was almost six feet tall and looked like she came straight from the Olympic one-hundred-meter final. The nicest girl in the world. We were handball girls, after all. She's a nurse here now, by the way. Anyway, after school Sabiya went to talk with her. To make peace."

"And then?" I say.

"Instead she jumped up and headbutted Jeannette onto the ground."

"That's crazy," I exclaim.

"The lady had a violent temper, though she's certainly gotten better at hiding it. But she was cold with me when she started here, maybe felt threatened because I knew who she was. I can't help wondering whether the guy who was shot here the other night had been a part of the same scene."

She glances at her watch. "Shit, I have to run if I'm going to make day care, have to go all the way to Oppsal, you know."

"Same here, I'd better pick up the boys from the after-school program soon. They like getting home a bit early. But we can go for coffee another day if you like?" I say as she gets to her feet.

"Yes, I'd like that," she says, and her face lights up.

I stand up, as if to give her a hug, hold her shoulders firmly, and kiss her on the cheek.

"My goodness," she says, smiling coquettishly as she walks away with quick nurse's steps.

When she's about twenty yards away, she turns around and waves. I wave back before she disappears around the corner.

CHAPTER 19

CLARA

After brooding all night long, I get up around five. By then I've made up my mind.

To visit Agnes, I have to drive for an hour and a half.

First, I must take the ferry back the same way I came the day before. It's the same boat, the same ticket collector. He greets me cheerfully. I say as little as possible, and consider waiting in the car, but this business of staring at the fjord has somehow become a ritual. So, I get out and stand there, by the side railing.

Outside the home I sit in the car doing my breathing exercises for a long time. I open the car door, step out, and look up at the steep, black mountain behind the home. Above it the sky is a bright blue. An airplane flies through the sky, leaving behind a long white strip, and I have a brief flashback from my childhood. Whenever I saw an airplane flying far above me, I always fantasized about where the plane had come from, where it was headed, who was on board.

I have really no desire to go into the building.

My entire body tenses, trying to refuse.

And I've promised Daddy that I wouldn't.

But still, this is something I must do. And it must happen *now*. I must get it over with.

"Clara! Goodness! You're a sight for sore eyes!" says the woman standing behind the reception desk. It's clear that she thinks she knows me.

I glance at the name tag on her chest.

Her name is Bodil. She has short, heavily dyed, dark hair with long bangs drawn to one side. Several gold earrings in each ear. A fake tan, sixty or seventy pounds overweight. Huge thighs under the white trousers of her uniform. A few fading, grayish-blue tattoos on her forearms.

Could she be someone I went to school with? High school?

She looks like a grandmother of almost sixty years, but the women here around forty often do. I've wondered what it is that makes forty-year-olds in Western Norway look twenty years older than people in Oslo, on average. But when Henrik points out the same thing, I always object.

"Well, you haven't been here before?" she says, and glances down at her notepad.

"No." I have no intention of explaining anything whatsoever to this woman.

"Agnes lives in a separate building for long-term patients. It's right on the other side there. Come on, I'll take you," she says, walking energetically away in white sneakers. "Your mother isn't used to having visitors. She's heavily sedated and calm, for the most part, even listless. She probably won't say all that much. But she has started to talk. It's unbelievable, none of us expected it . . ."

I don't say anything and finally Bodil stops talking.

The corridor smells of medicine and cleaning supplies. I am longing to return to the balcony at home, the sheep bells, the tiny birds, and the rushing river.

But there's no way around it. I must go inside, stay for a while. Leave again.

Bodil opens the main door to the building with a key card. Here it smells of wet paint, and a wave of nausea rises in me.

When I was little, Agnes once made mutton and cabbage stew while she was painting the kitchen. She must have been in a manic phase then. The stew was left stinking on the stove for days, and the smell of boiled cabbage mixed in with the smell of paint. Since then I haven't been able to stomach either.

"We're going up to the second floor," Bodil says, and starts up the stairs. At the top she opens a door with a sign bearing my last name and walks in.

None of what I have envisioned is correct.

The fat, disgusting woman doesn't exist.

Maybe I just tried to make Agnes less dangerous, less like herself, so I would somehow manage to find the strength to visit her.

But the woman who gets up out of her chair has not changed all that much in thirty years. Her hair is less shiny, and a fine web of wrinkles has spread across her face, like a photo filter, but her skin is astonishingly smooth. Her eyes have lost their sparkle, but she is just as agile and slim, quite skinny in fact. Her back is just as erect, her hair still reaches far down her back. She is wearing a long flower-patterned skirt and a white blouse, just as before.

Is it the same clothing? Or have they bought new clothes in the same style for her?

Either way, it feels as if she has just been lying here like a wilted Sleeping Beauty for thirty years.

I'm unable to get a single word out. In the end, she is the one who starts talking.

"Well now, is it you?" she says. She puts on a slight smile and looks straight at me, through me.

The hair on my forearms stands up. I glance over at Bodil.

"Well, I'll be off, then," she says. "Call me if you need me."

She closes the door behind her.

"Yes," I say. "Shall we sit down?" I nod toward the tiny, round birchwood table by the window with two matching chairs. She sits down, perching on the seat edge of one of the chairs. Now it seems to me as if there's something hateful in that pale gaze of hers.

"It's been a long time," I begin as I sit down.

Then everything comes to a halt.

I've planned what I'm going to say. Gone through it over and over again, last night, this morning, on the way over here.

But sitting in front of her, after all these years, I feel paralyzed.

"Thirty years, two weeks, and three days," she says, and an abyss slides open in front of me. I fold my hands in my lap and lean forward, feeling dizzy. "Did you come from Oslo?" she adds, tucking her hair behind her ear with one thin hand.

I nod.

"Your twins, how old are they?" she continues. "They must be eight now? Still innocent, then . . ."

Oslo? The twins? How does she know all of this?

I clear my throat. I must get her to change the subject. "I don't know how much you remember . . ."

"Everything," she says, with a beaming smile. "I remember everything."

It's like falling through a trapdoor and onto a stone floor below. The breath is knocked out of me. I am unable to say anything. I want to stand up, leave, but don't have the strength for that either.

She suddenly looks at me in terror.

"Clara . . . ," she says, fingering the alarm she has around her neck. "Clara with a *C*."

Her chin drops down to her sternum. In the course of a few seconds, she has reverted to the version of herself she has probably been for the past few decades.

"Agnes? Agnes?" I say. And then, in the end, tentatively: "Mommy?"

Calling her that never came naturally to me, and it doesn't now either. It's like having a rotten potato in my mouth. Agnes looks at me with apathetic eyes.

I sit for ten seconds, twenty.

Then I stand up and leave without giving her another look.

As I walk back through the corridor, it happens again. The nausea. The trembling. It all comes back. I stop walking and lean against the wall.

"Are you all right?" asks a nurse who walks past me.

"Yes, of course," I say, smiling, as I straighten up and continue walking down the hall. I don't want her to mistake me for a new patient.

But I'm there now. In the car flying off the cliff. Again and again.

CHAPTER 20

LEIF

1981

That summer was the worst anyone could remember. There was snow on the ground almost until Norwegian Constitution Day on May 17 and frost at night after that. Then it started raining and blowing.

There was only one hay harvest, late in the summer, and there was scarcely enough even for feed. For the first time I had to buy feed for the animals.

The strawberries we used to sell on the side of the highway from a pallet table under a striped parasol, or deliver to the local stores, just turned into mushy, pale lumps that we left to rot in peace under the ground foliage.

The apples were small and wretched, unripe without a trace of red, not even worth pressing for cider.

This was the downside of the small farm life. Not all the work. Not the paltry income. But the risk that one day it would all go to hell, landing us in financial ruin. And no safety net.

In the evenings I sat at my desk with a calculator and tried to figure out how to make it work. The numbers glowed red in my face. I had already burned through our savings.

Just when I didn't think it could get any worse, the sheep were infected with scrapie and had to be slaughtered.

What was I supposed to do? Selling the farm I'd inherited from my father, the farm that had been in our family for more than two hundred years, was out of the question. Although I had never done anything but work on the farm, I tried to find work at the factory in the next town, at the store, at a repair shop. But there were several of us in the same boat, and I never received more than halfhearted assurances that they would see what they could do.

At night I lay in bed staring at the knotholes in the pitched ceiling, listening to the rain lashing against the rooftop, the wind pounding on the walls of the house.

It was the sound of home, the sound that had always calmed me and made me happy. Now I just grew anxious.

Several of the men in the village decided to enlist in the UN forces stationed in Lebanon, and they'd been after me to join them. Everyone knew it had been a bad year. But I just scoffed every time somebody mentioned Lebanon.

Now I started seriously considering enlisting, mostly because I had no other option.

We needed the money. And it was only for a limited time.

"I can take care of the children," Agnes said.

I considered saying that would be nice for a change but held my tongue.

Maybe it would bring her and the children closer together.

Twice I had seen Agnes strike Clara. I'd told her in no uncertain terms never to raise a hand against the children again. And that was a long time ago. It seemed like she was in a good period now.

"Fine," I said the next morning after having lain awake all night. "If you think it's a good idea."

We didn't tell the children anything until it was all settled, until I'd signed the contract with the armed forces, with whom I'd had no contact since completing my compulsory military service.

Clara absolutely did not want me to go.

I tried explaining that Daddy would be away for only a few months and that he would think of her and send kisses home from the sky every evening. Daddy just had to help keep some nice families safe, and then he would come home and never go away again. And Mommy would be home, Mommy and Lars and the animals.

She crawled up into my lap, something she'd outgrown, wrapped her arms tightly around my neck, and refused to let go. "You can't," she screamed, again and again, so it hurt my ears, all the while clinging to me tightly, so tightly. I tried seeking out Agnes's eyes for support, but she looked away. I had a sinking feeling in my gut. Was this the right thing to do? What was the point?

And as I took my seat on the tiny aircraft that would carry us to Fornebu Airport, where a Hercules would fly us to Rhodes, where we would change flights one final time and board the plane that would take us to Beirut International Airport, as I fastened my seat belt, closed my eyes, and leaned back, it was as if a curtain opened, and I had an overwhelming feeling of having made the biggest mistake of my life.

I was homesick already. I missed the wind, the rain, and the sun; the creaking of the floorboards and the crackling in the woodstove; the two warm bodies that were my own.

I had never felt so alone, even though the others sat around me, drinking beer, smoking, and telling bad jokes.

Nobody talked about what awaited us.

CHAPTER 21

CLARA

When I get home after visiting Agnes, I fill a bucket with ammonia, green soap, and scalding hot water, and spend an hour cleaning, hard and fast. Greasy crud on the kitchen cabinets and the kitchen fan, dust under the wooden bench in the hallway and under the chairs in the living room.

The whole time I can see her. Her shriveled face. The skinny hands. The colorful skirt, just as faded and outdated as she is.

It's all far too familiar.

I put on my black running tights, a tank top, sweatshirt, and running shoes, and go for a run down along the river and up along the waterfall. It's steep. I was too busy to find the time to exercise much while I was working on the bill, and I can feel it in my legs and my breathing, but I give it my all, up the curving path, between moss-covered rocks, through the spruce forest and the small birch clearings.

The run is logged on Strava via my pulse watch. But I'm alone. There are a few Strava users in the village, but not many, and they run on different routes. It's mainly just Henrik and I and the boys who walk here, a couple of times every summer. People would have to cross our property to get to the summer farm, and they don't do it. And many people would rather drive four-wheelers on gravel roads than go walking. It irritates Henrik. He drones on about how pristine nature must be left undisturbed. Then I always defend the people here, pointing out that gravel roads aren't pristine nature, even though in principle I can't say I fully disagree with him.

Every square foot, every crevice, and every huge root curling over the path, every anthill and every rock face—I know all of it. The natural landscape here is almost more me than I am myself. But from time to time I have to jump over trees that have fallen across the path.

It doesn't look like Daddy has been up here this year. During our vacation I'll have to come up with the chain saw and clear the path, which is disappearing more and more every year.

I'd seen it clearly when I arrived at the farm the day before.

The broken flagstones on the roof, the peeling paint on the porch, the broken windowpanes that had been covered up with a sheet of cardboard, the bucket in the hallway collecting the water dripping from the ceiling.

There's so much here that's falling apart, and the disrepair has accelerated during the past year.

I must deal with it. But not today.

The waterfall is huge. It foams and roars, the sound mingling with my blood pumping harder and harder through my body. I push myself as much as I can. When I reach the top, I lean forward, gasping for breath; lactic acid has flooded into all my muscles.

After a while I straighten up, jog along the lake on the summer farm and over to the small waterfront below our cottage, the tiny gray house farther up the hill that has only a single window with small panes facing the water.

There's a rock here where I usually sit down. I can often sit here for hours staring at the water without getting bored. It never ceases to amaze me how quiet it is here and how savage it becomes just a short distance away, where the smoothly flowing water suddenly becomes a thundering, wild waterfall.

Then I feel the wind pick up, it blows straight through me.

It's only at the water's edge that I can talk to him. Only here that I can really feel close to him, as if no time had passed at all.

"Lars?" I whisper. "Today I went to see Agnes . . . yes, Mommy, you know."

"Ooh," he replies. "Isn't that dangerous, Clara?"

"Yes. I think maybe it was stupid of me."

"Did you tell Dad?"

"No . . . I can't do that."

"Hmm," he says thoughtfully.

Lars was so little and sweet when he was lying in his cradle, waving at us, gurgling, and laughing. I loved to sit holding him in the crook of my arm, rocking him back and forth. When he got bigger, I carried him around everywhere, took him outside with me, pointed at everything, and told him the names of what we saw. Flower, Lars. Cow, Lars. Barn. Tractor. Barn bridge. Grass. Daddy. Mommy. Farmyard tree. Wheelbarrow. Cat.

I taught him almost all the words. I led him around by the hand when he started to walk. I taught him how to ride a bike.

He's one of those thin, blond kids with big, blue eyes that always look surprised, as if he doesn't fully understand what world he has come to.

When he's happy, he leaps backward with long steps while making small, strange pumping movements with his arms, almost like when the kids at school do the bird dance. He's more interested in birds than anything else in the world. He knows almost all the species in Daddy's bird book, and he can recognize them by their song alone.

At night he often wets the bed, even though Mommy gets angry and says he should have finished with all that a long time ago. He's not allowed to lie in bed with her, but he can lie in bed with me when he comes padding in at night. Here at the summer farm we always share a bed. And I always sing to him before he falls asleep.

Through the window a little bluebird flew, a bluebird flew, a bluebird flew, I sing. Then I sing, *Found a little boy with eyes of blue, dippedy-dippedy-doo.*

The words *dippedy-dippedy-doo* always make him laugh.

Mommy often brings us here, especially now that Dad is in Lebanon. Every time the phone rings I jump, afraid that something has happened.

I didn't want him to leave. He was the one who read me Jules Verne in the evenings, who took me on walks in the woods and taught me the names of birds and trees and how if we should lose one another, I must hug a tree and call for him. He was the one who took me to the summer farm and taught me to love being in the mountains.

But he left anyway. Now it's just Mommy, Lars, and me here.

Mommy says she married Dad because of the nature here, even though she's almost always inside the house. When we're here, she likes to go up to the top of a mountain and stand there screaming or lie in the heather, looking up at the sky.

Breathing in the sky, she calls it. Then we must leave her alone, not disturb her.

We usually sit playing farm with pine cones and rocks. I'm really too old for this, but I do it anyway, for Lars's sake.

This morning is clear and shiny. The dew is still on the grass, but the sun has just washed the closest mountain—the one Mommy likes to scream from—with a golden sheen. Soon, the sun will light up the entire summer farm.

Lars went outside before me—he had to pee. At the summer farm there's no outhouse, so we pee anywhere.

I dawdle a bit before going outside. And when I step out the door, he's nowhere to be seen.

"Lars," I call. "Lars? Lars?"

I walk around the farm, calling loudly. The pounding of my heart accelerates, I run up to the cottage, tear open the door. There are three beds in the one-room cottage, one in each corner except for the corner where there's a stove. Lars and I usually sleep in the bed that's the broadest and the shortest. Mommy usually sleeps in the darkest corner, in the longest bed.

"Mommy," I shout. "I can't find Lars."

She grunts something or other, and I run outside again.

I would have seen him by now if he were somewhere nearby. He must have gone down to the water. He loves going there to skip stones, but I taught him that I must always go with him. He can't swim and the currents are strong because of the waterfall plummeting down at the far end of the lake.

I run down to our little beach, which is really nothing more than a sandbank between the grass and the water.

There are fresh boot prints in the sand. And isn't that a shadow out in the water?

Once I heard a lifeguard on TV talking about how people usually think that children will float and that there's plenty of time to save them, but in real life children will often call for help, so their lungs fill with water and they sink like stones.

Now I try to remember what I have taught myself.

Deep breaths. In. And out. In. And out.

I tear off my jacket, kick off my boots, inhale, and dive in. Sediment from the muddy bottom. And then a shadow below. My eyes sting. I close them, open them. Yes, it's Lars, my brother, on the bottom. But he doesn't see me; he floats farther and farther away with the current.

Soon, I will need to breathe. I open my eyes and swim in Lars's direction. He's closer—I can almost touch him. Then he's dragged away from me again. I kick my legs and manage to get my arm around him. He squirms.

The current pulls us toward the waterfall. Soon, we'll disappear into the huge, roaring whiteness. Then I remember something Dad said.

The current is the weakest at the bottom.

I take a firm grip around Lars's neck, kick my way downward and away while trying to use my free arm to navigate.

Downward and away.

The huge pressure around me relents a bit. The rush-covered, muddy bottom is just below us; I touch down on something with my toe. But now I *must* have air. A little more, a bit farther, a bit farther, keeping us down, down. It seems like we are starting to approach the other side. It's not wide, the lake, just endlessly deep and turbulent.

Lars is a heavy weight dragging me down. But we must keep moving upward, up, up, up.

Like that, there, I crawl onto shore. Coughing, hacking, I open my eyes. I'm so dizzy, everything is spinning. I lie down for a couple of seconds, then sit up again.

Lars is lying on his side beside me. Is he alive? Is he breathing? I roll him over onto his back and start blowing into his mouth and pressing on his chest. I breathe and press, breathe and press. Again and again.

"I have to go," he says then, puts his arms around my neck and gives me a hug.

"Wait a minute, Lars," I say.

"Sorry, I can't."

A gust of wind rushes through his body. Then he's gone.

Now I stand up, brush myself off. The buildup of lactic acid has receded.

I take a walk around the farm. Everything seems to be in order.

I didn't bring the key, so I can't go inside, and must make do with placing the palms of my hands against the wall and leaning against the cottage, one second, two.

My great-grandfather built the cottage. The woodwork is over a hundred years old.

All the flesh has been worn off the bones of the wood siding, eroded by storms and rain, frost and heat, winters and summers, year after year. Only the raw nerves remain inside there. They press against my palms, so we are almost one, the old house and me.

I stand there like that for a second or two, absorbing the pulse of the dead, gray wood. All the tree rings in there resonate against my palms.

Then I straighten up and start the walk down.

CHAPTER 22

HENRIK

A quick little click, a few seconds of waiting, and then Sabiya opens the door to her room.

I take a step inside, the door closes.

Two warm arms around my neck, a thinly clad body against mine, a mouth against my own.

I've tried to the best of my abilities to repress the vision of Sabiya and her husband on Ullevålsveien Street. This seminar up here at Lysebu, at the most beautiful time of year, is like a gift for both of us. A whole night together, our first. We will not let anything ruin it.

I did feel a little bad about saying no to Clara when she asked if she could stay out west a little longer. Had it been only an ordinary seminar, I would have agreed and stayed home. But I couldn't give up this day. And my mother, the only possible babysitter, is in Stockholm with friends.

"An hour and a half until dinner," I say, throwing myself backward on Sabiya's bed, reaching out to her with my arms. "An eternity!"

"We just have to be careful," Sabiya says, and waves a key card. "See, you get your own. For tonight. But remember to be quiet in the hallway. And tomorrow morning you have to leave before anyone wakes up."

"I know, I know," I say. "I *have* stayed at a hotel before."

"You . . . ," she says, with a shy smile.

"Haven't you?" I ask, half joking, half serious.

"Oh yes," she says. "But less frequently than the rest of you, I'd say."

We fall silent for a few seconds.

"You know, I wasn't allowed to spend the night at camp or on school trips or any of the other things most kids did. And I'm barely allowed to do it even now . . ."

I should have used her comment as an opportunity to learn more about how it was and is to be her, but I'm too impatient. I ask no more questions, lie on top of her, take hold of her wrists, and kiss her on the throat.

She twists her head back and forth, laughs, protests. But I know it's just an act.

When we are lying there afterward, breathing heavily, the compulsory question comes, the one I knew would be asked sooner or later.

"Have you ever been unfaithful before?" she asks, and looks at me inquisitively.

"No," I say. "And I never thought I would be, either. But that was before you showed up."

On my way to dinner I stop by the reception desk. And in the shop that sells pottery, honey, and God knows what else, on the other side of the lobby, is a woman I recognize.

Melika Omid Carter.

She must be around fifty years old now but looks almost the same as she did twenty years ago, when she would race around Grünerløkka in a sassy little Jeep visiting her restaurants. The set of her mouth is harder. The crow's-feet around her eyes are more pronounced. Otherwise, she's the same. Fit, slender and firm, expensive blue jeans, tight black top, wide leather belt, her wavy hair flowing down her back. Heavily made-up eyes, gold earrings. A little vulgar, mostly sexy, well preserved. One of those hot, mature women most of my buddies would have happily fucked given half the chance.

It's crazy seeing her wandering around here, as if she'd jumped off my list and into real life. I feel a touch of how I used to feel when I was a little boy and my father had visitors I recognized from the newspaper or television.

After adding her to my list, I'd done a search and found a feature article about Melika Omid Carter in a glossy magazine.

She's Iranian American. Her family immigrated to the US when she was little. She came to Norway as a teenager and has since built herself up from being poor, lost, and unable to communicate to a savvy, tough-as-nails businesswoman.

She's just opened another trendy café, but she also owns yoga and meditation studios, has her own exercise blog, and owns a line of fitness wear. The woman is a role model, the kind of immigrant even the members of Anton Munch's own party must approve of, nodding their acceptance, the kind of immigrant who maybe even votes for them.

Carter is known for her network and for her extraordinary business acumen, her gender and country of origin notwithstanding. And her name is on my list.

Now she's standing with her back to me, studying a selection of soaps, and then she walks out of the shop and down the corridor, pulling a small roller bag with one hand.

Nobody is in the dining hall yet. I google Melika Omid Carter and Lysebu, hits from the past six months. And yes, there it is.

A monthly yoga instructor course, something there's clearly a big market for.

On her blog she writes about how beautiful it is at Lysebu, how fantastic the food is, how lovely the pool is, that kind of thing. A garish contrast to what I've read about her in the hospital files.

The names on the list had slid quite smoothly and effortlessly into place. I hadn't been completely honest about what I would use the examples for, but my colleagues seemed relieved to have a chance to at least do something.

Including Faisal Ahmad, there are five cases.

Five families. Five cases. There should be at least twice as many.

In the past few days I've found the names of two or three journalists who have written about domestic violence, people I can contact. It feels as if producing this one-page document is the most useful thing I've done in a long time. There's some irony to that, given all the time I spend saving lives. I'd shown the preliminary list to Sabiya, who had seemed impressed. And rightly so.

Askildsen arrives in the dining room and takes a seat at the table. Bente and Roger are right on his heels.

"So, this is the old frontline soldiers' home? Not too shabby," Askildsen says.

I was the one who suggested Lysebu instead of the tacky Holmenkollen Park Hotel just down the hill, where there is a better view, but worse food and less style.

There is of course an element of extravagance over this annual gathering, that we spend the night at a hotel in our own city. The budgets are tight. But Askildsen, no matter how asocial he is otherwise, believes in the importance of these outings. Maybe because, unlike the rest of us, he lives alone; I suspect we are the closest thing to a family and friends that he has.

Sabiya is wearing a blue-and-white summer dress with a V-neck. She sits down directly facing me. We have one of the round tables by the window. I try not to look directly at her too often, try not to seem especially interested in her, talking with the others instead. Everyone chatters away about the usual things, a happy mixture of private life, soccer, vacation plans, and gossip about doctors who aren't here.

I sit in silence for the most part, absorbed in my own thoughts and unable to follow the conversation. I'm glancing around me constantly, on the lookout for Melika Omid Carter.

The others don't know who she is, what she has done. I'm itching to tell them. But my list is unofficial, and anyway this is not a suitable occasion. It's best to keep my mouth shut about the list and take part in the small talk instead, before they decide that I'm arrogant.

But suddenly, a silence falls over the table. Everyone looks at Askildsen and Sabiya, who is sitting there with a glass of white wine.

"You can't be serious?" Sabiya says.

"All right, then," an offended Askildsen says.

"What are you arguing about?" Roger asks.

"MeToo," says Bente, who's been listening to their conversation. "What else?"

"Aren't you a fan of MeToo, Askildsen?" I ask.

"I'm just afraid that every tiny thing is going to be blown way out of proportion, that it will lead to a kind of mass suggestibility," he says, obviously embarrassed and at the same time glad to have the chance to explain. "Then everything will be interpreted through that paradigm. And I don't like women turning themselves into victims when they're independent beings on an equal level with men. That's at least what I've always assumed."

"Ooh," Bente says, and glances excitedly over at Sabiya, as if she's watching a tennis match.

"Honestly, nobody's victimizing themselves. It's the opposite," Sabiya says.

"But listen," Bente says. "Do you remember all the stories about old Dr. Skjølberg?"

"He was crazy, basically," Roger says.

"Did he mess with you, too?" Bente asks.

"No, Jesus," Roger says, and blushes. "But I remember . . ."

"Hey, the man's not here," Askildsen says. "Behave . . ."

There's a bit of snickering and a few seconds of silence.

"I agree. To hell with the ghosts of old chief surgeons. Let's talk about the elephant in the room instead," Roger says. "That a murder was in fact committed on our watch, and everyone appears to have forgotten about it—"

Sabiya breaks in. "It's nice to talk about something else occasionally! There's been no other topic of conversation besides this murder recently."

"For me, at least, it seems wrong to behave like nothing out of the ordinary has happened," Roger says.

"Nobody is saying we should do that," Askildsen responds. "But a whole year ago I arranged temps to cover shifts for all of you so we could have this little gathering. And the unit nurses have been included for the first time, something that would never happen at many other workplaces . . ."

"Yes, of course," Roger says. "We're happy about that. That's not the point."

Askildsen tries to salvage the conversation.

"By the way, do you know the history of this beautiful place?" he asks, and without waiting for a reply, starts telling us about the Hammerich couple who organized the Danish relief initiative for Norway during the Second World War.

"So, a toast to Lysebu, and to Henrik, who suggested coming here this year," he concludes.

Everyone raises their glasses and toasts, Sabiya murmuring a little to herself.

"To the Hammerichs. And to us!" I say.

CHAPTER 23

Clara

It was Henrik who suggested we should try to have children. I was less enthusiastic. I was afraid of failing, as my mother had done. My fears weren't alleviated as I lay on the bed at the ultrasound clinic, where Henrik had dragged me for an early test to confirm I was pregnant, since I felt neither nauseated, nor tired, nor different in any way.

"Look at that," the midwife said.

Two small chambers with two small hearts thumping and beating.

"Wow," Henrik said. "Is that . . . *two?*"

"Yes, indeed," the midwife said. "Perhaps twins run in your family?"

"No," I said, and sighed.

"No," Henrik said, and laughed.

Several ultrasounds followed, oodles of them throughout my entire pregnancy, and sick leave started in week twenty-two, although I would have preferred to keep working. My stomach pulled me toward the ground. My hands and feet started swelling. My body hurt all over. I started itching.

All night long I lay awake scratching. It was apparently common, they said.

The birth was not especially memorable. With electrodes attached to my body to monitor both babies, I lay there, all tied up, a prisoner of all the electronics. It wasn't anything like I'd imagined. But at least

I didn't scream. The babies came out. The itching disappeared. And I breastfed them and let them lie on my chest. All those things.

Things went well. I wasn't my mother. I handled it.

When the boys were six months old, I started working again. They'd started fighting. They lay side by side, two round bundles in diapers and wool who couldn't walk, but what they could do was hit each other on the head. They screamed and hit and hit and screamed, and I didn't know what to do with them.

Henrik was much better with them. He had a natural gift, lifting them up and tossing them in the air and gurgling and tickling them and making faces. He got them to stop screaming and hitting, made them laugh and laugh and laugh.

The boys grew. Their fat baby cheeks disappeared as they became tall and slender.

They turned two, three, four, five, yelling at me angrily when I came to pick them up from day care.

"No, Mommy," they said. "Daddy! We want Daddy." And even though I did not in any sense want to have two mama's boys clinging to my apron strings, this disturbed me. Maybe there was more of Agnes in me than I wanted to believe.

From the time they were three until they were five, the boys' eternal fighting and arguing was replaced by an overwhelming symbiosis.

They didn't use *I*; it was always a collective *we*.

"We and Andreas," Nikolai said when he meant himself and his brother.

"We and Nikolai," Andreas said.

If one of them was unhappy about something and cried, the other always talked on behalf of his brother. When they were old enough to get up in the morning without us on the weekends, one of them would wake up the other and they would pad downstairs together, chattering all the way down the stairs to the television in the basement. And I exhaled. Now they didn't need me any longer, not really. I'd done my part.

In addition to having each other, they have a playful and loving father. Although the children are an exception, Henrik is most warm and good-natured with strangers, when it doesn't cost him anything. The closer to him you get, the cooler he becomes.

We argue about debris left in the pockets of trousers put in the wash, about sorting the trash, about where we should go on vacation, about how we should speak to the boys, about whose fault it is that the garden looks the way it does.

Lately there's been less open fire and more silent, strategic warfare.

I quickly lost interest in all the sex business. It became repetitious; there was nothing new and exciting about it anymore. Besides, I was always tired. That was perhaps not very original, but it was true.

And then, after several years of complaining about too little sex, several years during which he squeezed up against me at night when it was unthinkable for me to bring myself to do anything but sleep, when I twisted away and he grunted, dissatisfied and insulted, it was suddenly over.

He stopped trying. In and of itself it was fine. Maybe he was just tired of being rejected.

But at the same time, he began to appear more satisfied. More cheerful. And he looked different. Not much, but enough that it was noticeable. The little bulge above the waistline of his trousers disappeared. And his hair had always been a little too long, but he started having it cut more often, so once again it looked appropriately scruffy and charming.

I understood that the curse Grandmother Edith had inadvertently placed on us had come true.

Henrik appeared to believe that he was good at covering his tracks.

He wasn't. There were receipts in his workbag. Suddenly, there was a condom in the lining of his toiletry bag. And the code on his phone wasn't exactly difficult to crack. It's 2205, the same code he uses for most things. On his phone I found some intimate messages in his mailbox from a couple of women I'd never heard of before.

I hate infidelity. Ever since I was a little girl and my mother left my father, it has seemed to me to be the most pathetic thing in the world.

All the same, I found out that the only way to handle the humiliation was to pretend I didn't know.

CHAPTER 24

HENRIK

Sabiya calls it a night at ten thirty. Roger leaves shortly thereafter. At a quarter to eleven I say good night.

First, I go to my own room. There's a balcony outside and a magnificent view of purple mountains with shades of green and gray. The information folder on my desk includes a photograph of a tasteful swimming pool. Open until midnight, it says.

Perhaps a trip to the pool first would be an agreeable kind of foreplay?

Meet me at the pool in 10 minutes? A swim before bed? I text.

Ten seconds later: OK, but keep a safe distance. Albeit punctuated with a smiley face.

I quickly change into swimming trunks under running clothes. If I should happen to meet someone the following morning, I can say I've been out for a run, that I woke up early and couldn't fall asleep again. I pick up my key card, a towel, and my phone, and walk quietly out of the room.

In the gallery running between the buildings, the one with a low ceiling and glass walls and a garishly painted, life-size wood sculpture of a mother and two children, I think I can detect the characteristic scent of Jean Paul Gaultier cologne.

I really hope Roger isn't down there. Then we'll just have to turn around. It would be extremely awkward splashing around together.

Luckily, Roger is not in the pool.

Only Sabiya is there, floating on her back in the water.

The room is dark, except for a rectangle of ceiling spotlights above the pool and the flickering lights from a few large, thick candles in hurricane vases. The lighting makes the water surface glitter.

We're alone. But the long wall contains enormous windows offering a view of the grounds. There's just enough darkness outdoors and light indoors to allow people to see us from the outside even though we can't see them. This was not a particularly prudent plan after all. But I throw caution to the winds. It's late, everyone has been drinking, there's certainly nothing wrong with going for a swim with a colleague.

Sabiya stands, motionless in the light, with the water coming up to her breasts. She smiles, her hair wet and drops pearling on her golden skin. She looks like a million bucks. Brigitte Bardot, Ursula Andress, Charlize Theron, Angelina Jolie, none of them can hold a candle to her.

I walk toward the sauna, hesitate as I grasp the classic wood-block door handle.

"Will you join me?" I say, and nod toward the sauna as Sabiya swims past. I'm a bit nervous about people seeing us from outside. In the sauna nobody can see us or what we're doing.

"Rather not," she says, and stops moving for a moment. "I get claustrophobic—it's too hot and stuffy."

"Agreed," I say, even though it's not true, and release the door handle.

"Wouldn't you rather come in?" she says, and glances up at me with a gaze I can't quite read, before she pushes away from the side again, rolling over onto her back. Her arms paddle backward, her feet kicking up and down in the water.

I strip down to my swimming trunks, walk to the stairs in the corner, descend into the water, and start swimming after her.

There's a strange odor in the room. Something burned, like incense, an odor I recognize, even though I'm unable to identify it. It makes me feel a bit unwell amid all this bubbling, luxurious pleasure.

I gulp down a deep breath and dive under, trying to see without swim goggles. It's not easy. Light and shadow twirl in a kind of dance and I get dizzy, as if I'd consumed far more alcohol than I actually have.

For a moment I think I see a shadow fall over us from above, but when I come to the surface again, turn around, and gaze up from the edge of the pool, there's nothing there.

CHAPTER 25

Clara

It's exactly eight o'clock when I knock on her open door.

Mona expects us to be on time. Not one minute early, not one minute late. Exactly on time. Rumor has it that in an attempt to outwit those individuals who would invariably arrive five minutes late for the Thursday 12:00 meeting, she quietly changed the time to 12:05. Now everyone arrives exactly on time: 12:05.

"Hello, Clara," Mona says. "You can shut the door behind you."

Can you stop by my office at 8:00, if you're in the office by then? read the subject line of the email that had dropped into my inbox one hour earlier.

The email itself contained only her signature.

Secretary-General Mona Falkum

When I was first hired here, I'd just graduated. I had beaten out applicants with more experience, presumably because I appeared to be a better fit, whatever that means.

At first, I tried to take part in the social life of the ministry; the deputy director general impressed upon me that it was a good idea. I attended lunch on Fridays when lots were drawn for the weekly prize of a bottle of wine and later in the day joined in for drinks. I volunteered to run in the Holmenkollen relay with my colleagues, who were in bad shape and had poor competitive instincts. They were all more interested in the beer they would have afterward at Youngstorget Square.

It wasn't long before I dropped all of it.

Instead, I started arriving first and leaving last.

I brought case documents home with me and read them in bed. Obvious solutions and connections emerged before my eyes, and I went to my boss and presented my arguments.

He smiled. "Yes," he said. "That's one way of looking at it. In theory. In practice there are a number of obstacles."

A fifteen-minute monologue would follow.

Later I tried this with some of my colleagues. They smiled the same smile, which said: You will understand with time. I thought that if I just acquired more authority, if I just found a better way of making my arguments, of presenting them, then people would understand. In the meantime, I carried out my work duties impeccably.

Being an executive officer in a ministry is like walking into an impenetrable forest. You spin this way and that. Try a path here, a path there. But again and again you find yourself entangled in more underbrush, again and again the paths lead nowhere.

And then fifteen years have passed, and you understand that you haven't accomplished anything at all.

Mona is sitting behind her desk, red in the face and her mouth set in a grim line. Her silvery-gray, short hair, which has always made me think of James Bond's boss M, is like a helmet on her head. She is wearing a black suit jacket decorated with a silver costume brooch. The pins are her trademark.

"Munch stopped by and launched his plan for you," she says once I've sat down.

"Ah," I say expectantly. I would like to know what she knows before saying anything. She is after all the one who invited me here.

"Yes, you aren't seriously planning to become a state secretary?"

When she pronounces the title, she enunciates every syllable.

"I don't know," I say, which is the truth.

When Munch first mentioned his proposal, it had seemed ridiculous, like a joke. But since then I'd started to like the idea. When I came back from Western Norway, I asked Munch if the offer still stood. It did. For the time being.

Being a state secretary is a chance to gain far more real influence than I've ever been anywhere in the vicinity of having.

Besides, it's something new. I like doing things that others don't do, that nobody expects of me.

Munch's political party is not my party.

But maybe I can bring about change from the inside. Maybe it will be more effective than all the bureaucratic maneuvering in the world.

Mona attempts a disarming laugh.

"Clara, you are one of the most capable coworkers I have. If you're going to quit to . . ."

She stops, searching for words.

". . . to go over to the dark side?" I say, with a little smile.

"Something like that, yes . . . Well, I don't understand how you can even consider it. After fifteen years as a skillful civil servant? Become a *politician* . . ."

She says it with the kind of contempt in her voice that only truly high-level civil servants can permit themselves to show when there is a real crisis in the works. Normally, they all behave as if they have mutual respect for one another.

"I know you worked hard on the bill, but the time wasn't right. You can't just change course like this. That's not how it works. And yes, that kind of thing *has* happened before. But it hasn't been a particularly successful move."

"No?" I say, mostly to show that I'm listening. It's clearly like throwing gasoline on the fire, because she continues with even more zeal.

"Inger Louise Valle, she was also a lawyer and later minister of Justice. It ended with her being demoted to minister of Local

Government, after which she stepped down. Minister of Justice Anne Holt got sick and retired to write crime novels. State Secretary Haktor Helland came from a position as director general at the Ministry of Children and Families and went down in the maelstrom following the Rød-Larsen fisheries fiasco. And a transition like this is hardly a socially strategic move . . ."

"Ah," I say. "I'm not necessarily so . . ."

". . . concerned about what people think of you?" she finishes with a sigh, and then we smile a little, both of us. "What *are* you concerned about, then?"

"Getting something done. One way or another," I say.

"Good God," she explodes, and her irritation shines through. I can see it in the tense severity of her face as well. "Don't you think everyone wants that? And do you really think you will get more done as a girl Friday for Munch?"

She leans back in her chair as if to take a better look at me.

Mona Falkum is not always nice, that's clear. And she definitely has her own agenda.

When she continues, it's as if she's read my mind.

"Nice people don't end up as senior staff—remember that. Anton Munch stopped your bill. And what about the day he's pushed out? I shouldn't tell you this, but I know you're discreet. Munch is good. And apparently, easy to work with. But I see more of him than the rest of you and I've started noticing things. You can't trust him. There's more than one side to him. Do you understand?"

I nod.

Mona gets up and walks around her desk to put her hand on my shoulder.

"Clara . . . If you change your mind, I'm going to forget that I've heard about this. It's foolish to jump the gun. But the position of deputy director general will be vacant in the ministry soon. I will potentially have considerable influence there. If you don't change sides, that is," she says, looking at me pointedly.

I don't reply, don't know what to say.

"Promise me that you'll at least think about it?" Mona asks.

"I'll think about it," I say, like an echo of my recent response to Munch's suggestion, and get to my feet.

CHAPTER 26

HENRIK

Shortly after 8:30 a.m., I'm awakened by sirens and shouts and the sound of cars pulling up outside my hotel window. Immediately I'm filled with foreboding.

I jump up, grab my key card, and run down to the reception area where I find some of the others standing around, looking dumbfounded.

"What's going on? I must have overslept," I say, feeling like what I've been up to is written across my forehead.

I had decided to stay up all night, not miss a second of my time with Sabiya. But around half past three we fell asleep. By six o'clock we were already awake. Sabiya made it clear it was time for me to leave.

After that I had crashed, exhausted, on the couch in my room, still wearing the same running clothes I'd been sneaking around in the evening before.

"We don't know for sure," Roger says.

Three uniformed police officers walk through the door and continue into the hotel. They appear to be part of a patrol unit or something. What's going on? Immediately my pulse rate accelerates.

"It must be something serious," I say.

Outside the window there's an ambulance and several police cars. They've driven all the way across the courtyard and parked on the other side.

"I heard someone say they've found a dead body," Bente says. "And that's just sick . . ."

"How do we know it isn't one of our people?" Roger asks.

"That's actually a good question," I say. "But we're all here, after all . . ."

"What about Sabiya, has anyone seen her?" Bente says.

My skin prickles.

"Haven't seen her, no," Roger responds.

I try to think back. "Me neither."

Could something have happened to Sabiya after I left her room? Something that had already been discovered. Hardly. But still . . .

I have to know. "Why don't I try calling her?"

I take out my phone, call. No answer.

"I'm going to look for her." I head for the stairs up to her floor.

At first, I climb the stairs calmly. Then I break into a run.

My heart is beating quickly, my mouth is dry. Everything's fine, I tell myself. It's not her, she's in her room, busy with all her usual foolishness, makeup and hair-drying and all that; it takes time, Sabiya is particular about such things.

But when I knock on her door, nobody answers. I try peeking through the tiny peephole, but all I can see is a blurry haze. I get out my phone, call her again. No answer. But I can hear the phone ringing inside her room. Is she there? Or is it just her phone?

Suddenly, I can see it clearly, Sabiya lying on her bed, strangled or beaten to death. Maybe her handsome husband is nuts after all, and has found out about us, showed up here, attacked her.

And then it's my fault.

I feel like throwing up. I shouldn't have had so much to drink yesterday. Shouldn't have gone to the pool. Should have gotten more sleep. Shouldn't have been an unfaithful prick.

On top of this there's the police and death and all of it, again. And Sabiya is missing. Damn, damn, damn. As I'm standing there with my head bowed and the palms of my hands pressed against the wall, somebody comes around the corner.

Sabiya, alive and well. Sweaty and red-faced, dressed in her running clothes.

"Henrik? What are you doing?" she asks.

"Sabiya? Are you . . . here?"

"Yes," she says, surprised. "Where else would I be?"

"My God, I thought you were . . . dead."

"Dead?" she says. And starts to laugh, scornfully. "Dead, yeah, right . . ."

I'm so infuriated I almost smack her.

"What the hell . . . Someone was murdered at this hotel last night," I say. "And I couldn't get hold of you, not in your room, not on the phone . . ."

"I went out for a run. But . . . murdered?" she says, her eyes opening wide. "Seriously?"

"Yes, according to Bente. Now can you understand why I was worried about you? Didn't you see the police cars? When you were outside?"

She shakes her head.

"I came in through the back."

Roger rounds the corner, stopping in front of the door to the left of Sabiya's room.

"Medical consultation?" he says knowingly.

Neither of us reply. Sabiya had boasted about getting a room on a floor far away from everyone else. So much for that.

"Don't let me interrupt," he says, and goes into his room.

"What's that supposed to mean?" Sabiya says, watching him skeptically.

"Sabiya." I place one hand against the wall beside her head. I lean toward her. "I . . ."

"Henrik," she says, shaking her head, looking at me coldly. "Not. Here. Not. Now. OK?"

"What the hell," I say, as the anger flares up again, but before I can say anything else, she ducks under my arm and darts into her room.

The night we spent together had been exactly as I'd hoped it would be. Warm, intimate, close. But in the morning, she seemed uninterested and dismissive, only concerned about getting me out the door as quickly as possible.

And now, when I couldn't find her and thought she was dead, she laughed right in my face.

How can she change so quickly?

Here I am, wagging my tail, only to be rejected. And there are police officers everywhere.

"Have you given a statement?" I ask when we're walking outside together. I'd taken her aside at lunchtime and demanded a rendezvous in the park. The staff meeting had of course veered off topic and turned into a discussion about the murders. But we couldn't leave Lysebu before the police gave us permission.

"Not yet," she says. "What about you?"

"No. But I'm planning to say I was in my room all night. And you?"

"That I was in my room." Sabiya's eyes are evasive. "It's the truth."

"Are you going to say I was there too?" I cringe at the tone of my own voice.

She shakes her head without saying a word.

"By the way, Bente heard that the body was in the sauna," she says. "Really."

"And that it was Melika Omid Carter."

"What?" I stop walking and stare at her. "Are you kidding?"

"Do you think it's something to kid about?" She sounds hostile.

We're surrounded by hope. Environmentally friendly, buzzing beehives. Greenhouses filled with plants. A tiny gazebo, with poles like an exotic birdcage or a cheese dome over a white marble bench, lowered into place on white gravel in between the trees, where they probably take wedding photos. But the idyllic setting now seems almost grotesque.

"And listen, about our trip to the pool," I say. "Maybe it's best we don't say anything about that? Same with our list?"

"*Your* list . . ."

"Fine. *My* list. But we should get our stories straight."

"That woman deserved to die," she says without answering my question, a strange gleam in her eyes. "I treated her child at the outpatient clinic once. One of the worst cases I've seen."

"But could it have been her husband?"

"He's a filthy rich, Iranian-born businessman. He lives in Los Angeles; she's alone with the children. It's *her*, believe me. People like that come from all walks of life and all nationalities and every period in history. I guarantee you that Melika was one of those who'd been abused, subjected to things that you wouldn't even be able to imagine . . . And she has, against all odds, overcome it all, only to become someone who does the exact same thing to her own children."

"What a fucking family legacy."

"Precisely," she says gloomily.

When we get back, the others are sitting at the small tables just off the lobby, each with a cup of coffee. Everyone is a bit green around the gills.

"Where's Askildsen?" I ask.

"Inside negotiating with the police about when we can leave," Roger says.

"It would be nice if they found the man who's running around murdering people," I say laconically.

"Yes . . . Or the woman," Roger says.

"What do you mean by *that*?" Bente says. Her voice sounds like she's choking back tears.

"Just that we don't know who it is," Roger says. "It *could* be anyone, male or female."

"Highly likely, sure," Bente scoffs.

"But most likely it's one of us, isn't it?" Roger says. "It's logical. Two murders and we've been there on both occasions . . ."

"Come on!" I interrupt. "If it had been one of us, we would have certainly chosen other crime scenes, don't you think? For that matter, if I were the one killing these people, I wouldn't have done it at Ullevål or Lysebu. I would have done it in their homes. Or anywhere else where they wouldn't be linked to me."

Roger agrees. "You're right about that. But still . . . ," he goes on, "two murders in two weeks with all of us nearby? Of course we'll be suspects. And I really don't like it."

"Me neither," Bente says as she dries her eyes.

I feel an increasing sense of anxiety. The half truths I've told the police are starting to bother me. What an unfaithful, lying asshole I am.

Then Askildsen walks out, his jacket over his arm, pulling his roller bag.

"They've arrived, the police from last time. Elin and Morten. So, this murder is clearly being linked to the last one. You must go in now, Henrik. Sabiya is after you, Roger after her. Bente and I can go home. We'll be contacted later."

"Is it true she was lying in the sauna?" Roger asks, and looks at Sabiya and me.

"I think so," Askildsen says, and sighs. "But I got the impression she was killed last night . . ."

Roger wrinkles his nose. "She was lying in there baking all night long?"

"Jesus," I say.

"Yeah, that's enough," Sabiya agrees.

"We don't know that." Askildsen returns to Roger's question. "There's apparently a timer or something that turns the sauna off automatically, so they don't have to go by there in the evening when they close the pool. But listen, I suggest we don't speculate too much yet. It's bad enough as it is."

"But if she was shot? Wouldn't we have heard it?" asks Bente, ignoring him.

"Haven't you heard of silencers?" Roger asks. "Like at Ullevål?"

"If it's a victim of foreign origin, *again*, and she was shot with a pistol, *again*, and the culprit just vanishes into thin air, *again* . . . then there *must* be a connection here, right?" I say, without mentioning there are further similarities between the victims.

"Henrik, remember that you're supposed to go in now," Askildsen says.

"Of course." And I get to my feet.

CHAPTER 27

ROGER

I don't like that I'm one of the people going in to be interviewed, one of the people they are clearly prioritizing. Am I still a suspect?

"OK, Roger, can you tell us what you did later that night, after the dinner party broke up at 10:45 p.m.?" the policewoman asks me, and pushes a tiny pouch of snus into her cheek. I wouldn't have thought that was allowed during working hours. It makes a bad impression.

"I wasn't tired, so I wandered around inside the hotel. And then I went for a little walk outside, here on the grounds."

"Alone?"

"Yes."

"How long were you walking around?"

"I don't know, a half hour, maybe?"

"Were you ever anywhere near the pool area?"

"Not really . . ."

"Not really? What does that mean?"

"Well, like I said, I went for a walk through the buildings, exploring the facilities. And at one point I walked down the stairs of that wing there, but I stopped when I realized there was nothing but the spa and pool in that part of the hotel. I went outside afterward."

"So, you didn't go into the changing room or farther inside?"

"No, I didn't."

"Did you speak to anyone?"

"No," I repeat.

I can tell they suspect me.

I've been too close, several times. I must do something to alter their impression.

"But . . . I saw somebody."

"Tell us," the policewoman says.

"When I came up from the basement, I saw Henrik go down to the pool room. And when I was walking outside, I passed by the huge windows facing the swimming pool. And then . . ." I hesitate, as if I'm uncertain about whether I should say this.

"Yes?"

It's Morten who's talking now. Encouraging. Interested. I like him.

"Well, from the outside I could see Henrik and Sabiya inside, in the room with the swimming pool. She was swimming. And he was just standing next to the pool looking at her."

"You were standing outside watching them? Did you stand there long?"

"No, half a minute, maybe. But when I thought about it afterward it seemed strange, considering the night at Ullevål. I saw them together then, too."

"OK, now you're going to have to give us more details," Elin says.

"Henrik and Sabiya," I say. I lean forward and take a deep breath. "I saw them. Together. Outside. When I was outside. But they've probably told you about this?"

CHAPTER 28

HENRIK

The children have turned on the sprinkler under the trampoline. They're jumping up and down in the spray that's rising through the black jumping mat, leaping sideways like joyful dolphins, doing backflips and somersaults, hollering and laughing. The sun creates small rainbows in the water ascending from the ground.

Their small bodies in the sunlight, in the water, as beautiful as sculptures, so full of the future.

It seems like I can see them growing and getting taller with every passing day. At the same time, it's as if they were just born.

Against my own better judgment, when Clara was giving birth to the twins, I'd tried to hold her hand, place a washcloth on her forehead, breathe with her, all that. But she just waved me away. As strong as ever. And if there was one thing she didn't need help with, it was breathing. She'd been practicing that with a nerd-like single-mindedness for years.

"How much does it hurt, on a scale of one to ten?" the midwife asked when Clara's cervix dilated from two to eight centimeters in the course of an hour.

"Five, maybe?" Clara said.

"Do you know whether you have a high threshold for pain?" the midwife asked.

Clara just shrugged.

"Yes, she definitely does," I said, sort of feeling that I should intervene. As soon as I'd said it, I regretted it, realizing that I had just put words into the mouth of this long, slender being with an enormous bulge in the middle of her body.

It seemed like the humiliation of lying there, naked, dependent upon the doctors and the midwife and me, was the worst part for her. Maybe that was why she didn't make a sound while she was in labor, although she managed to convince them to allow her to give birth without an epidural, in contradiction with all recommended guidelines for giving birth to twins.

A moan, once or twice. Otherwise, nothing. Not a word, not a scream.

It didn't resemble any of the births I had witnessed as a student and during my internship.

When I went up to Lysebu yesterday, I'd been giddy with spring fever and joyful anticipation. Things at home were fine. Clara was holding down the fort, my project was underway, a whole day with Sabiya awaited me—and I'd distanced myself a bit from the Faisal and Mukhtar Ahmad incident.

In the course of a single day everything had unraveled.

I see the water, the leaves on the bushes lifting, the sun peeking between the branches, but I see it through a haze.

And the water spraying, the laughter, the creaking of the trampoline, all these summer sounds, I hear them all as if from a distance.

There's an evil omen here running through everything beautiful, harmonious, safe. The contrast—to everything I've been reading about in recent weeks, everything I've seen over the years, the scope of which I am only now beginning to grasp—the contrast is just too great.

And then I recall a verse from a Swedish poem. Written by Pär Lagerkvist, I think.

All is mine, and all shall be taken from me,
Soon all shall be taken from me.

Again, I sense this feeling of connections I should be able to discern, like the minnows the boys try to catch with a landing net when we're swimming, which always just slip away.

There's so much evil in the world.

If you kill someone who kills or injures others, are your actions justifiable?

Andreas is lying on his back on the wet trampoline, trying to nudge a ball toward his feet. Nikolai is filling the wading pool with water. It has seats like a hot tub, a plastic piece of inflatable junk. Grandfather Leif bought it for them for their birthday; I wrinkled my nose, but the kids love it, of course.

Soon, they're busy with their usual breath-holding contests. They've been doing that since they were three or something. It's unbelievable how long they can stay underwater.

"Did you have the night shift?" Andreas asks. He looks at me sympathetically, noticing probably how tired I am. I shake my head.

"I've just been away at a work meeting. And I slept poorly at the hotel."

This afternoon, for once, all four of us are having dinner together. Clara came home and prepared the meal, while I helped by setting the table and talking about the latest murder.

On the menu is salmon with spinach, one of her standard dishes.

Clara doesn't like to cook. I imagine her breathing a sigh of relief every time she manages to throw together a meal and can cross the item *dinner* off her internal checklist. Salmon clearly makes her feel like she's been especially conscientious, as if she hasn't heard that farmed salmon isn't that good for you.

As usual, she's fried the fish for too long. It's burned and has fallen to pieces, while the pink flesh inside is raw and trembling. The potato wedges are swimming in oil. The spinach is wilted and sad. It is only by exercising extreme self-control that I manage to refrain from commenting.

"Yuck, I don't want salmon," Nikolai says.

"Me neither," Andreas says. "Why do we always have salmon?"

Clara looks at them over the rim of her water glass, silent and expressionless, as she always is when the world disappoints her. It's my job to get them to change their tune.

"Oh, come on now, pip-squeaks," I say. "Don't you want to get big and strong so you can crush the other boys on the soccer field? Then salmon and spinach are the best things you can eat—they'll give you super-duper powers."

I've repeated the same tired truth for years. I know they don't believe it any longer, but at least it gets each of them to take a bite of fish.

"Can I have ketchup on it?" Andreas asks.

"Oh, for God's sake," Clara says, shaking her head and sighing. She has an aversion to ketchup; you'd think it was created by Satan himself.

"No ketchup on salmon and spinach," I say. "It ruins the whole super-duper effect. People have been doing research on it for years . . ."

"Daaaddy," Nikolai says, erupting into laughter. Then Andreas starts laughing as well and soon a smile is even twitching on Clara's lips.

"Eat up now, then you can leave the table," I say.

"Yippee!" they say in unison. They wolf down the last bites, throw down the silverware, and dash off.

"Well done," Clara says, and raises her eyebrows. "Eat and run . . ."

"OK, then I suggest you try convincing them next time," I say.

Neither of us says anything while I finish eating. Then I get up and start clearing the table. Clara is leaning over the dishwasher and loading it with dishes.

"I've had a job offer, by the way . . . ," she says.

"Wow," I say. What can it be? A law firm? They often recruit from the Ministry of Justice, I know that. But Clara has been in the ministry world for too long to be a candidate of interest for them. "Where?"

"At the Ministry of Justice . . ."

I am about to mock her but bite my tongue. Clara's been employed at the ministry for an eternity. "A promotion, then?"

"To state secretary," she says, and smiles a girlish smile. "Woll's resigning. And Munch wants me to take his place."

I freeze, holding the frying pan in one hand, my mouth wide open.

"But you're a civil servant. Is it common to change sides like that?"

"No. But it's happened before. And it will happen again," she says. I can't help wondering if the biblical turn of phrase is a coincidence.

I place the frying pan in the sink and sit down on one of the stools. "Not this time, certainly?"

She shrugs and goes back to putting dishes into the dishwasher.

"Wait a minute," I say. "Are you saying that you're considering it?"

"Maybe," she says, again with a half smile. "So, you think it's really nuts?"

"Yes, I do. Don't those people work an obscene number of hours? And you'll be giving up a permanent position for an appointment—you could be sacked anytime."

"You don't have a permanent position either," she says, which is true. At Ullevål nobody gets a permanent position until they turn fifty. Even then, it's not certain. It depends on whether you've had a permanent position elsewhere first and if you're lucky.

For my own part, it's not that important, but most people are interested in securing permanent employment. The uncertainty of such a system creates an unhealthy work culture, where nobody really dares to criticize anything.

"Wouldn't you rather enjoy life? Have a little downtime? Travel, drink good wine? Take long vacations?"

"No," Clara says, and looks at me, baffled.

I'm never certain whether she understands my sense of humor when I tease her about this.

Make the trip "home" to Western Norway, sure. Vacation, no.

Clara is and remains a clever girl from the countryside, a competitive person, a career woman. She has definitely never been full of joie de vivre.

"You don't like having a boss. Besides, do you sympathize with these people at all? I thought you didn't like Munch."

"I don't really, no. But I don't have to like him. I'm working on a plan to blow it all up from the inside."

She sounds enthusiastic, for once.

I shouldn't just shoot it down. I should listen to her, support her, let her work out the madness of this idea in her own way.

But I'm not that smart.

"No," I say. "It won't work. Even for you."

Immediately I realize both my mistake and that it's too late to take it back.

"Fine," is all she says in an ominous tone, her face completely impassive.

CHAPTER 29

CLARA

The door to the cabinet minister's office is shut.

"He'll be with you in a minute," says Vigdis, who's sitting at her desk responding to requests for participation in various things.

Yes, to the First of May speech next year. Yes, to the annual meeting. Yes, to a hearing.

No, to contributing a favorite recipe to a cookbook. No, to choosing a playlist on a radio station.

I wait beside the polar bear, leafing through the newspapers on the table. Glaring headlines about the two immigrants who were murdered dominate all the front pages.

One of the papers appears to have a source on the police force, some type of "deep throat" who issues statements about this, that, and the other thing, probably to the extreme chagrin of the police.

Two main theories have formed, the newspapers summarize, which also point toward a group of colleagues at Ullevål Hospital who, oddly enough, were present at both murder scenes.

The first theory is that an extremely racist, disturbed individual is going around shooting immigrants, like a copycat of the Swedish Laser Man killer from the 1990s.

It's the dry season in the world of news, and one of the papers has run the old Laser Man story again, for the benefit of younger readers.

In the period from August 1991 to January 1992, the Swede John Wolfgang Alexander Ausonius shot eleven people in Stockholm and Uppsala.

Just one of the victims died, but the rest of them sustained permanent disabilities. The only thing the victims had in common was their dark skin color.

Ausonius had a German mother and Swiss father. As a little boy he'd been bullied because of his black hair and dark complexion.

The shootings triggered the second-largest police hunt in Swedish history, and after six months of searching, Ausonius was caught red-handed while committing a bank robbery. Since then he was diagnosed with antisocial personality disorder.

The newspaper has given the story a new twist in disclosing that now, in 2018, Ausonius has been convicted of the murder of a woman in Frankfurt committed back in 1992.

If there really is a person who is tempted to follow in Laser Man's footsteps in Oslo, it could stem from the acute tensions of late between various factions, involving right-wing politicians and the massive media coverage of the Islamic community and gang-related trouble, the newspaper comments.

Theory number two, on the other hand, focuses on gang-related homicides in Oslo's immigrant community.

The murder of Ahmad fits this theory.

The murder of the Iranian American entrepreneur Melika Omid Carter isn't a very good fit. But maybe she, too, had ties to these communities, although there's no clear evidence to support this conjecture.

The police couldn't say anything more and didn't want to speculate.

The media has tried to get Askildsen to make a statement about the fact that he and his coworkers were in the vicinity of both murders, but he is refusing to be interviewed.

In several of the newspapers, commentators have written about the case in the Op-Ed pages.

The police must solve this now, before the city explodes, one of them writes.

"You took my pen," somebody yells angrily behind me. "It's mine! Mine!"

I turn around. Two anemic young girls somewhere between the ages of four and six, their hair in braids and dressed in tutus and striped stockings, are sitting and drawing while the Cartoon Network rolls on the TV screen behind them.

Munch's daughters.

"Everything OK, girls?" the secretary says, and stands up to arbitrate.

At that moment the door opens.

Woll walks out. We look at each other for a second or two.

Then I walk inside, close the door behind me, and take position center stage, in front of the cabinet minister's desk.

"Jesus, Clara, these murders are doing me in," Munch says. "It's all the press is writing about, it's all they care about, and it's complete chaos. But enough about that. How are you doing? Have you made up your mind?"

He leans back in his chair, looking at me expectantly.

I have considered and doubted and reconsidered.

Mona's right. Henrik's right.

All common sense would seem to dictate a clear no.

The most important argument is not based on consideration for my family, the civil service staff, or myself, but that I don't identify with Munch, his opinions, or his party. And that the guy at times acts like a fool.

"Yes," I say. "I've made up my mind."

"And?"

"I'm ready."

"Well, what do you know!" he says, trying somewhat unsuccessfully to turn on the charm. He gets to his feet and shakes my hand. "I knew it! Even you couldn't pass this up."

His cell phone rings. It's lying in the middle of the conference table beside me.

Anna-Karin calling.

I hand him the phone. He glances at it, makes a face.

"Hello," he says. "Of course. Yes, we're at the mall now, the girls have been trying on clothes. We're having some iced tea at a café here. Yes, we're really enjoying ourselves," he says, sending a semi-abashed look in my direction. I study my fingernails and pretend not to notice.

"Teacher planning day," he says after he's ended the call. "My wife had to work. So, I had to take the kids. And I swore on my life that I wouldn't bring them here . . ."

"I understand," I say.

Sure, I understand. I understand that he's a doormat and that he's just as big a liar as all the others.

"We'll formalize your state secretary appointment as soon as possible," he says. "Oh, by the way, Clara, are you a party member?"

I shake my head. "No."

I'm not one to join organizations, and I've never been a member of a political party. If I were to join one, Munch's party would not be anywhere near the top of my list.

"Figured as much," he says. "Then you should join."

"Must I?"

"Well," he says, stalling a bit. "Nobody can force you. But the party would prefer it."

"Fine."

"You'll also be subjected to a thorough security-clearance review. They will ask you if there are any issues in your past that could create difficulties, but it's just a formality. And then you'll be appointed in a cabinet meeting next Friday. Welcome aboard!"

CHAPTER 30

Henrik

"But why do you want to be a secretary, Mommy?" Andreas asks.

Clara has just told the boys that today she will be formally appointed by the king to the position of state secretary at the Ministry of Justice, after I strongly advised her not to accept the offer.

"You don't say," I'd replied and tried counting to ten when she dumped the news on me the evening before.

And then I managed to keep my mouth shut. Because I am a modern man, after all, who doesn't delude himself that he can or should decide what his wife should do. A man who welcomes his wife's advancement at work, who takes a lot of responsibility at home.

The problem is I would also like to be heard.

And even though it's not possible that Clara can work much more than she did when she was working on the bill, that was at least temporary.

My work is in shifts. I want to have a life; I can't be a full-time father.

"I'm not going to be an ordinary secretary," Clara says now. "I'm going to be the kind who helps the person who is the minister of Justice."

"What's his name?" Andreas asks.

"Anton Munch," I say, enunciating all the syllables.

"That's right," Clara says.

"An assistant, then?" Nikolai says.

"Kind of, yes," she says, and picks up her packed lunch from the kitchen counter.

She will probably be the only state secretary who brings her lunch to work. Liverwurst with a dill pickle, salami with cucumber, the same thing ever since school.

"But wouldn't you rather be the boss?"

"I'll be the boss sometimes," Clara says. "I'll be able to decide more, I hope. We control the fire department. And the police . . ."

"The police are trying to find the person who killed the guy at Dad's job," Nikolai says.

"And that lady at the hotel," Andreas adds.

Clara looks at me in irritation, as if it's my fault they're exposed to the news.

"And Daddy will have to be more of the boss here," I say. "Because now we'll be seeing even less of Mommy than usual."

"Oh my God," Clara says, and looks at me in despair. "We talked about this."

"That's a bit of an overstatement," I say. "I was *informed*, yes."

"But, Mommy, why don't you want to spend time with us?" Nikolai asks.

"Yeah, why do you want to be with that Anton guy instead of us?" Andreas asks.

"Thank you very much," Clara says, sending me a cold glare. "Of course I want to spend time with you," she tells the boys and smiles. I raise my eyebrows and whistle. Clara's face turns red, but she says nothing, just ignores me, the way she always does when she's angry. "But Mommy has to work," she adds. "To earn money, so I can buy food and clothing and toys for you . . ."

"Yes, exactly, that's the only reason," I say.

"And now I'll be doing things at work that are a little bit different from before," Clara continues. "But I'll be working in the same building and with the same people. Do you understand?"

"Are you going to be on television and stuff?"

"Probably not."

"On the radio? In the newspaper?"

"I don't know. Maybe," she says, and I can hear that she is growing impatient. "But I have to go. Bye now."

She bends over Nikolai and hugs him, repeats the procedure with Andreas, slings her bag over her shoulder, and leaves.

"Bye now," I shout demonstratively and then, in a saccharine-sweet voice, "Good luck today, dear."

This politician business has made her blossom. She has a new and unusual fervor in her eyes.

To my great surprise, the evening before, my wife, the former great social media skeptic, had even set up a Facebook account. She will now share videos, selfies, party propaganda, and other forms of amusement there. It was apparently one of the cabinet minister's demands, that she become active on social media.

Besides, her phone is buzzing from the time of the six o'clock news broadcast on the radio in the morning until after the national evening news on television. Munch apparently wants her to follow the news around the clock.

The most surprising thing is the enthusiasm and eagerness with which she addresses all of it.

"When are you planning to sleep?" I asked when she was sitting under a blanket on the veranda, answering messages. She'd just had a half-hour conversation with Munch and seemed to be full of energy and happy.

"Don't know," she answered, shrugging and taking a hit from her evening joint. That apparently never changes, and I feel a pathetic pleasure over the fact that at least *something* is the same as before. But won't she be obliged to give up smoking now that she's a state secretary?

When I reach my office, I open the file containing my list. Since Lysebu I've started getting cold feet about the entire business. I've already spent far too much time on this. I'm going to get fired if I keep this up. Besides, something dismal, something disturbing has infected my wonderful project.

Melika is on the list.

My list gives me an obvious motive.

In addition to this, it's coming between Sabiya and me. Or *something's* come between us.

She no longer has time to meet me by the hill near Frognerseteren. We have very little contact on Strava. If I comment, I receive no answer. If I arrive at the office and she's there, she always has some excuse for leaving right away.

I don't know what her avoiding me like this means. But it makes me uneasy.

Yes, I *must* put this list away, at least until everything has calmed down. Maybe I should even delete it. The problem is that I've sent it to Sabiya by email. It's in the system. It's in her mailbox.

It's impossible to concentrate. And today I *must* work on the article.

Then Askildsen comes in and without waiting for an invitation sits down in Sabiya's chair. He is lanky and lean, but not in the flexible, athletic way. More bluish pale and thin. Round eyeglasses.

"Henrik," he says, wiping his balding pate with one hand. "These damn murders . . ."

"Yes?" I say, and make a special effort to sound natural, relaxed, sincere, but my heart is pounding hard and fast in my chest.

"Do you know anything at all about them that I don't know?"

"No . . . What would that be?"

"I can't say. I just have a feeling someone's hiding something from me."

He looks around, his gaze lingering on the view for a few seconds, before turning to face me again.

"Sabiya isn't here, I see. The atmosphere around the unit isn't bad these days, is it?"

"No," I say, and swallow.

"Good. Well . . . do your job, Henrik."

It sounds like a threat. He closes the door behind him before I have a chance to reply.

I lean forward a bit, hold my head in my hands. What does he know? Does he suspect Sabiya? Does he suspect me? Does he know about the list?

The conversation was the kind that would seem fine had it been transcribed, but the tone, facial expressions, and pregnant pauses were unpleasant.

I sit quietly for a little while, thinking.

Then I do the one thing I had decided *not* to do.

I take the key off the top bookshelf and unlock the top drawer of Sabiya's desk. Then the drawer in the middle. Finally, the bottom drawer.

No sign of it in any of them. Not under the mess on Sabiya's desk either.

The Glock's no longer there.

One second. Two. Three. I go through the entire process again in reverse. Close the drawers, lock them, put the key back in its place.

As I'm sitting there, I can feel the panic hit me, like a huge wave rolling into land when a boat that is far too large has sailed by far too close to shore.

This is scaring the living daylights out of me.

What is happening? Is someone after me, someone who's playing games with me? And what's up with Sabiya? In both cases, we were together at the time of death. Is she messing with my head? Who is she really? What should I do now? I have no idea.

So, I do what I always do when there's a crisis. I call Axel, my brother from another mother or whatever it is they call it now.

"Hey," I say. "I need to get away for a bit. You have to come with me to the cottage this weekend."

"To Kilsund? Now?" he says in surprise, which isn't strange, since I haven't done anything this spontaneous since I met Clara, or at least not since the boys were born.

"Yes," I say. "It's not even a request. Go pack!"

CHAPTER 31

CLARA

The email communicating that today I will be appointed to the position of state secretary of the Ministry of Justice is sent out internally just after 9:00 a.m.

Two hours later the cabinet ministers and the prime minister convene the cabinet in the Royal Palace.

When the session is adjourned, I am no longer a senior adviser.

"Congratulations, Clara. Perhaps you can use these?" Vigdis asks, with straightforward professionalism. She is standing in my doorway holding a few flat-packed cardboard boxes.

This is something she has a lot of experience with, from all the cabinet ministers who've had to clear out in a hurry, many of them with no more than a few hours to pack up their things before their replacement is standing on the doorstep, ready to be immortalized with a bouquet of flowers and a key card and a big smile, while the ousted ministers will take the elevator down and walk out into the street where there's no car waiting and nobody cares anymore. I would wager she's dreading the day she will have to pack up Munch's collection of helicopters and emergency response vehicles.

"Yes, thank you," I say, and accept the boxes.

"Woll's office was emptied out and cleaned last night, so it should be ready for you. I'll put a cart outside here, for when you're ready to move your boxes. Things are a bit heated in there these days. The cabinet minister is all worked up because of these murders, you know. We could use a levelheaded woman, Clara, it's a good thing we have you."

"Thank you very much," I say. That was certainly a warm and appreciative welcome.

When I put the first of my boxes on the cart outside the door, a few of my colleagues from my department are standing in the kitchenette directly across from me, leaning against the counter.

They don't say a word. They just look at me.

When I roll the cart into the cabinet minister's section, the little adviser and my two state secretary colleagues are standing in the middle of the room in front of the polar bear and laughing loudly.

I catch something they're saying about the party office. And something about how it's damn well not to be believed. Vigdis is sitting near them, working; the smile on her face is calm and indulgent.

My politician colleagues catch sight of me, stop laughing, and fall silent.

At that moment Mona comes out of her office. She stops and observes us with a tight-lipped smile.

"Well, Clara, here you are with your new gang."

One of the other two state secretaries mumbles something. This time it's impossible to catch what he says.

Munch comes out of his office; the door is straight across the hall from Mona's. Between them sit Vigdis and the other assistants.

"I need someone to make an appearance on the evening news and talk about the shortage of firefighting helicopters for forest fires. Tonight. I'm stuck attending my mother-in-law's seventy-fifth birthday in Bodø this weekend."

The others stare at the ground. Nobody wants to be the front man for this issue. The firefighting helicopter debate has received a great deal of media attention in recent days, and the coverage has been scandalously critical.

"Clara, would you like to give it a shot?" Munch asks, and looks at me.

"Fine," I say. "I don't know anything about firefighting helicopters, but . . ."

"Doesn't matter, neither does anyone else here," he says, with a sidelong glance at the rest of the political team.

"It's Friday—we have the wine lottery," Vigdis warbles. "Does one o'clock work? You're the guest of honor, Clara, you'll be there, won't you?"

"Of course," I say.

At that moment my phone buzzes in my pocket.

CHAPTER 32

HENRIK

Father called, he wants me to open up the cottage in Kilsund. Can you take the kids this weekend? I text to Clara.

OK.

It's quite generous of her to let me leave without notice, particularly considering I didn't give her the chance to extend her stay in Western Norway.

Of course, Axel can go with me. He has the weekend off and the children are with Caroline.

As we drive on the highway headed south, for a short while I'm able to suppress my panic and look forward to reaching the craggy coastline and the salty scent of the ocean, the unending horizon with nothing to see but a few rocky islands and a ship from time to time.

The cottage has been shut for the entirety of the long autumn and the winter and spring, besieged by all kinds of stormy weather, and smells stuffy. Not bad, but stuffy. I open all the doors and windows.

There are faded blue curtains, old brag-book photos of fishermen holding up the day's catch and other highlights in black and white or sepia on the wall, yellowed pine paneling, a varnished pinewood floor, a modest assortment of knickknacks, and a huge nautical map on the wall.

Everything is as it has always been, unaltered since my grandfather built the cottage in 1952.

Two years later he bought the twenty-one-foot fishing boat we still have. Every summer we sail it to the annual Kilsund regatta. My grandmother Edith won it in 1959, and I won the eight-to-twelve-cylinder class on two occasions.

That's something we agree on, my father and I, that down here nothing is to be changed. My uncle took possession of the house after Grandmother Edith passed away and almost ruined it with updates before he relinquished it to us. Kilsund is to be preserved.

I love coming here to go rowing, or simply to sit and look out across the water, paint the odd wall, do repairs. The kids enjoy going out on the boat, fishing for crabs from the pier, diving off the crag. Often, just the three of us will come out here while Clara stays behind to work.

Axel knows this place as well as I do.

Back in the day, our mothers were both put on mandatory bed rest and lay side by side, nurturing their growing baby bumps at the former Woman's Clinic and talking each other's heads off. Ever since then, the two of them and the two of us have been inseparable. For years Axel and I lived together in a rental. Now we live just two minutes away from each other, and we always celebrate events and holidays like New Year's Eve and Norwegian Constitution Day together.

Christian Ferner-Hansen, Axel's father, became Dad's best drinking buddy and friend around the time the two of us were born. Our mothers loved talking about them behind their backs.

Sometimes I believe this is why they are still married, Mother and Father, and Jenny and Christian, because Mom has Jenny, and Dad, Christian, and vice versa.

Running away from the world gives me a wonderful feeling. But I know it will work only for a day or so. And not even the view of the red sunset behind the rocky islands and drinking whiskey with Axel on the stone steps will be enough to quell the nagging anxiety burning like acid in my chest.

I down one drink, and then I down a second and a third. We talk about soccer and geopolitics, about why nobody makes legendary rock and roll albums any longer and whether the eight-hour series about Genghis Khan is the best of Dan Carlin's *Hardcore History* podcasts. Yes, it is, in my opinion. I can't get enough of those Mongolian equestrians who came from nothing and conquered the world, but Axel prefers the one about the fall of the Roman Empire, which he claims is really about the United States.

Four drinks. Five drinks. Finally, Axel looks at me with concern.

"What's going on with you, Henrik?"

"It's nothing," I say.

"You almost never get wasted. Is it Clara?"

We rarely talk about relationships. For that reason, such questions, when they are asked, seem blunt.

"She's suddenly become a state secretary," I say. "In other words, everything's as usual."

Axel stares out across the ocean and smiles. "You can say that again. Tough lady, that one. A carnivore among herbivores. Sort of a female Clint Eastwood."

He's always liked Clara.

"Better from a distance."

Now Axel straightens up and stares at me. "Do whatever you want, just don't get a divorce."

He's still disillusioned after the breakup of his own marriage. Tidal waves of disappointment and bitterness continue to wash through him.

Now it seems that Caroline's new man is the main problem.

"Some idiot wanting to meddle with the child-rearing always comes along with it. The other day my children reprimanded me for not putting my coffee cup on a coaster on the table. Understand?" Axel waves his arms. "*A coaster* on the table? Who do they think I am? They got that from this bourgeois creep from Tønsberg. A full-fledged upstart. He's proof that hipsters are about as independent as teenage girls. I stalked him on Facebook. It's all about electric bicycles, Interrail, and organic wines!"

"I've heard worse," I say.

"It wasn't until afterward that I discovered Caro and her girlfriends all use the same divorce lawyer. The guy is known for securing especially favorable terms for the ladies. It's costing me my damn shirt! You're better off carrying on with someone on the side. But don't forget, make sure she's married, that she has just as much to lose as you. That's where I went wrong."

"She *is* married," I say suddenly.

"Oh?" Axel says, and glances at me in surprise. "A promising start . . ."

I do a Google search for Sabiya, find her profile photo from the hospital website. There she is, dark-skinned, smiling, radiant.

Sabiya Rana. Attending Physician, Department of Pediatrics at Ullevål Hospital.

MD 2008.

Shoulder-length, wavy black hair. Red lipstick. A sly, cryptic look in her eyes.

"Here," I say, handing Axel the phone. I sit gazing at the view. The moon is hanging so low in the sky that it's almost on the surface of the water; the sky above is powder pink. A few hundred yards away some idiot has built a fire on a promontory, even though the temporary ban on campfires in the open is in force here.

He inspects the photograph for a long time. "So that's what you've been up to . . ."

"Is that all you have to say?" I ask, a little offended.

"Great, whatever works for you," he says, hedging.

"Sure?"

"But that there isn't my thing."

"That there?"

"I know someone who was carrying on with a Kurdish lady. And eventually, there was, to put it mildly, a lot of drama. They might come across as completely secular, but they also have a lot of extra baggage."

"Now you're really generalizing," I say in irritation.

"Caro always accused me of that, too. And of course I'm generalizing. Everybody does. Your pulse rate goes up if you encounter a gang of immigrants on the subway. When you encounter an old lady, not so much. That's generalizing—a gut feeling. And your gut feeling is often right."

"I've also got a gut feeling," I say.

"And?" he says expectantly.

"The media is going on and on about a racist Laser Man or gang war in the coverage of these murders. But that's just hype."

"Because?"

"Because nobody's picked up on the fact that what connects the two murders—except for the immigrant background—is that the victims were both child abusers. For the Pakistani victim at Ullevål, it was clear. The Carter lady's cut from the same cloth. It's not pretty."

"Immigrants are overrepresented statistically speaking for such things," Axel says. "Like it or not, it's a fact."

"Sabiya was completely distraught. It was as if she felt ashamed that the Pakistani was one of her fellow countrymen. Afterward I found out she was a member of one of those girl gangs that robbed other girls at Oslo City in the old days, long before she became a pediatrician. What do you have to say about that?"

"Like I said, a lot of baggage."

I draw a breath.

"We share an office. And one day when Sabiya wanted to emphasize how important it is for us to maintain a low profile about our involvement, she showed me a pistol that she kept locked in a drawer, just in case her ultraconservative husband happened to find out about us. Now the Glock is gone. And the police investigation indicates both victims may have been shot by a . . ."

Here I pause for dramatic effect.

". . . Glock."

"Holy shit," Axel says, and gasps for breath. Apparently, he has no ready response for this.

When I get to my feet to follow the path leading down to the outhouse, I feel almost sober.

On Sunday afternoon Axel drops me off at home. I get out of the car with my bag over my shoulder.

The boys are running around in the garden. I pick up Andreas, swing him around, and give him a squeeze. He smells of sunscreen, of summertime little boy. He squeals and laughs, a joyous laughter.

The same procedure with Nikolai. Then we go into the house.

They ambush me in the hallway, wanting to play-fight. I allow myself to be pulled into it, but soon they are lying on either side of me, wanting to cuddle, so I pull them close, absorbing the heat from their small bodies.

And while we're on the floor like that, Andreas with his forehead against my chin and Nikolai with his index finger against my chest, the doorbell rings.

Both the boys and I jump.

"I'll get, it, I'll get it," Andreas says, and runs toward the door with his brother on his heels.

"No, me," Nikolai shouts.

They carry on like this all the time. Everything's a contest. Who can eat more hot dogs, who can ski the fastest, who's better at math, who loses the most teeth the most quickly, who falls asleep the latest, and who's the first to wake up.

I don't want to miss out on any of this. And that's first and foremost why I hang in there, not because of Axel's advice.

Nikolai reaches the door first, but Andreas shoves his way in front of him, pushes down on the door handle, and opens the door.

Outside are three police officers. They are in uniform, light-blue shirts, ties, the whole package, and there are too many of them to be delivering news of a death in the family. Besides, I know them.

For a few seconds, it's completely quiet. Like a silent movie.

Andreas and Nikolai, who throughout their entire childhood have howled *police, police, police* in sheer joy every time they've seen a patrol car or an officer in uniform, who at times have insisted they were going to be policemen when they grew up, run back to me, without a word.

They sense danger, instinctively.

I stand up, catch each of them by the arm, hug them to me. Now Clara also comes out into the hallway.

"May we come in for a bit?" one of the policemen asks.

Without waiting for an answer, all three of them step into the front hall with their boots. Just as well, I don't want them standing on the steps where the neighbors can see them.

"What's going on?" Clara says in her coolest voice from behind me.

"Henrik," the policewoman says, ignoring Clara. "We would like you to come with us to answer a few questions."

Nikolai emits a tiny whimper.

"Go to your mother, you two, we have to borrow your daddy for a while," the policewoman says, looking at him.

"Go ahead," I say to the boys. I don't dare ask any more questions while Clara is listening. "Go to your mommy. I'm just going to help the police for a little bit."

Andreas darts over to Clara and stands with his arms around her leg, like he did when he was younger. Petrified, he doesn't move, just stands there stiffly, staring ahead.

Nikolai, on the other hand, starts screaming.

"Daddy, Daddy, Daddy," he howls, and tugs at me. I lift him up, carry him over to Clara. He's gotten big. And heavy.

"You ride with us, Henrik," the policewoman says, and I nod, not wanting to encourage any more conversation here in the hallway. I kiss the boys on the cheeks and try to tell them I love them, but my words are drowned out by Nikolai's howling.

"Talk to you soon," I say to Clara. It doesn't occur to her to give me a marital kiss for the sake of our audience.

Then I lumber along behind the police, trying to move as naturally and calmly as possible.

CHAPTER 33

CLARA

I don't usually call in the morning. Today I'm on the line before eight.

"Hi, how are you doing?" I ask.

"I'm muddling along. I stopped by the consumer co-op yesterday. Afterward I bought new windshield wipers for the car. And salt lick for the sheep. Spent money like there was no tomorrow. But I haven't seen Bella for two days. That worries me."

"I'm sure she'll come home," I say, and summon my strength. "But listen, Daddy . . . The police took Henrik in for questioning yesterday, and now it looks like they're going to keep him there."

"My God . . . What are you saying? Is this about the Ullevål murder?"

"Yes. And the murder at Lysebu. It's just a misunderstanding, some kind of police error. I'm sure it will all be straightened out soon. But would you mind coming to stay with us? I'll pay for your ticket, of course."

There's a moment of silence.

Daddy has always preferred to be in his own home.

Before his parents died and he had to take over the farm, he was at sea for a couple of years. By the time he took over the farm, most of his spirit of adventure, not to mention the chance to travel anywhere, had disappeared. Whatever might have remained of such a spirit had vanished during his six months in Lebanon.

Since then, apart from five or six nights spent in our house over the years, for christenings and such, he hasn't slept anywhere but home at the farm.

"Yes," he says. "Of course I will."

CHAPTER 34

HENRIK

They are emanating something different, Elin and Morten. It's as if the chummy, lighthearted tone of collaboration between us has just been an act, a mask they have taken off to reveal their true essence. Or maybe it's now they're playacting.

I don't know and it really doesn't matter. They're not my friends, after all.

The only thing that matters is getting out of here as quickly as possible.

"We've come across some interesting email correspondence," Elin says as soon as they have wrapped up the endless formalities and I have again agreed to be questioned and waived my right to a lawyer, even though I'm beginning to wonder if I might actually need one. "It appears you've been trying to collect information about different patients who have been victims of domestic violence, and doing so without the knowledge of your superior. Is that correct?"

"Yes, that's correct," I say, attempting a sincere and open tone of voice.

"In an email to Sabiya Rana dated May 23, you write, and I quote, 'Here's a list of the abusers: scum of the earth—they ought to be water-boarded and crucified IMHO.'"

Oh my God. Read out loud in her voice and intonation, my off-the-cuff remark to Sabiya sounds completely deranged.

"That's how I was feeling then," I say, and clear my throat. "You have no idea how much evil those people are responsible for. Yes, it makes me furious. Yes, it was a careless comment. But no, it doesn't make me a murderer!"

She leafs through her papers a bit.

"Is it also correct that Melika Omid Carter was one of the names on this list?"

I nod. Cards on the table now.

"Yes, she was," I say, still calm.

"OK. Let's go back to Ullevål Hospital on May 10," Elin says. "The Pakistani father was killed by a shot from a pistol. He was found at 10:27 p.m. The time of death must have been between 10:15 and 10:20. We were notified at 10:35 and were at the scene at 10:45. We know all this. What we don't know is where you were between 10:15 and 10:30."

"I was at the unit," I say. "I told you that before."

"You were there the whole time? Inside the building?"

I nod. Can't start changing my story now.

"Well," Elin says. "It's surprising you still claim that, even though we've tried to give you the chance to correct it. Because you were observed outside with Sabiya around 10:05. The two of you were standing close together and looked upset, according to our witness."

Who had seen us? Who had talked? And why hadn't we just told them the truth?

"Yes, that would be correct. Sabiya was upset. She went outside to get some air. And I followed her. I just forgot about it."

"Do the two of you ordinarily go outside in the middle of a shift?"

"No. But it wasn't exactly an ordinary shift, not after that little boy came in. Anyway, Sabiya was upset, completely beside herself, in fact. I'd never seen her that way. So, yes, I tried to calm her down."

"The witness says that it looked as if the two of you were, and I quote, 'out of it,' and at the same time, it seemed like you had 'an intimate connection'?"

"Yes, of course. What happened to the boy was extremely distressing. And I was especially worried because Sabiya seemed deeply troubled . . ."

I cringed slightly. But what the hell, I must simply tell them everything, save my own skin, as I'd decided on my way home from the cottage.

"You want to change your statement in other words, from the previously stated series of events, in which you were inside the building at all times? Now you are saying that you went outside with your colleague?"

She's about to paint me into a corner.

"Yes, but just for a few minutes," I say, and even I can hear how pathetic it sounds. "Five at the most. Then we went inside again."

"Well, there's a discrepancy there," Elin says.

"Is there?" I say. Already I'm feeling completely exhausted.

"How did you get back into the unit after your conversation with Sabiya?"

"Sabiya used her card. We went in together."

"She used her card, yes, 10:12. That's right."

"Yes, exactly," I say, and lean back. "We both went inside then."

"But the problem is that you used your card to enter at 10:21. In other words, nine minutes later. So, the question is: What did you do outside for nine minutes after Sabiya went back in, *without* you? Also, why are you insisting you went back in together? When it's impossible that you did so?"

An avalanche is released around me and inside me, it thunders away, and I have no chance to stop it.

This is not right.

"In theory, those nine minutes are enough to get to the prayer room, shoot Mukhtar Ahmad, go back, and punch in at 10:21," Morten says.

"In theory," I mumble. I fold my hands, squeezing them together hard, all the while trying to appear calm. The air-conditioning must be out of order; sweat is running along my temples and down my cheekbones.

CHAPTER 35

CLARA

The morning meeting begins on a jovial note.

"Clara! The weekend's winner," Munch says. "You're off to a flying start."

"Thank you," I say. "I've at least had a crash course in firefighting helicopters . . ."

"Sorry you had to give that one away, Anton," the adviser says. "A classic winning case."

"Not until Clara got hold of it," the head of communications says, to his credit.

The evening news assignment on Friday had snowballed. First, I was sent to appear on the six o'clock news. Later I was asked to return for the evening segment. After that, I was called in to appear on a variety of news broadcasts on Saturday and Sunday.

At first all I said was that we recognized the need for more firefighting helicopters and would address it as soon as possible, a statement that doesn't really satisfy viewers, especially when there are ongoing forest fires in several locations in Eastern Norway.

I called Munch.

I called the executive officer and deputy director general and the director general.

I called the Directorate for Civil Protection.

I called Munch again.

By Saturday afternoon I reported the news that we would be mobilizing fifteen new firefighting helicopters designated for the rural areas and that the state would cover the cost of the helicopters.

"Yes, good job, Clara," Mona says. "All we need to do now is find out what we're going to do about this killing spree. Fewer murders are committed in Oslo than people think. One or two a year. Now suddenly, we've had two, one right after the other. And if it turns out the Laser Man theory holds water, people will demand action. We must show that we won't stand for the systematic execution of immigrants."

"I'll take care of it," Munch says.

"Shall I send you some speaking points?" the head of communications asks.

"No, that won't be necessary," Munch says. "The Laser Man theory is just humbug on the media's part. I've personally received a briefing on the case from the head of the investigation. And I know that the police are now certain the weapon came from one of the gangs in Oslo."

Everyone is looking at him. And then it's as if he summons his strength before launching into an angry monologue he has clearly been longing to deliver, all the while turning his cell phone around and around in his hands. The long side down, the short side down, then the long side, then the short side.

Hard and fast, as if the phone were a deck of cards.

"It's escalating all the time. You don't have to look any farther than Sweden to understand what will happen if these people are permitted to carry on. Gang killings are an ordinary occurrence. They won't be stopped by lectures on morality and personal ethics or by allocating more funding to youth centers! It seems like the police have given up on combating organized crime. These people only understand one thing: brute, physical force. They must be under surveillance twenty-four hours a day. Stop their cars. Ransack them. Bring them in on petty charges. Send a clear message that we don't accept this."

"Exactly," the adviser says.

Munch takes a breath, banging his iPhone against the table in a steady rhythm.

"The other party thinks they can solve this through dialogue with groups who couldn't care less about Western values. They have attacked us for years whenever we've tried to point this out. Now it turns out that we were right all along. If people absolutely refuse to follow Norwegian law, they can pack their things and get out. Criminals must be put in prison, the police must be armed, and illegal aliens sent home on the next damn flight out of here."

"Exactly," the adviser repeats with enthusiasm.

Mona sighs heavily beside me.

"It's a provocation that there's no support from the other parties on this. Had these thugs been running around waving plastic toy pistols, both the media and the other parties would be shouting about how we must prohibit this unnecessary use of environmentally hazardous plastic toys. But when they're running around with actual firearms, we are the only ones who seem to care."

At first there's silence. Nobody knows how to respond.

A lot of what Munch is saying is sensible. What's shocking is his tone, as if he's giving a well-rehearsed performance at his own morning meeting, that and how he insists on drawing categorical conclusions about the recent murders.

He's not finished, either.

"I would like to use this case as an example of the rotten culture in that social environment. Like how they're going after one another now . . . Wait, what the hell," he exclaims, and stares at his phone.

The entire screen has suddenly cracked. It looks like there's an intricate spiderweb embedded in the glass.

"Oh dear," Vigdis says. "I'll call the IT Department right away and order you a new one. Give it to me, Anton."

"Thanks," Munch says, staring in sorrow and shock at his iPhone screen, as if he can't fully grasp what has happened.

"Just give it to me," Vigdis says gently, and like a helpless child who has broken his toy, he finally hands his phone over to her.

"No matter what, you should be careful how you talk about this case," Mona explains. "It's not very smart to have the nation's minister of Justice speculating about the causes in a double homicide case when we don't know anything yet with certainty. If we are absolutely going to comment, it should be in extremely general terms."

"You don't say," Munch replies sarcastically.

"At least have a talk with Police Commissioner Monrad before saying anything. This is a police matter, after all, even though you will no doubt be obliged to handle her."

"Yes, speaking of populist . . . We don't need that woman. We have our own police contacts," the adviser says.

"You're mistaken about that," Mona says wearily and runs her hand through her short hair. She tends to do that when she's irritated, which she often is during these morning meetings with the political leadership and the head of communications. "Monrad's sharp. And has full oversight. You should definitely have her on your team."

"By the way," I say. "My husband and his colleagues at the pediatrics unit at Ullevål have coincidentally found themselves in the vicinity of both murders and are trying to help the police to the best of their abilities. I believe Henrik is speaking to them right now."

"Small world, isn't it," Munch says without showing a modicum of interest.

"Terrific that they're helping out," Mona says.

I exhale silently. I have intentionally avoided using words such as interrogation. And neglected to mention that Henrik has been at the police station since yesterday.

Several times in the course of the meeting, I've glanced at my cell phone.

Has Henrik called? Or the media?

Nobody has called. But with every passing hour, this is turning into an increasingly volatile, ticking time bomb.

"Next item," Munch says impatiently, and I breathe a sigh of relief. "There's a dinner at the Royal Palace on Wednesday evening. I should be there. But I'm flying to Brussels Tuesday evening and won't be back until Thursday. Sorry, Mona, I didn't realize there was a conflict before now . . ."

He puts a finger to his lips and looks over at his secretary, who shakes her head and rolls her eyes, smiling loyally.

Everyone laughs a little. Everyone knows that such dinners are Munch's least favorite thing and Mona dislikes his sloppy attempts to play hooky.

"OK," she says, with a sigh.

"So . . . Clara," Munch says, and looks directly at me. "If we can get you clearance in time, could you step in? Feel free to bring your husband, the doctor. Then the ministry will be represented."

I shrug. Nod.

Out of the corner of my eye, I can see Mona shaking her head.

"A clear breach of protocol to send a state secretary."

"Any more business? Anyone?" Munch says. "Going once, going twice? Nothing? Off you go, then."

The meeting is adjourned.

I glance at my phone. An unknown Oslo number. A voice mail message. I listen to it on the way into my office.

Henrik. Who asks me to call him at a specific number.

"Clara," Henrik says breathlessly when I get him on the line. I'm sitting behind the closed door of my new office. "You won't believe this. The police won't be releasing me anytime soon. Right now they're taking a short break from questioning. I don't think they're allowed to hold me for more than forty-eight hours without formally charging me. But can you let Askildsen know that I'll be away from work for a while? And ask him to tell the others that I'm ill or something; I don't want everyone to know where I am. Say that it's a misunderstanding. Will you call my father, too? He must help me. Tell him to call me. OK? I have to hang up now . . ."

He sounds agitated, almost panicky.

"I'll call right away. And Henrik?"

"Yes?"

"It will be fine."

"You think?"

He sounds like he's on the verge of tears.

"Of course. Just hang in there."

CHAPTER 36

HENRIK

The room we are sitting in is small and sterile. It would have been suf-
ficiently minimalist even for Clara.

I've read that interrogations nowadays are carried out in more
relaxed interiors, where those involved sit in ordinary armchairs with a
small table between them. Nobody sits facing each other on opposite
sides of a table, because all the research has shown that the person being
questioned just shuts down and stops talking.

Well, be that as it may, this interrogation is being carried out in the
old-fashioned manner.

The room is furnished with a table, on top of which are water and
glasses and cups and a coffee dispenser, and the chairs we are sitting on.
A single window offers a view of a birch tree, which like everything else
has begun to turn brown after a month of intense heat and no rain.
Yellowish-brown leaves sail past as they fall to the ground.

I have picked up a few things from my father and Christian, and
from the year I studied law. As is the case for all other professions, things
are not exactly as they might seem.

Interrogation is not always carried out 100 percent by the book,
although the police will try to make it seem like it is. Although the
intention is for the process always to be respectful and open and all that,
mistakes are made and slipups occur in this field as they do in all others.

The police have often been more concerned about nailing some-body than about precisely whom they nail.

Now I watch them, trying to meet their gazes. Elin has put on makeup; it makes her look older and more severe.

"I went inside with Sabiya!" I say loudly. "I give you my word, just ask her. I wasn't outside for very long, that would have been crazy."

"I want to remind you that you've just changed your statement, about how you were outside. And your card was used to enter the build-ing at 10:21 p.m.," Elin says calmly.

Silence. The sound of a fan going around and around, spinning the way my head is. I get dizzy, my fingers grow numb, I feel like I'm about to collapse onto the floor at any moment.

"Let's review your statement from Lysebu." When I don't reply, Elin continues in a monotone, reading from a document: "'I sat outside until around eleven. And then I went to my room and slept like a log until I was awakened by all the commotion early this morning and went down to the reception.' But when questioned, the maid who cleaned your room said your bed hadn't been slept in. How can that be?"

"I slept on the couch," I say desperately.

"You slept on the couch, then we'll make a note of that," Elin says.

"No. I was with Sabiya," I burst out suddenly. "In her room."

Elin and Morten exchange glances.

"When questioned, Sabiya Rana told us the two of you have been having an affair for the past year."

She told them. Without saying a word to me.

"Yes," I say frantically. "And that's correct. But I'd promised her never to tell anyone about us. I took that promise seriously. I was afraid my wife would find out, but more than anything I was afraid of Sabiya's husband, the man she needs a pistol to protect herself from."

Morten has been sitting in silence for a long time. Now he clears his throat and leans forward.

"From the bullets and caliber, we can establish that Melika Omid Carter must have been shot with the same pistol as Mukhtar Ahmad. It is highly probable that it's a Glock 17 9-millimeter with a silencer."

"All right," I say.

"The Glock 17 is a pretty common firearm," he informs me. "It is used in the armed forces. And sometimes a pistol will go missing there. After the murder we investigated criminal groups that have been involved in conflicts with Ahmad and his circle. We discovered that a stolen Glock 17 with a silencer has been in circulation in that community for a number of years."

My nausea subsides somewhat.

"The illegal 'owner' of the firearm has been interrogated. It turns out that he knows Sabiya Rana and has admitted to giving her the gun in November of last year."

So, they are really tying this to Sabiya, that's why they want to talk to me, because they suspect her. Thank God.

"Did Sabiya ever show you this weapon?"

This is when they want me to deny it, so they can corner me.

"Yes," I reply, loudly and clearly. "She did."

"Did you tell her what you thought about having a firearm lying around the office?"

"I probably should have. I tried. But I was afraid of what her husband might do."

"When she was questioned, Sabiya admitted to having kept a firearm at the office. She has at her own initiative confirmed the story of how the pistol came into her possession. It's not our job to decide what the consequences of this obvious violation of the Norwegian small arms law will be. We are investigating a murder. What interests us is that the man who gave Sabiya the firearm naturally knew that she had it, but not where she kept it. You on the other hand did."

"Yes," I say, and consider telling them about the sight of Sabiya and her husband on Ullevålsveien Street, that with time I am coming to believe that Sabiya lies quite a bit. But how can I put this in a way they will believe?

"Sabiya also says that the pistol was suddenly gone when she went to get it right after the murder of the Pakistani father."

The air is heavy and stuffy.

More than anything I just want to cradle my head in my hands. Elin stands up, walks in a circle around the room, tugging at the belt of her trousers, as if preparing herself for another round in the boxing ring. Morten leans forward, evidently ready to take over in the meantime.

I close my eyes and drive the thumbnail of one hand into the cut on my fingertip on the other, to give myself something else to focus on.

"Yes, and as for Lysebu," Morten says. "The witness who saw you outside the hospital at 10:05 the evening Mukhtar Ahmad was killed also saw you in the pool at Lysebu at 11:00 p.m., when Melika Omid Carter was shot. Is that correct?"

"Yes," I say.

"Were you in the sauna?"

"No."

"But your fingerprints were on the door handle of the sauna door. Can you give us an explanation for that?"

I can't. Not just now. All I'm capable of doing is to submit to the urge to cradle my head in my hands.

"We find ourselves in a unique situation in that you have no alibi for either of the murders. You have changed your statement in both cases. You knew where the murder weapon was kept. You have expressed a wish that both victims would die. And you have a motive," Morten says.

Elin puts her hand on my shoulder.

"I understand your rage, Henrik. I see a lot of horrible things on the job as well. But you're a law-abiding man who has committed acts that must be punished. Deep down, you know that. Can't we just put the cards on the table?"

"I didn't kill them," I whisper.

CHAPTER 37

CLARA

"These two murders represent a trend that must be stopped," Munch says with great pathos. His slightly bloated face fills the entire screen.

Mona, Vigdis, the head of communications, and I are standing in front of the television on the wall directly across from Mona's office.

"Oslo, and particularly the east side, is in the process of becoming a lawless city, resembling more and more parts of the world we don't like to compare ourselves with and less and less our own safe capital. The behavior of these gangs toward ordinary people is extremely threatening. The murders of the father Mukhtar Ahmad and the mother of two, entrepreneur Melika Omid Carter, constitute the last straw. We must put an end to this killing spree and the change it represents before our country is destroyed. We've been working to implement harsher sentencing and to arm the police, give the police a more visible presence, and remove the prison waiting lists. This work will be made a priority in the time ahead. I have requested a crisis package for the police to use to crush the gangs wreaking havoc in our city."

"What do you have to say about the shocking murders that have just been committed?" the interviewer asks.

"A mother and a father have been slain. Several children have lost the most beloved person in their lives. This is unacceptable. I will make sure the police mobilize all available resources for the purpose of stopping these gangs."

"'This is unacceptable,'" Mona parrots. "Is it possible? I have forbidden all use of that phrase."

"You're strict, Mona," the head of communications says.

"It's necessary. It's on a par with the saying 'richest country in the world.'"

"Anton hasn't been himself lately. He's been sleeping poorly," Vigdis, his maternal protector, says.

"Where is he, by the way?" I ask.

"In Parliament," Vigdis says, the only one who knows his whereabouts at any given time.

Everyone is still staring at the television. The broadcast cuts to Cathrine Monrad. Big, blonde hair, heavy makeup, huge earrings—again it strikes me that she doesn't look like a police commissioner.

"That one," Vigdis says. "Isn't she a little . . . inappropriate?"

"Hush," the head of communications says.

"Police Commissioner Cathrine Monrad, are you willing to comment about Minister of Justice Munch's statement?" the journalist asks in a booming voice.

When Cathrine Monrad looks gravely into the camera, her gaze doesn't falter for an instant. "It's extremely unfortunate that the minister expresses himself with such certainty about the ongoing investigation of this serious case. Especially when we are considering every alternative. I take strong exception to the minister of Justice's remarks."

"Uh-oh," the head of communications says.

"There'll be trouble now," Mona says, crossing her arms. She moves about restlessly.

"Wait," Vigdis says, and squints toward her cell phone when the news segment is over. "I received a text from the minister."

"Has he gotten a new phone? Or does he get glass splinters in his fingertips when he texts now?" I ask, unable to restrain myself.

"Now, Clara," Vigdis says, and sends me a long-suffering look. "Yes, he has a new phone. I arranged it immediately, of course."

"What does he want?" Mona asks.

"He wants me to call Cathrine Monrad and bring her in for a reprimand."

"Now?" Mona asks in surprise.

"This afternoon, yes, before he leaves for Brussels."

"OK, I'll see what I can do, even though it's not a good time . . ."

Mona usually attends such ticklish meetings with government agency directors. She is after all responsible for personnel matters.

"Well," Vigdis says with an apologetic smile. "He says here that he wants Clara to be there and only Clara. I see he has an opening at three this afternoon. Do you have time, Clara?"

"Yes," I say as indifferently as I can. "I guess I do."

"Ooh," the head of communications says, making a face.

"All right," Mona says, struggling to maintain her composure. "If that's how he wants it, then . . ."

"I'll call Cathrine Monrad," Vigdis says, and smiles the smile she puts on when she must make particularly disagreeable phone calls.

CHAPTER 38

HENRIK

In terms of appearance, this place isn't bad. In a way, it would have been better if it had been. Since the Norwegian prison system is quite humane, people often think that being in jail isn't a hardship.

They are mistaken.

The room itself and the interior remind me of the military. Especially the blue bedding, except that it has the words *Department of Corrections* on it, and not *Armed Forces*.

Otherwise, the cell has thick gray walls, a metal door, a mirror, a sink, a closet, a window with bars, a ceiling light and reading light, a heater, an air vent, a cooler for food. And a simple steel toilet.

The biggest problem is there are no distractions. They have of course taken my phone. I've been given a pen and paper. At first, I tried jotting down a few words for myself, to try to acquire an overview of the case. But it made me a bit paranoid, afraid that what I wrote would be intercepted and used against me. In the end I tore the sheet of paper up into tiny pieces and threw them away.

In the distance I can hear the sound of someone playing ping-pong.

Every sound is intensified here, since there's nothing to see.

I haven't been inside a cell since my first, failed year at law school when I was doing pro bono work. And being locked up instead of visiting as an ambulatory hero is something else altogether.

There's so much I don't understand.

Who saw me outside the hospital and in the pool? What more could they have seen? Why in the world does the entrance log show that I entered the building nine minutes later than I did? What happened to Sabiya's Glock? And all this circumstantial evidence, is it enough to put me away for good? It can't be. Or can it?

Imagine if I end up sitting here indefinitely?

That thought is almost intolerable.

A little break from daily life. Nobody hounding me, no bosses, no patients, no children or wife or neighbors, how wonderful that would be, for a little while. I remember thinking that when I heard about people who had done time for something or other. Nothing you *must* do. Just relax, read, sleep. A kind of time-out from the daily grind.

Jesus, what an idiotic idea.

It's of course impossible to relax when you're locked up in a tiny room with no other company but the many thoughts that are constantly getting tangled into an enormous knot.

Why didn't I understand before that the freedom I have taken for granted for forty-three years is the biggest and most important blessing I have?

What are the boys thinking? Will they find out where I am? Will they think I've abandoned them, let them down? Will they be afraid about what will happen to me? Nikolai and his nightmares—what will this do to him?

And Sabiya, what is she really thinking? Does she suspect something? What has she understood? Did she set me up?

What if she calls Clara and tells her everything?

Clara's new job, will that go down the drain now?

I should have done everything differently, right from the start. Or not started the affair in the first place.

The door is unlocked, and the guard, a guy with the physique of a bodybuilder, sticks his head in.

"You have a phone call," he says.

"OK," I say, and get to my feet.

It must be Clara; she's the only person I want to speak with now. But it's not her.

"Henrik?" my father says on the other end. Tears fill my eyes. I rub my sleeve across my face, a bit in disappointment that it's not Clara, a bit in relief that it's my father.

William Fougner always finds solutions. Things tend to work out when he's around. Now I start sniffling like a little kid.

"Dad," I hear myself say in a thin voice. The word sounds strange. It feels like it's been a hundred years since the last time I called him that. "You have to help me."

Silence.

"I'm going to make a few calls," he says finally. "Find out if the media knows anything, try to get them to postpone releasing this. And then I'm going to see if Christian can help."

Christian, Axel's father and my father's best friend, is known to be the toughest defense attorney in the city.

"Thank you . . ."

If anyone can get me out of here, it's him.

"Clara wants to visit you, but you're not allowed any visitors at this time. And if she were to show up there, this case would most likely explode, so it's not a good idea anyway. But when we meet you must tell me everything. From start to finish. Do you understand?"

"Of course," I say.

CHAPTER 39

Clara

Cathrine Monrad is tall, even taller than I am. She's not in uniform. Slender and fit in a leopard-print suit and with long blonde hair flowing down her back. An expensive, pale scarf around her neck. She looks more like a glamorous Swedish crime novelist than a division director.

"Hello, Cathrine Monrad," she says to me, in a Bergen dialect.

"Clara Lofthus," I say, and shake her hand. "Nice to meet you," I add, as it occurs to me that it might be wise to start out by showing a little courtesy.

"Congratulations on your new position as state secretary," she says, and inspects me, as if she is trying to discern whether I still think it's something worthy of congratulations. "Will it just be the three of us?" she asks, and looks around.

"Yes, today we will be keeping things a bit intimate," Munch says. He pulls out a chair for her before walking around to the other side of the table.

The meeting room has the capacity for twenty people around the table and is far too large for three people. Scheduling the meeting here is more than anything a kind of master suppression technique.

I follow him, so the two of us are seated side by side, with Monrad directly across from us.

Mona Falkum should be here. One member of the civil service staff should be here at least. I had tried to say as much, but Munch wasn't interested in listening to me.

One of our former cabinet ministers had always included civil service staff members in every meeting. When he stepped down, he said that he'd never regretted this practice. The more trust he demonstrated, the more loyalty he would receive in return, was his philosophy.

Munch, on the other hand, is treating the civil service staff more and more like the enemy with every passing day.

"Well, then? I see you're out there making statements about me to the media," Munch begins. "And here I was under the impression that as the director of one of my subdivisions you were supposed to be loyal to me, a cabinet minister?"

"In principle, yes," Monrad says.

"In *principle*?" Munch repeats, stressing each syllable.

Monrad takes her time. She pours a glass of sparkling water, then a cup of coffee. Takes a sip of coffee, places the cup down on the table.

"Well," Monrad says, and sighs. "It is very unfortunate that you insist on this connection between gang-related crime and these two murders. That can be dangerous. And when it comes to loyalty, my loyalties are first and foremost supposed to be with the public and the best interests of the nation."

"Our nation's finest," Munch snorts.

"Yes," Monrad says. "When you make such a statement, it's like throwing gasoline on a fire. It produces both unnecessary anxiety and high-risk situations without any basis in the facts. The gang situation is bad enough without our stirring things up further for no good reason. I gave the journalist my best assessment. It's my duty to adhere to a strict policy of professional ethics. If you'd contacted me, I would have warned you."

"You couldn't have just given me a call?" Munch asks.

He's playing stupid now; all three of us know he would have done the same thing regardless of what she said or did beforehand.

Anton Munch thinks only about what benefits him personally, says only what people want to hear, or more precisely: what he thinks his *constituents* want to hear. He doesn't give a damn about the rest of the population.

That's how they all are, even though Munch is perhaps worse than average.

It's also accepted that politicians use strategic communication, that they don't say what they think, but what they *believe* will be beneficial. And strategic communication quickly becomes so manipulative that it ends up being a lie.

All these years I've looked down on this in contempt. Now I am personally a part of it, have voluntarily stepped into the lion's den.

What am I thinking? That I'm going to change something?

"For the love of God," Monrad says. "The point is to avoid getting people all steamed up when it's not in our best interests. When you've already taken such a public stance, it unfortunately doesn't help if I give you a call. The police commissioner must step forward. In the media. And preferably right away."

How typical of such self-aware division directors to refer to herself in the third person.

"And as far as loyalty goes," she continues. "It's pretty invidious behavior on your part to attack a government institution without any dialogue with us whatsoever."

"Well," Munch says. "I have an absolute requirement for all of my subordinates, regardless of whatever needs they otherwise might have . . ."

As he says the word *subordinates*, I lean as discreetly as I can away from Munch, pick up the phone I'd put down on the chair beside me, and lift it a few inches above the seat, making sure that it's still well hidden under the tabletop.

Munch and Monrad are busy staring each other down and don't notice that I punch in my pin code and type a few keystrokes.

There. I put the phone down again.

". . . demonstrate loyalty in front of the media. At all times. No matter what."

They glare at each other.

"And this is not the first time you've done such a thing. We don't need to go further back than the evening news recently, for example."

Cathrine Monrad shakes her thick blonde mane and emits a wry laugh.

"With all due respect, we are receiving so many different instructions, targets, and assignments from you these days that we don't have time to concentrate on the work we're supposed to be doing. It's a problem."

"What does that have . . ."

"As far as this matter is concerned, there *are* as stated good security-related grounds for my shutting down these theories of yours. If the official Norway, represented by the minister of Justice himself, states that gang members are responsible for these murders and it proves not to be true, it can lead to sanctions nobody wants. And I can't refrain from taking action just to indulge you. There are enough people doing that."

Silence.

Monrad is right. With Mona being the one honorable exception, people here don't dare contradict the cabinet minister. People are afraid of retaliation and trouble. And in their eagerness to protect the cabinet minister from any pushback, they in fact fail to protect him.

"Cathrine," Munch says, slowly and clearly. "If you continue in this way, it will be impossible for me to trust you. Do you understand what I'm saying?"

"Well . . . ," Monrad says, her face red, glancing over at me for the first time. "What does your state secretary think about that threat?" she asks with a trace of derision in her voice.

"Allow me to summarize," Munch says. He's not interested in an answer from me. "You must change your style with the media. Or even better, stop having any style."

"Are you serious about this?" Monrad says.

"Yes, it's really not your job to be a politically correct media whore."

Silence. The sound of invisible glass crashing to the floor.

"OK," Cathrine Monrad says, and gets up. "This meeting is over."

She lifts her beige coat off the chair and drapes it over one of her arms, throws her bag over her shoulder, and leaves, without looking at us or shaking our hands, even though we've gotten to our feet.

But when she reaches the doorway, she turns around suddenly.

"Had you contacted me, I could have told you that an ethnic Norwegian man is now in police custody and will be charged for these crimes."

For a second or two she looks at me. I straighten up and meet her gaze, defying the impulse to cower in my seat.

I can see that she knows. She could have said it.

But she didn't.

Then she walks down the corridor, her heels slamming against the floor.

"What the hell was the last thing she said?" Munch mumbles as he gathers up pens and papers and his phone. "I'll give my contact a call and find out what's going on."

Half an hour later I'm called into his office.

Munch is sitting rigid with anger behind his desk.

"Clara . . . is this true? Is your husband really the suspect? For double homicide?"

"Yes. But he's innocent."

"You seem sure about that."

"Believe me, it's a mistake. He'll be out soon."

He gives me the once-over and sighs.

"Everyone warned me not to give you the state secretary position, and they were apparently right. A lot of people would make short shrift of you now."

"You must do what you need to do."

"The problem is, that won't look good either . . . ," he continues, as if he's talking to himself. "Twenty-four hours, Clara! That's what you get. If he comes out a free man, we'll forget about this. And this conversation. But of course, you understand that if there's any basis to the charges, I have no choice."

That evening, when I'm safely home, I open the Strava app.

I know about her. I've known all along. About the others, too. But I haven't said anything, and Henrik thinks that I don't know anything. He thinks he's so smart, because he doesn't text her or chat with her, and he has no idea that I've discovered his Strava account. All I did was look through the lists of the running routes he uses the most frequently and I found him. DOCTORH.

And after I found him, I also found MRSSPLENDID. She couldn't have come up with a more pathetic handle.

Did Henrik think it was enough that they didn't follow each other on there? When they are constantly giving each other kudos and commenting on each other's posts and pictures? When the time periods for their runs always coincide? And the heart rhythm info shows that they've taken twenty-to-thirty-minute breaks at the same time?

I'm not using the app now to find proof of his infidelity but to find out what the damn sanctimonious MRSSPLENDID does in the evenings.

I access her running routes. It looks like Sabiya runs the same route at 8:00 p.m., the same routine, several times a week.

It's 7:35. It will take me fifteen minutes to get to the neighborhood where Sabiya lives.

"Can you watch the children for a while?" I say to Dad. "So I can go for a short bike ride?"

It's good having Dad here, seeing him with the boys. Now I notice how much I've missed having him around us every day.

"Of course," he says, and after telling the boys, who are both sitting immersed in their respective iPads, I jump on my bike.

Nobody could possibly believe Henrik has done what he's being accused of.

And Sabiya has been keeping that pistol locked in her desk drawer.

It was even in the papers, that the victim was shot with a Glock.

Sabiya was nearby at Ullevål. And at Lysebu. Every time Henrik was close to the victim, she was close to him.

If I can find evidence that Sabiya was up to something she shouldn't have been, that could be enough to release him from jail and bring him home to us.

Ever since Cathrine Monrad's final remark at the end of the meeting earlier today, I've understood that I am already on borrowed time. She could decide to tell others about Henrik to undermine Munch.

The soles of my feet are burning.

Twenty minutes later I'm standing between the trees in the grove located behind Sabiya's garden. The lawn is well tended, the grass looks like ready-made artificial turf that has simply been unrolled. Nicely trimmed and short, completely different from the anarchy of our lawn. A deck stained gray and white, decorated with huge pots containing pink daisies. A white, recently stained or painted house. Big windows.

I catch a glimpse of the living room inside. Light, airy, neat.

In Norway, successful, well-assimilated immigrants like Sabiya refer to themselves as "Desis," or at least that's what Henrik told me. And no Desi would dream of living in Grønland—he said that once, too. Such neighborhoods remind them too much of the overflowing, garam masala–stinking digs they grew up in.

No, Desis live in modern, spacious villas or detached houses outside of the city.

And of course, that is just how Sabiya lives.

I see her walk across the room inside. Tight black jeans, a white silk top. She picks up a blanket from the couch and folds it. Picks up some toys from the floor. Leaves the room, comes back, sits down with her phone, gets up again.

Her husband comes in. The two of them stand in the middle of the room, having a conversation. Does he know about Henrik and their heated make-out sessions in the forest? Or about the pistol in the drawer in her office? Definitely not.

For a brief second I feel like going inside and telling him everything. But now it's more important to link Sabiya to the murders than to stir up trouble for her at home.

Sabiya disappears and comes in again, now dressed in snug, black running gear: tights and a lightweight jacket with a hood. She nods at her husband, disappears again.

I step back in between the trees.

Immediately I see her come out the door on the side of the house, the soles of her shoes crunching against the white gravel on the driveway where their two cars are parked. A white Tesla, recently washed and pretty. And a little BMW, the electric kind. Also white. Flawless cars, a flawless house—they must be earning well, both of them.

Everything looks perfect.

CHAPTER 40

SUSANNE

"Mommy, Mommy, Mommy," he howls. Maybe he thinks it will get me to stop, but it just makes me slam his head even harder against the floor. Maybe the downstairs neighbors can hear us—I don't give a fuck, even though I'm sure they're the ones who called the child welfare authorities, got them to show up here and start snooping around and asking questions.

They must take the kids away if they find me intoxicated or beating them, and up to now I've managed to avoid that, because I'm smarter than they are, smarter than anyone thinks I am. People think I'm dumb because I look the way I do, with all the makeup and the Botox and my hair and clothes. I'm not.

I'm just not like them.

"No, Mommy," his sister cries, trying to drag me away. "Stop it, that's not allowed. No! No!"

I turn around and hit her as well. She falls on the floor. Damn brats. I pick them up, one in each arm, lug them out into the hallway and up the stairs.

Thump, thump, thump. They are howling, but I open the door to the storeroom and throw them inside, close the door, and fasten the hook. They have mattresses they can play or sleep on, crackers if they get hungry. And the room is soundproof. The man who lived here before me apparently used it as a home cinema. Probably sat there watching porn.

The guy who's visiting gets restless when we run out of booze, wants to go downtown to score some more cocaine. I agree to drive him to the subway, because I really haven't had all that much to drink. Then at least I'll be rid of him.

When I get home, I hear thudding sounds. Christ, they can't carry on like that. As I stomp up the stairs, my head feels like it's about to explode again. When I open the door to the room, the most horrendous stench in the world billows out at me.

The boy has shit his pants and stuck his hand in his diaper; there's shit everywhere, on his hand and on the wall and on the mattresses and on his sister.

"Damn it all," I say, and slam the door shut. I go into the bathroom, turn on the faucet in the bathtub, and take off my clothes, hanging them on the hooks inside the door.

Then I take the white powder out of its hiding place and put it on the tiny mirror.

I said I didn't have any more. Didn't want to share, not with him, not with anyone. I carefully place the mirror on the rim of the bathtub.

Then I go downstairs again, pour myself a glass of chilled rosé, an expensive wine. I hadn't wanted to share that either.

When I return to the bathroom, I put the glass down beside the tiny mirror before I gently lie down in the water. I will probably fall asleep. I often become drowsy when relaxing in the bath like this.

There's a creaking sound in the house. It must be the wind.

I lean back, take a selfie, and send it to a couple of friends, absolutely not to the guy who was here earlier this evening. Actually, I hope he never comes back. Too small a dick, too little money, too little intelligence. Only his ego is enormous.

The warmth spreads through my body, but I can still feel a draft from the bathroom door in the part of my torso that's above the water.

I must have forgotten to close it properly. I should get out and do it but don't relish the thought of getting out of the warm bath now.

I turn toward the door to see how much it's open.

That's when I see her.

A strange woman wearing black running tights and a black sweatshirt, standing silently in the doorway of the bathroom.

How did she get in? And what does she want?

I'm about to scream, but she places her index finger against her mouth and nods toward the wall closest to the hallway.

"Hush," she says. "There's no point in screaming. Nobody can hear you."

I don't reply and try to sit up. The water sloshes; I'd filled the bathtub too full and some water lands on the floor. The woman comes closer.

I should just get up and leave, knock her down, anything, but I'm unable to do either. I'm not even capable of thinking.

"Who are you?" I ask, in a whisper, as if trying not to provoke her. "And what are you doing here?"

"I'm here to take you out," she says. Her voice is quiet and hoarse. She speaks differently, isn't from around here.

Then I feel something cold and metallic against my temple.

A gun.

"Hey," I say, sitting up an inch or so. She stops me by pressing the muzzle of the gun against my temple even harder. I peer up at her at an angle, without moving my head too much. "I have no idea who you are or what you want. But can't we talk about this instead . . ."

"This is for those two," she says, and nods toward the hallway again.

"For the children?" I say, my voice rising to a falsetto. "But why?"

"So they will be spared. It's about time they were rid of you."

She leans toward me.

She's pretty. Her eyes are elegantly made up.

And very blue. I've never seen such blue eyes before.

"And for Lars," she says.

PART 3

CHAPTER 41

HENRIK

"Does the accused consent to being remanded in custody for four weeks, as petitioned, or is the accused requesting release?"

"I am requesting release," I croak, and clear my throat. My voice is hoarse.

"Is the accused willing to make a statement?"

"Yes," I say.

In this kind of hearing, the judge has all the case documents. Christian explained this to me.

The accused, who in this case is me, gives no further detailed testimony but usually confirms the statement already given to the police. The judge then reads aloud what has been transcribed and asks whether the accused accepts it as his legal testimony.

The police prosecutor takes the floor to provide grounds for his motion. Then the defense attorney provides the grounds for release, if the accused is requesting release.

Then the judge takes a little time to determine his ruling, which is read aloud in court.

The accused can appeal, accept, or file a motion for a stay pending appeal.

I know all of this already, from my meaningless first year at law school before I quit. We'd gone on an excursion to municipal court and sat for days observing arraignments.

Christian requested a closed courtroom in the interest of privacy, but his request was denied. Apparently, such requests are seldom granted. I glance around me nervously. Luckily, I don't see any familiar faces or anyone from the media. Christian explained to my father and Clara that they shouldn't show up here to avoid drawing further attention to themselves.

That probably suits both of them just fine.

Elin and Morten are here, I see. Police investigators don't usually attend hearings, unless the case is important, Christian has explained.

I have slowly begun to realize that this *is* an important case.

The judge reads from the police prosecutor's recommendation: "Given the aggravating circumstances of the case, the risk of the destruction of evidence and of repeat offenses, the police request a four-week extension of custody without the right to visitors or to receive or send mail."

An hour and a half earlier I had been driven to the municipal court in a police car, led down into the basement where the cells are, and met briefly with Christian. He had just received the case documents; they normally receive them an hour before. After a short conversation I was brought up here and into the courtroom.

It was so reassuring to see good old Christian Ferner-Hansen that I found myself struggling to swallow down something thick forming in my throat.

He has ridden his bicycle, for sure, all the way down here from Ivar Aasens Road. A couple of times I've seen him riding his bicycle downtown, even though he didn't see me. Every time I see him, I find it touching. Christian is like a force of nature as he rides away on his old bicycle with his coattails flying out to the sides and the wind in his thick gray bush of hair.

During the past year he has more or less retired. He probably takes even longer walks in the forest now, on the Puttedalen trail or straight up from the Fyllingen Farm to the summit of Kikuttoppen Ridge with a view to the south facing Bjørnsjøen Lake, Appelsinhaugen Hill, Tryvann Lake, and on a clear day, a glimpse of the Oslo Fjord.

But now he's brushed the dust off his revolver and returned to the fray to rescue me. And I can't sit here daydreaming about the forest.

The police prosecutor has brought an annotation, a summary of the case, and a petition for my imprisonment on remand, which the judge now reads to us.

All these empty phrases from my law studies twenty years ago and from the hours spent under Father's desk acquire another luster now that they are about me, my life, my future.

The judge cites the gravity of the case, how the investigation is in its early stages, and that holding the accused in custody is therefore necessary, especially given the danger of destruction of evidence. The accused can, should he be released, contact witnesses and try to influence them.

For my own part, I sink farther and farther down in my chair.

My sense of the unreal nature of the events unfolding is heightened. A pounding begins in my temples, and I take a sip of the water they've put in front of me. I haven't eaten and haven't had enough to drink. I'm becoming dehydrated and exhausted. Every movement requires enormous effort.

When combined, all the circumstantial evidence they have against me makes for a pretty damning case.

All those stupid white lies of mine become entangled into a tight knot I'm unable to undo.

The worst part is that I can no longer remember what's true or false. It's all a huge mishmash.

CHAPTER 42

—————

Clara

A few weeks earlier

It's only May 10, but it feels like the first day of summer.

In the evening, when finally, it's cooler, I sit at home on the couch in the living room, with the laptop on my knees, going through my inbox, trying to make a to-do list for the coming weeks. It's slow going.

Munch has shut down my bill.

And Daddy has had a stroke.

Everything's going to hell.

Then my phone on the couch beside me starts blinking.

Henrik cell, it says. There's even a heart after the two words. One of the boys put it there. I must see about removing it.

"Yes?" I say.

At first there's just a few seconds of silence.

"Henrik?"

He clears his throat.

"Can you go check on the boys, make sure they're safe and sound?"

"What do you mean?"

Then he tells me about the little boy and about the guy wearing the blue Chelsea jersey who is on his way to the prayer room.

I check on the boys.

Nikolai is lying in bed on his stomach. Today he's sleeping in just his underwear, a green pair with dinosaurs on them. Andreas is lying on a mattress on the floor. He has his own room but prefers to sleep in his brother's room. We might as well have moved his bed in here. He still sleeps in Captain Sabertooth pajamas, light gray, faded and covered with skulls and crossbones.

They sleep soundly at night. There's no chance they will wake up.

I report back to Henrik. We hang up.

A four-year-old.

A boy a bit younger than Lars had been. So tiny and so big. A boy who understands so much and at the same time, so little.

I've read enough reports and studies and guidelines about these kinds of injuries that I can picture the tiny body, not unlike the two fast asleep upstairs, not unlike Lars back then, just a little darker and smaller.

A little body who suffered in silence and endured, persevered, who believed that was how life was supposed to be. How life *must* be.

A little body who loves his mother and father, who believes it must be his own fault that somebody does such things to him.

Images fly past my eyes. Things I don't want to remember. Daddy sitting and looking at Lars in the pink bathtub, Daddy calling me.

How I came. And looked. And understood.

It's more than I can stand.

That's when I decide.

I will have just a brief window of opportunity. I've already checked on the boys. No need to look in on them again.

I pop into Henrik's pretentious home office, find his extra key card for work that I know is lying there. The code is the same one he uses everywhere: the boys' date of birth, 2205. In the hallway I grab my backpack, turn on the alarm, lock the door, and go out to my bicycle.

Four minutes after I ended our phone conversation, my bicycle tires are crunching over the gravel in the driveway.

Inside me a motor is spinning now, fueled by an anger that has been smoldering like an ember, which has always been there, lying dormant, like a volcano.

The ember has once again burst into flames.

This late in the evening the air is cool and crisp, saturated with the scent of hedges and flowering shrubs and the first lilacs, so early this year.

It's still not dark. It barely gets dark at all this time of year.

I pedal as fast as I can. There's not much traffic, few people are out. I try doing my breathing exercises as best I can while riding a bicycle. It's not ideal, but it's all I have time for.

When I reach Ullevål Hospital, I enter through the garage behind a nurse who is about to start her shift, and park my bicycle there.

In one of the basement corridors, there's a huge cart with clothing in it that has clearly come from the laundry room. I pull on scrubs—a shirt and pants—so I can walk by unnoticed. Visiting hours are over, after all. In the corridor there are also hampers for dirty laundry. I've seen them before when the children and I were here with Henrik. All hospital clothing is laundered at nearly boiling temperature.

I take the back stairs leading up from the basement to the fourth floor where Henrik's office is located, avoiding the manned reception area. Henrik has complained about the lack of surveillance cameras at Ullevål, something that irritates the staff when dealing with aggressive patients or next of kin. But if they've actually installed any security cameras at the hospital, the lobby would be a clear first choice.

The office wing is dark. Nobody's at work now. Nobody ever is at this time of day, even though the floors below are bustling with activity. I pull on a pair of disposable gloves, slide the card through the slit, punch in the code, and open the door. I don't want to turn on the lights; instead I use the flashlight on my cell phone.

Henrik's and Sabiya's desks are in the third office on the left. Computer, keyboard, paper. I recognize Henrik's mess. The home-wrecker Sabiya's desk is neat. There's a photo on it, showing three dark-haired children, whom I recognize from the pictures on her Facebook profile.

In the corner nook where her desk and Henrik's meet, it becomes gradually messier and there I spot a scalpel with a mint-green handle; we have several scalpels of the same type lying about at the house. I put it in my pocket; who knows what might come in handy. I also take a small pink hairbrush, almost a child's size. A thick layer of dark hair is tangled between the bristles.

Then I look at the drawers beneath Sabiya's desk.

It must have been a perverse case of a heart filled to bursting and in need of a release when Henrik one winter evening confided in me about poor Sabiya, the smartest and sharpest of all, who was trapped like a rat in her marriage to a horrible husband.

"And you know what?" he said at the end of a long monologue.

"What?" I said.

As expected, that was all it took for him to blurt that out as well.

"But you have to promise not to tell anyone . . ."

"Jesus, spare me . . ."

"Well, after the leukemia course, we were sitting there talking about how it had gone and were about to leave, and we just needed to catch our breath for a moment after all the parents and questions and . . ."

"Get to the point."

He gave me a hurt look, as he always does when I say that.

"Well, suddenly, she pulled a pistol with a silencer out of the drawer of her desk, and . . ."

"A *pistol?*" I exclaimed, genuinely surprised.

"A pistol, yes. A Glock, I think. And then she aimed it at me."

"Isn't she afraid someone will find it?" I asked.

"The drawer is locked, of course. But the key is on the top shelf of our bookcase."

Why did he tell me all of this? Did he feel *so* certain that I didn't know about his lover? Did he think it was the kind of information about colleagues that faithful husbands shared with their wives?

He continued: finally he dragged the explanation about her husband out of her. He emphasized that he'd asked her to remove the Glock from their office, and added that they would sometimes refer to it as "the animal," just between the two of them.

Since then I haven't asked about it and he hasn't mentioned it. But I doubt he's presumed to make any demands whatsoever on his precious lady friend.

The pistol is there for sure, if she hasn't moved it on her own initiative.

First, I try opening the drawers beneath Sabiya's desk. They're all locked.

Then I reach up and run my hand across the top shelf. There's no guarantee the key is still there. But sure enough, there it is, toward the back of the shelf.

I open the drawers under her tidy desk with the photograph of her pretty children on top.

Nothing in the first one. Nothing in the second.

But then, in the third drawer, beneath a printout of a PowerPoint presentation, among toothpicks and paper clips and receipts and a bead necklace one of her children probably made for her—she must have jammed all her junk into the drawer—there is a pistol with a silencer on it.

I pick it up, check the magazine, tuck the weapon into the waistband of my pants, pull my shirt down over it, slam all the drawers shut, lock them, and put the key back in place.

Then I go back out into the corridor.

Only twenty-three minutes have passed since Henrik called me, seventeen since I jumped on the bicycle at home. But the man in the Chelsea jersey might have long since finished his prayers.

It all hinges on my making it to the prayer room before he leaves.

Once I heard a musician say that before he begins to play his instrument, he must reset himself, reduce himself to nothing. Only then can the music come through him, only then is he transformed into merely a channel the music flows through.

And now and again, when I'm out running and everything is in sync and I get into a rhythm, then I can forget that I'm a body running.

I just keep going.

And that's what I am now, a vibrating nothing with an ember in my stomach, propelling me forward, in pursuit of him, like a dog on a scent. Down into the basement. Out through the garage. To the right. Out back, toward the dreary area, where there is a smoking shelter that resembles a bus stop. All the way to the blue door Henrik once pointed out to me as the entrance to the prayer room.

The scalpel in my pocket wouldn't make a sound. That's an advantage. But I would risk ending up in a tussle with the guy. Better to use the pistol. I draw it out from the waistband of my scrubs, hold it with both hands against my body, push down the door handle with my elbow, and shove open the door with my shoulder.

I must be quick now. And hope that the silencer works.

The area of the room is about sixty square feet.

Lying on a prayer mat is a guy wearing a blue Chelsea jersey with his back to me, praying. I can hear him mumbling to himself.

Astaghfirullah.

Astaghfirullah.

Astaghfirullah.

I let go of the door, let it slide shut behind me.

He twists around to see who has come in.

His gaze. At first irritated. Then astonished. And then afraid.

I take three steps forward, still holding the Glock up in front of me.

"What the hell . . . ?" he says.

211

"This is for the boy in there," I say. "And for your other children. And for Lars."

And then I fire.

An orange flame flies out of the barrel of the pistol, and I hear a soft popping sound. It looks like I've hit him in his side. He crawls forward.

Again I pull the trigger.

Now it appears that I've hit him in his back. But he's still moving. I walk over, take hold of his arm, roll him over onto his back, and shoot him in the heart—or where I imagine it is—at close range.

Then his gaze vanishes inward.

For a second or two all my anger and all my anxiety are replaced by a tiny, giddy feeling of euphoria, like bubbles in a glass of champagne rising to the surface, a joy I've never felt before, at least not in thirty years.

A crystal-clear second of silence, until my flight response kicks in.

I can't stay here.

I pick up two of the cartridge shells off the floor. The third is nowhere to be seen and looking for it will take too long.

The last shot made a dark hole in his jersey. But oddly enough, for three gunshots there's very little blood. I bend down and lift his blue jersey, revealing a flabby stomach covered with black hair. It feels like he has a pulse, that he's lying there throbbing and burning. And where the bullet entered, there's a bump filled with a bluish-red liquid.

What did I shoot him with?

I shove the pistol into the backpack before I exit through the blue door and start walking back to the main hospital building.

Fear, like all other feelings, is first and foremost an illusion.

It was poor planning on my part to leave the bicycle in the garage; I don't like wandering around here now. But I must bring the bicycle home with me.

I enter the building using the key card, go to the basement, peel off the scrubs, toss them into one of the hampers, and walk back to the parking garage.

As I calmly ride the bicycle out, the grounds are as quiet and peaceful as they were when I arrived.

Ten minutes later I am wheeling the bike through the gate in front of our house. It's only then that I remove the disposable gloves, cut them up into small pieces, and flush them down the toilet.

The boys are sleeping in the same positions as they were an hour ago. I open the window wide to let in some fresh air, bend over, and kiss first the one and then the other.

I turn around in the doorway.

"Good night," I whisper.

Then I go to find a place to hide Sabiya's Glock 17.

CHAPTER 43

Henrik

It is the police prosecutor's turn. Yet again he presents the chain of circumstantial evidence connecting me to the murders and crime scenes.
I feel nauseated, unwell, as if I were hungover and being driven blind-
folded, full speed ahead, down a road full of hairpin turns.

It looks as if the judge becomes more convinced with every point
that's hammered in.

I'm done for. I'm Harrison Ford in *The Fugitive*, Aden Young in
Rectify.

Finally it's Christian's turn. He has a year-round suntan. He is mus-
cular and lean. A healthy lifestyle, except for the wine on the balcony
or in the sunroom with Jenny in the evenings.

Now he takes his time.

"As humans we are created in such a way that as soon as we reach
a conclusion, our brain will start searching for grounds to support it,
regardless of whether or not the conclusion is correct," he begins.

"The confirmation trap is a concept with which Norwegian defense
attorneys are familiar. Usually, I would never speak about it at such an
early stage, but in this case, it seems as if this phenomenon has oddly
enough already infiltrated the investigation, which has unfortunately
acquired an extremely one-sided focus, solely intent on finding evidence
in support of its hypothesis. Some serious errors have been made in
this investigation. Among these, the police asked my client to enter

the crime scene and identify Mukhtar Ahmad before the area had been cleared by the crime scene investigators, in clear violation of principles pertaining to the preservation of an uncontaminated crime scene. But let us not spend time on this now. There is otherwise more than enough to address."

An almost inaudible hum of astonishment passes through the courtroom.

"The police believe that the accused is guilty. They have submitted a chain of circumstantial evidence. What does this evidence tell us? First, that the person in question harbors hate and contempt for child abusers, as exemplified by an email dated May 16, 2018. If we were to imprison every Norwegian who shares his opinion, our prisons would fill up very quickly . . ."

"Stay with what's relevant to the case," the judge rebukes him.

"Forgive me, your honor. Further, the prosecution attributes importance to the fact that Fougner changed his statement regarding his whereabouts at the time of both murders. This seems strange, until we understand that he did this to avoid disclosing confidential information of a personal nature. We may all have our opinions about extramarital affairs, but God knows, I believe I speak for many of us when I say that the issue of infidelity has no place in the judicial system."

Christian walks around the room, wearing the customary robe over his street clothes.

"And then there's the weapon. Sabiya Rana informs Fougner that she owns a firearm that she keeps in their shared office. Should he have brought this to the attention of his employer? Yes! In retrospect we can say of course he should have. But for the same reason that he said nothing about his relationship with Rana—his strong feelings of loyalty—he chose not to. Does his knowledge of the firearm make him a murderer? No and again no. There is absolutely no forensic evidence to support such a claim. His DNA has not been found at any of the crime scenes, or on the murder weapon, which hasn't been located. The conclusion is that the likelihood of his being convicted of this crime is extremely small. And I would remind the court that the conditions for imprisonment on remand stipulate that the probability that the accused has committed the crime of which he or she is being accused, *must* be greater than the probability of innocence."

The old fox draws a breath.

I am relieved, but far from certain that it will be enough.

CHAPTER 44

CLARA

Ever since the first time, the Glock has been safely hidden behind a beam in the old, unfinished attic of our house, where otherwise all there is to be found are bird skeletons and hymnals and newspapers from 1912.

This is the second time. And everything is different, more carefully planned.

I like the thought that I have managed to steal something back from Sabiya.

I did some reading and found out the Glock 17 is used by the armed forces and is also popular among private pistol enthusiasts because it is a reliable and relatively inexpensive firearm.

This type of gun has gone missing in several contexts over the years, through thefts of the armed forces' warehouses, private citizens, or stores where firearms are sold. But with an eye to the long-term plans I have begun concocting, I hope the Glock has been registered by the book, ideally by Sabiya herself.

The ammunition is 9-millimeter, the same used by the police. To purchase ammunition, you need a firearms permit. I don't have one. This can be purchased illegally. But both alternatives are too risky. I must make do with the bullets in the magazine. They should last for a good long while; the magazine was full when I took the Glock.

I fired three shots in the prayer room. Now fourteen remain.

The ammunition is called Federal Hydra-Shok. It's expensive.

I read all this online when I stopped at a random internet café at the Oslo train station. Doing searches for this type of thing at home or at work was out of the question.

Melika Omid Carter is a clear choice from Henrik's list, the one I found when I logged on to his home computer the morning before I went to Western Norway. I had noticed that he was up to something, and I wanted to know what it was.

I did my best to memorize the list and wrote the names on a Post-it, which I hid along with the Glock in the attic.

Carter is also an immigrant, and people will believe she was killed because of that, and for the time being they are free to believe this. Because of her ethnicity, Carter is on Sabiya's radar, just as Ahmad had been.

When I read about Carter in the *Business Times* a while back, I thought she was impressive in many ways. Tough. Hard as nails. But Henrik's project memo shows that the woman is also rotten to the core.

Her children were covered with scars from beatings, and she also burned their tongues and bodies with a hot spoon. It's incomprehensible that they are still living with her.

It doesn't help that Henrik is making this list of his.

The only thing that helps is to *do* something, the way I did at Ullevål, the way I am doing now.

Melika holds a course in Oslo every month. On her blog she writes about the exclusive quality of the rooms and cuisine, that she always arrives the night before, has a three-course meal made of the most delicious, fresh ingredients in the restaurant with a view of the treetops and the city far below. Around eleven in the evening she swims her two thousand meters in the elegant swimming pool where she's almost always alone.

And, best of all: she will be holding a course at Lysebu Hotel on the same day Henrik and Sabiya will be there.

Munch will be attending a conference at Lysebu Hotel later in June. His security people have checked out the grounds and reported back to me that there's just one surveillance camera at Lysebu, right by the entrance. I will manage to avoid that. Several back doors, one leading to the pool, will be locked when Munch arrives, but are otherwise usually left unlocked.

At the cybercafe I also found an old blueprint of the hotel, an enclosure in an application from Lysebu to the municipality for approval to build an extension. It had been meticulously filed in the municipality's electronic public records and provided a good overview of the building.

At exactly 10:40 p.m. I enter the side door. Henrik and the gang are probably still drinking cognac in the dining room.

A short flight of stairs down, and I'm in the basement.

Down here the ceiling is so low that I almost knock my head against it. The hallway is narrow and white, a miniature version of the catacombs at Ullevål.

The door into the changing room is also unlocked. Hospitable and laid-back, in true Danish Norwegian spirit. No security guards, no key card, just open doors. The changing room is empty. Ten lockers with keys, none of them locked. I put on disposable gloves and shoe covers, and a cleaning smock to wear over my clothes. I'm already wearing a baseball cap. It's discreet and effective. My reflection in the mirror confirms that I look like the cleaning staff I'm trying to impersonate. Then I leave the changing room and go into the pool area. It is now 10:45.

I start puttering, *becoming* the service employee Clara at work.

One of the long walls is made up of huge windows. On the other long wall is the door to the changing room I just came out of, and a stall containing yet another rainfall shower. The sauna is dark, except for the soft green light filtering out under the door.

The most remarkable thing is the end wall outside the door to the women's changing room. An oval, white sculpture is installed there. A mother and her children. The Madonna association is clear. A child in each arm, gazing up at her adoringly, the good mother.

Had I been the type to believe in such things, I would have taken it as a sign.

Along the edge of the pool, forming a partition between the water and the wall with the sculpture, is a row of birch branches. When I place my hand against one of them, a thin layer of birch bark falls off the branch, like a shower of dust. The tree reminds me of the invasion of young birches that have sprouted on the summer farm in recent years, which I'm having a hard time keeping at bay.

It's quiet, just the hum of the ventilation unit, the muffled sound of people in the distance, maybe from Henrik and his coworkers in the dining room.

And then finally, Melika Omid Carter arrives.

Even wearing a bathing cap and swim goggles, she is recognizable. She stares at me, clearly surprised and irritated to find somebody else here. Then it's as if she revises her plan, pushes the swim goggles up onto her forehead, walks into the sauna, and closes the door behind her. She carries a tote bag over her shoulder.

In the dim green light of the sauna I can just discern the outline of her body through the tinted glass wall as she puts down the tote bag, unfolds her towel, and lies down on the lowest bench.

The clock on the wall above the pool shows the time is 10:50.

I retrieve my own tote bag, walk over to the sauna, go inside, close the door behind me, take position, leaning against the bench where Melika is lying, raise the pistol and aim.

She lifts her head, stares at me in surprise.

"This is for your children," I say. "And for Lars."

The recoil feels more powerful this time, even though I'm prepared for it now.

I shoot her right in the heart—I'm sure of it—at close range. There's not as much blood as the last time, only a splattering of small red dots, which I step straight into.

I have plastic shoe covers on my feet. They don't leave behind shoe prints. But due to the size of the footprint made through the plastic cover, they will understand that I'm a woman. And even though my feet are larger than Sabiya's, they are small in terms of my height, just a size seven. Perhaps that will confuse them a bit.

When I step out of the sauna, the water in the pool is blue and serene.

Again, I glance at the clock. I was in there for one minute.

In the changing room I tug off the smock and put it in the tote bag. Since Melika took all her belongings with her into the sauna, there's no visible sign of her presence in the pool area. With a little bit of luck, she won't be found until tomorrow.

Then I leave, as calmly and naturally as if I were a hotel guest. I carry the tote bag over my shoulder, put my hands in my pockets to hide the thin disposable gloves I'm still wearing, and then walk down the corridor, up the stairs to the floor where the group room, the lounge, and the automatic coffee machine are located, where it is still silent and deserted.

Now the door is locked from the inside. I unlock it, walk outside, huddle against the wall, remove the disposable gloves, and put them in my pocket.

I walk calmly across the grounds toward my bicycle, which I left at the edge of the forest.

CHAPTER 45

HENRIK

Christian is not finished. He raises one finger, as if warning everyone to listen very carefully.

"In closing I would add a significant detail. Last night there was another murder in Oslo, which the police prosecutor conveniently failed to mention in his closing argument. A woman in her thirties was murdered in her home."

"That's not relevant to this case," the police prosecutor protests.

Christian smiles. "It's not relevant to the case of the accused, no, I can agree with that. But the fact is that the victim, Susanne Stenersen, was on the so-called list of abusive parents, the list that the police investigators are claiming amounts to a motive on the part of the accused."

Out of the corner of my eye I see that Elin has leaned forward and is listening attentively.

"Naturally, this could be a coincidence, although it's not very likely. Henrik Fougner could still have committed the first two murders. But the preliminary forensic investigation shows the woman was shot with ammunition of a rare type—Federal Hydra-Shok—also found in the bodies of the two previous victims. Therefore, in all probability the same weapon has been used for all three murders. The police have, as we know, spent a lot of time undermining my client's alibi. But I have difficulty imagining a more watertight alibi than being in jail. I would therefore request the immediate release of the accused."

"Does the police prosecutor have anything to add?" the judge asks.

"No," the prosecutor replies. He looks tired.

Christian, on the other hand, struggles to suppress a tiny smile.

I glance over at Elin and Morten. Judging from their expressions, it would appear they had not anticipated this. I would wager the police are aware of the details Christian is sharing with the court, but they had certainly not expected him to know about them.

The details haven't been released yet to the media.

The old scoundrel must have made a call to some office or other at the Grønland police station "just to make a few inquiries."

And one of his police contacts had leaked it, told him another case has come up that's very similar.

"OK, thank you," the judge says. "The court will now take a brief recess before convening again in fifteen minutes for my ruling."

CHAPTER 46

CLARA

After three-quarters of an hour, I'm home again.

This is the third time, and there was something almost routine about the entire episode.

I punch in the code on the door handle, press it down, and push open the door, which locks automatically when it slams shut behind me. The house is silent. I just want to go upstairs to the bathroom and take a shower.

But my father is sitting on the stairs, as quiet as a mouse in the darkness.

"Where have you been?" he asks, looking at me inquisitively.

"For a bike ride. I told you. Didn't I?"

"You did," he says in a strange tone of voice, as if he knows exactly where I've been and what I've done.

"Let's talk in the kitchen so we don't wake the boys."

"As if ten wild horses could wake those two," he says, and stands up resolutely. We go to the kitchen and sit down on two of the Wegner wishbone chairs, which I bought and Henrik thinks are too mainstream.

"Did they get to sleep all right?" I ask.

"Yes, of course. But I stayed with them in the bedroom for a while anyway," he says, and smiles.

In the past year he has aged, but he still looks younger than he is. His hair is thick and short; he has maintained the military haircut, trimming it himself with the electric shaver. And he has the same nice, brown skin color that he has year-round. It makes him look healthy and strong and vital, even though he isn't.

"Do you want a cup of tea? And a sandwich?" I ask, and put the kettle on.

"Yes, please," he says, and walks slowly into the living room.

He has more difficulty walking in the evening, I've noticed, maybe because he's tired. I take out the bread and sandwich fixings. I can hear the evening news from the living room.

This murder is the one I feel the most satisfied about. Among other reasons, because Henrik has the world's best alibi.

And because the murder further incriminates Sabiya.

During my investigations of the people on Henrik's list, the majority of whom were ethnic Norwegians, I discovered that Susanne and Sabiya were virtually neighbors. The pieces had then fallen into place.

I had to kill Susanne at a time when Sabiya was out for a run. A time for which later, when the noose was being tightened around her neck, she would be unable to provide a strong enough alibi.

I bought a burner phone ahead of time to alert the police about Susanne, so her children would be spared finding her. The burner phone was an old, tried-and-true trick, but it worked.

It was when I was tiptoeing up the stairs from the first to the second floor that I heard the faint thumping sounds from the almost-soundproof storeroom.

I shot Susanne in the temple. That was the most practical option, considering where I'd found her.

A thin stream of blood flowed from her head, turning the bathwater the same shade of pink as the rosé in the glass on the rim of the bathtub. Then I took out the small bag from the pocket of my tights and removed three strands of Sabiya's hair.

I chose the strands of hair in the bag because there were hair follicles on the ends of them, which would ensure Sabiya's DNA is found.

I had been certain that Sabiya's weapon would be evidence enough for the police to connect her to the murders immediately after the killing at Lysebu.

It wasn't. And with Henrik in jail, I realized I needed something more compelling.

I had put one strand into Susanne's hand that was dangling over the edge of the tub. I placed another strand on her shoulder. The third I left floating on top of the pink-tinted water. The three strands would be enough for the forensic investigators from the homicide team to discover them, but not enough to raise any suspicions. And it would be impossible to confuse them with Susanne's strawberry-blonde hair.

Here the bitch would find herself up against a real challenge.

On the way home I notified the police, identifying myself as a neighbor who'd heard children screaming on the floor above. I said it sounded like the children were locked up and home alone.

Then I smashed the telephone and threw the pieces down into a manhole, just to be on the safe side.

That's how I freed the children from their prison in the storeroom. That gave the entire incident a little added significance.

One more name can be crossed off the list, even though I just do it in my head.

I managed it, this time, too. I should be happy.

But there are more names. Seven more on the list. And then there are all the other names and children. How many children are locked up in storerooms?

What started virtually on an impulse at Ullevål has snowballed. Now I'm no longer able to stop.

It's like when I was a little girl and went skiing down Langebakken Hill and everything was just white and hard and shining and I went faster and faster, and my body turned into an arrow racing downward and I knew that I should probably snowplow soon. My pulse rate accelerated, my heart pounded harder, but I didn't snowplow, I didn't stop, I kept racing onward.

Now that I think about it, maybe it's been lying in wait inside me ever since Daddy went to Lebanon. I can still remember, from the time before he left, the feeling of joy.

A kind of effervescent sensation of soap bubbles in my body.

After Daddy left, I was never happy again. Not really. When he came home, I was relieved, but not happy, not then and not since.

CHAPTER 47

LEIF

1982

The day I came home, the fog hung almost all the way down to the ground, and the grass in the garden was slippery and overgrown. The front door was locked, and nobody opened when I rang the bell, so I had to go around to the back and knock on the window there.

Finally, Clara's face appeared. I signaled to her that she had to go to the front of the house and let me in.

"Hi, sweetheart," I said when she opened the door. I got down on my knees, but she just stood there looking at me. It was cold in the hallway and smelled of garbage.

"Can Daddy have a hug?" I asked, and then she gently pressed her body up against mine. I hugged her and she emitted a tiny squeak. But still not a word.

"Where's Mommy, Clara?"

"Upstairs."

"And Lars?"

"In there," she said, and nodded toward the living room. I stood up, took her by the hand and walked toward the living room, where I could hear the television, even though it was the middle of the day. I looked through the door leading into the kitchen. There were dirty dishes on the counters and table and no clean plates or glasses in the cupboards. Garbage and old newspapers were strewn all around, clean and dirty clothes lay in a glorious heap on the floor, and there were crumbs and grime everywhere. It looked like nobody had vacuumed or cleaned since I'd left.

"What the hell is wrong with you?" I shouted at Agnes later in the day. She was lying in bed like before, pale and withdrawn.

She didn't answer. I got started on the big cleanup job.

The children were silent and pale. The animals were thin and frightened and didn't seem well. The pigs weren't there at all. Agnes had sent them off to be slaughtered.

For several months I had more on my hands than I could manage, getting things up and running again, picking up the pieces, reestablishing contact with the children, and getting an overview of our finances.

I was told by the armed forces that I mustn't tell anyone anything about my time in Lebanon. I must especially not talk about the skirmish in Rachaya, that it could potentially damage the Norwegian operation. Apart from that, I heard nothing more from them.

At first, I stayed in touch with the other members of my squad, but meeting and talking to them made me feel stressed. I had plenty of other things to deal with, and the get-togethers soon petered out.

I worried about how the children had fared while I was away. Clara seemed very different. She showed no emotion; she didn't cry. She didn't want to be comforted when she hurt herself or if something was wrong, would never say what she was thinking, or feeling, or what she wanted. I tried to ask her about what had happened while I was away, how things had been at home, but she didn't want to talk about it.

"I looked after Lars, Daddy," was all she said. She took care of him now as well. She sat holding him while they watched *Sesame Street*, told him stories, helped him with the shoes he was still unable to put on by himself.

"Hush now, Lars," she said, and stroked his hair when something was wrong. She was like a little mother to him. A miniature adult.

Eventually, she started sitting on my lap again, putting her arms around my neck.

But she sat there without saying anything. I was the one who did the talking.

"I never should have left, I know that," I said. "But I'll never leave you again, I promise. Everything will be fine."

She didn't answer, but I saw that she was listening.

I was talking to myself as much as to her.

I slept poorly at night, waking up constantly, all sweaty and feverish. Often, I started trembling. And from time to time my heart leaped and bounced in my body. The first time it happened I thought I was going to die, that it was a heart attack. The next time I understood it would pass if I just lay down on the couch and hung on for a couple of hours.

The skirmish by the olive tree. The men who fell to the ground.

The green beret full of holes I found lying in the dirt that became the first item in my collection.

And then the episode a few weeks later. At the listening post by Jeita Grotto. Silence. Only the crickets and the barking of dogs could be heard. I used to scratch the goats between their horns.

The muffled bangs and machine-gun fire. The grenade that landed right beside me.

Afterward I saw that my hip was sticky with blood.

The splinter embedded deep in my flesh had entered just below my vest.

That was my second item.

These two things, the beret and splinter, were what I brought home with me.

That I had shot several people didn't bother me all that much, not in and of itself. I knew that it had been either them or me. Clara and Lars wouldn't have a father if I hadn't fired my gun.

And I was glad to be home. Of course, I was.

But at the same time, I longed to be back there, where everything was a matter of life and death, where there was never any doubt about what we had to do, where at all times we were working together on something serious and important.

Everything here at home suddenly seemed alien, as if I had landed on another planet. It frightened me. People frightened me.

In the evenings I often sat by the window staring out into the darkness. My shotgun hung on the wall in the storeroom. But after a while I started sleeping with it under my bed.

It was around this time that Agnes suddenly began to awaken, the way the flies hibernating in the roof on the summer farm will come to life if somebody lights the stove in there on a cold winter's day. She got out of bed, showered, brushed her hair, went to the new shopping mall and bought clothes, put on makeup. She looked astonishingly healthy, as if she hadn't been curled up under the duvet for months, silent and miserable.

She was on the upswing, I understood.

Not long afterward she came and told me she was going to start working as an assistant at the school. We needed the money. And then she would have a reason to get up in the morning. I breathed a sigh of relief when she left for work, with her purse over her shoulder and her hair in a pretty braid.

It's good that she's up on her feet again now that I'm feeling down, I thought.

CHAPTER 48

HENRIK

"It's not good that you got mixed up in this mess," Dad says. "But now we must try and keep it out of the media, even though I doubt that's possible. I have to say, I'm a bit concerned about Clara and her job."

That's pretty typical. Dad has always had a soft spot for Clara, thinks of her as his own daughter. He brags about how sharp she is, even though he thinks she's spent too many years at the ministry.

"Your mother is completely beside herself, by the way. You should talk to her," he adds.

"Fine," I say. "Just not today, please?"

"I can handle her for the time being. But Henrik. The most important thing here . . . You have married well. Very well."

"Dad," I say. "Please."

A lecture on infidelity is the last thing I need right now. And especially from him.

I believe my father loves my mother, that he can't imagine life without her. But he has a strange way of showing it.

There has been an inordinate amount of drama over the years. Phone calls late at night. Mother crying and carrying on, while my father remained silent. Or the time I came home from school early, when my mother was in Paris, and I walked in on the sight of my father's white behind pumping up and down between the thighs of Ninni Jessen. Moaning and giggling and whispering.

I tiptoed out of there before he noticed me. I have never mentioned it to him, just swore I would never be like that.

But that's exactly what I've become.

It all started when Clara and I moved into my parents' house. I sort of turned into my father, while he must have become gun-shy, because now he seems more interested in walks in the forest, expensive wines, and his buddies than the ladies.

"Well, Henrik, go clean up your mess," he says, and stops in front of our gate.

CHAPTER 49

CLARA

Everybody except Munch, who is in Brussels, is sitting and staring at the press clipping on their respective iPads. The front-page photograph of *VG* is a close-up of Cathrine Monrad with a portrait photo of Munch stuck in one corner.

The headline: "Media Whore!"

And then, underneath: "Will the Minister of Justice Be Forced to Step Down?"

"My God," the head of communications says. "Is it possible?"

"If anyone had any doubts about that characterization, she has certainly cleared them up now," the adviser says.

"If he's said half of this, then Monrad isn't the problem here," Mona says, and sends him a severe look.

"But how do we handle this? That's the question," the head of communications says.

"Has anyone spoken with the minister?" Mona asks.

"Not yet," he replies. "I tried calling him without any success. I'll try again. But, Clara, you were there for their conversation, right? Did he say this?"

Mona looks at me coldly, I notice.

"He was careless. I don't remember him saying all that, but . . ."

"I'll go call him," the head of communications says. "Go through the rest of the clippings on your own. This is the buzz of the day anyway."

"Of the month," Mona says. "Or the year. And on top of all that, they have yet another murder to write about. I don't understand what's happening."

"Yes," the adviser says. "Has the whole world gone off the rails? Killed in her own home? And no witnesses. How is that possible?"

"The neighbors on the floor below say they heard noises coming from Susanne Stenersen's apartment earlier that evening," Mona reads from some article. "Here they say this was normal, and several times they'd tried to notify the police and child welfare authorities that they thought Susanne's children were at risk, but nobody followed up . . ."

"Exactly . . ."

"Other than that, the neighbors said a man visited Susanne earlier in the day," Mona continued. "Susanne and this guy drove off around eight o'clock. They wondered what she had done with her children, because they could hear them inside. The neighbors were surprised she was able to drive because it sounded like there had been a party in her apartment before this. But Susanne came back ten minutes later. After that they neither saw nor heard her or anything unusual until the police arrived at 11:10 p.m. and scared them to death."

"My goodness . . ."

"The police have gone door to door, talking to everyone, but nobody noticed anything out of the ordinary, just some guy who was out walking his dog and saw a blonde lady on a bicycle. The police emphasize how important it is that people let them know if they've seen anything at all, yada yada. And oh yes, somebody called the police claiming to be a downstairs neighbor—that was how they were notified about Susanne. But the neighbors all say they didn't call, and the call can't be traced. Strange business."

We sit reading our respective screens in silence until the head of communications returns.

"The latest is Munch was given twenty minutes to respond and has already given the newspaper another statement. There he denies

235

categorically having said any of the things Monrad claims he said. She is inventing all of it to create drama and undermine him."

"My God," I exclaim.

It's an idiotic move on his part. However, it's also absurd that journalists tell you, of course you have a right to respond, but they will be publishing the article within the hour, regardless of whether you have commented, and regardless of whatever you may be doing. It's a pretty crude form of blackmail.

"I just hope Munch isn't lying," Mona continues, and there's a touch of schadenfreude in her voice as she gets to her feet and gathers up her papers. "I'll call Cathrine Monrad now and see if maybe I can do some damage control. And I suggest that from now on, for the time being, Clara responds to any questions that come from the media about this case," she says, glancing at the head of communications.

"Fine. I guess I'll get back to my twenty-five unanswered calls," he says.

"What's up with him?" I ask Vigdis as we head out the door, nodding toward Oddbjørn, the polar bear. Two men wearing coveralls from the ministry's service division are wrapping the stuffed bear in transparent plastic, the type I suspect is used to pack up corpses.

"They're taking him to be cleaned," she says as we watch them wandering away with the bear between them. "Apparently, vermin have started creeping out of his fur."

"Wow." I walk into my office, shut the door, and sit down in the super-ergonomic, black leather chair I have inherited from Woll.

I lean back and reflect for a minute or two.

Then I look up Cathrine Monrad's telephone number online. At first, I struggle to find the right wording, but finally I'm satisfied.

The phone makes a faint swishing sound as the message goes out.

Shortly afterward, Henrik calls and tells me he is a free man and on his way home.

CHAPTER 50

HENRIK

"Well, there you are, finally," Clara says as I walk through the door and she comes toward me. I'd gone out for a walk, couldn't bear to sit here at home and wait for the others. "Are you OK?"

"Not really," I say, noticing that I feel like I'm about to cry, that it's good to be home, but I feel emotionally battered, exhausted, incapable of summoning any feelings of joy. "What a nightmare . . ."

"What happens now?"

"I don't know."

"What was it that induced them to release you, finally?"

"Christian induced them," I say, and sit down on one of the stools in the kitchen. "You should have seen him. He was completely fucking fantastic. And concluded by pointing out that another murder of the same type had been committed last night, while I was in custody. And then there was some new forensic evidence, traces of DNA that ruled me out, as I understood it. Where are the boys, by the way?"

"In their rooms."

"Good, I'll go up."

"Fine. But Henrik . . . They're a little upset."

"Because of this?"

She nods.

"Don't expect too much from them."

"Hi, Henrik," a voice says, and Leif walks in from the backyard carrying a coffee cup.

"Oh, hi," I say. "Are you here? You startled me."

"Good to see you, Henrik." Leif offers me his hand.

"Likewise, thanks. But sorry," I say, and shake his hand. "I just need . . ."

"Of course, go upstairs and see your kids." Leif smiles at me warmly.

I trot toward the stairs, eager to see them, talk to them, hug them.

Again, I catch myself wondering how things have been at home while I've been away. Clara, who is otherwise an expert at everything imaginable, has always had to summon me when one of the boys threw a fit, pummeled her with angry fists, or screamed in a rage from low blood sugar. She has no idea how to handle their reactions. Usually, she locks herself in the bedroom or goes for a run. Now the boys are older and they seldom throw such tantrums. But I'm still the one who handles them best.

I knock on Andreas's door and go in.

"Hi."

There they are, both of them. Andreas is sitting with his iPad in his lap, Nikolai is bent over a LEGO pirate ship he's been playing with for a long time.

"Hi, Daddy," Nikolai says. Andreas doesn't say anything.

"Can I have a hug?" I ask.

Nikolai gets up, walks toward me hesitantly and embraces me carefully, on his tiptoes and a bit distant, as if he's afraid I might infect him with something.

"Hello there," I say, sweeping him off the floor and swinging him around.

"Ow, Daddy," he says, and laughs, but twists free. "Have you been in jail?"

It takes me a minute to collect myself.

"Have you?" he asks again.

"No," I say. "I'm just helping the police."

"You were gone for a long time," he says.

Andreas finally looks up from his iPad and glowers in my direction.

"Hi, Andreas," I say, and bend down to give him a hug.

"Don't," he says, and pushes me away. "You smell bad."

When I go downstairs again, Leif is perched unsteadily on a barstool in the kitchen. He's thinner, a mere shadow of his former self, I think.

"I have a dinner at the palace today," Clara says. "It would be nice if you accompanied me. Daddy can watch the children."

Everything about this suggestion infuriates me. As if I'm ready to be Clara's arm candy after spending four days in police custody under suspicion of murder. "I need a word," I say, and take her by the arm, pulling her with me out into the hallway. I shut the door to the kitchen and push her up against the wall.

It's a little excessive, especially with her father sitting on the other side of the same wall, but at this precise moment, I don't give a damn.

"Let go of me," she says.

"There, I let go of you."

"Good. Can I go now?"

"No," I say. "It's great that your father's here. But shouldn't he have the chance to settle in before being left alone to watch two boys who are a bit off-kilter as it is, while the two of us go to a ball at the palace, when I've just been released from jail . . . so you can cultivate your new network?"

"Are you done?"

"No. I'm just getting started."

"It is in fact not the case that the whole world revolves around you."

"No, everything is about Her Royal Highness, the state secretary."

"You're the one who messed around, putting your dick where it shouldn't have been . . ."

"What's that supposed to mean?" I say.

"You heard me," she says, speaking quietly as always. Clara *never* raises her voice, regardless, which often gives her added authority. But I can still tell that she's angry. "I've been holding down the fort here while you were at Lysebu, on a bender with Axel, and in jail. And today I must attend a dinner at the Royal Palace. And I hoped you would accompany me, now that you've been released. But I have absolutely no intention of forcing you."

"Wow," I say. I seldom hear Clara speak this many sentences in a row, other than on the phone with other people, and then it's always about the ministry. It almost softens me a bit. Almost.

"Good. Because I'm staying here, I'm not going to any palace ball."

"Dinner," she says firmly.

"Hmm?" I say.

"The palace dinner, it's not a ball."

"Whatever. I'm not going," I say, stressing every single word.

"Fine." She goes into the kitchen where she starts speaking softly with her father. I have a sinking feeling that yes, she will remember this, and yes, I will regret it. But to hell with it, I just got out of jail. There's no damn way I'm spending the evening making small talk with cabinet ministers and their wives.

I go out into the garden and sit down. It's only when I hear her leave that I get to my feet and go inside.

"I was thinking maybe we could have a barbecue or something," I say to Leif.

"Fine. I thought you were going to the palace ball with Clara . . ."

"Dinner, not ball," I joke.

"Dinner . . . anyway, Clara said we should order pizza. But I wouldn't say no to a barbecue," he says.

"That's what I thought."

Leif isn't the kind of guy who likes to barbecue. I've never seen a backyard grill, a suspended campfire pan, or even a disposable grill on the farm. But he has a dog's appetite for barbecued food, that I know. A pork chop, a hot dog, a beer, and he's happy, and now I want to make him as happy as possible. All I have to do is light the grill and marinate the pork chops, take out the hot dogs, and make a salad.

I set the table out in the backyard. Glasses, napkins, silverware, plates. Flowers on the table. Leif comes out of the house and sits down. The boys are running through the sprinkler.

It's muggy and hot. Thunder rumbles in the distance.

"How are you feeling, Leif?" I ask after we've eaten, and the boys have run off again. He must have lost twenty pounds since I saw him last, and he wasn't overweight to begin with. His face is sallow, and there are blue rings under his eyes as well.

"Not bad, could have been worse. In light of what happened."

"Yes, you mean . . . ," I say, probing, without any idea of what he's talking about.

"The stroke."

"Right, how long ago was that?" I ask, hoping that he doesn't notice that I am clueless, cursing Clara for not having mentioned it.

Yes, there had been something about her father when she went to Western Norway, but she hadn't said anything else. But then I hadn't asked all that many questions, either.

"Two or three weeks? A little more? I can't quite remember."

"How are you feeling?"

"Dunno, mostly I just feel . . . weak."

"It will pass," I say. "I promise. And thank you for coming to stay with them. It was an enormous help for Clara and the rest of us."

We sit in silence for a little while, staring into the lilac bushes. A bumblebee buzzes in and out of clusters of lavender blossoms. The lilacs make me nostalgic, remind me of Grandmother Edith, of her old higgledy-piggledy villa, which is now in shambles. And first and foremost, the summer when I met Clara, and everything still seemed possible.

"So you've been inside for a bit . . . ?" Leif asks, tentatively.

"Yes," I say, and try to imagine how my father would have handled this situation. I still feel wretched, even though I started feeling a bit better while I was preparing our dinner. But I would have felt even worse had I been at the palace making small talk with a glass of champagne in my hand. "It was insane. A police screwup of enormous proportions. Would you like a beer?"

Leif nods. I get two bottles of Carlsberg, open both, and hand one to Leif.

"I was only inside for a couple of days, but it was long enough. I feel almost a bit traumatized by it," I add, and immediately regret my choice of words; Leif is a veteran of the war in Lebanon. "They believe the same person is responsible for all the murders," I hasten to add.

"And what is the motive? Pakistani vendettas?"

"Well, that was the theory to begin with. But in addition to both the victims being immigrants, Carter also abused her children . . ."

"Is that common?"

"Well," I say, "more common than we like to think. In the best families. You'd be surprised. But immigrants are unfortunately heavily overrepresented, statistically speaking . . ."

We sit in silence for a while.

"How are the boys taking it?"

I shrug. "They're keeping their distance . . ."

"Just give them some time."

"Yes, I guess I'll have to," I say, taking another sip of my beer. "Fortunately, Clara stayed calm, cool, and collected throughout all of it."

"Yes," Leif says, and takes a sip as well. "She usually does. I wonder how she's doing at the palace ball . . . sorry, dinner."

The last comment is accompanied by a faint smile. I feel like giving him a hug.

"She's probably in her element. Let's drink to that," I say, raising my beer toward him. "To that daughter of yours who can accomplish whatever she wants."

CHAPTER 51

CLARA

Outside the back entrance of the Royal Palace is a long line of black cars, official state cars, diplomatic vehicles, and taxis.

On the invitation bearing the royal couple's coat of arms, the guests were kindly requested to arrive at the main gate between 7:20 and 7:40 p.m. That apparently means one is supposed to arrive at precisely 7:30 p.m., which is what I do.

A crowd of photographers and journalists is waiting to photograph the more celebrated guests. As I arrive, they start snapping away, several of them standing on the red carpet in front of me. After my weekend of dealing with the firefighting helicopters, I have clearly become somebody they recognize.

"Lovely dress, Clara," one of them calls.

The skirt is so long that it drags behind me when I walk. Vigdis had run out and found me a dress in a hurry earlier today, because I didn't have time to do it myself. It's amazing how quickly one becomes accustomed to having someone take care of such things. Even though the secretaries primarily run errands for Munch, they are also very useful to the rest of us.

Suddenly, somebody is answering the better part of my emails for me. Booking meetings for me. Rescheduling my dentist appointments, buying dresses, and informing me of the protocol for all manner of things.

Vigdis has among other things explained to me that formal dress means full-length dresses for women, not black and not white.

I hang up my coat in the cloakroom downstairs and take a trip to the ladies' room.

7:40 p.m. on the dot, in the ladies' room on the first floor, Monrad had written in response to my text. We have a pretty tight window.

Now it's 7:38. It's cold down here. The water from the faucet is cold on my hands.

I stand before the mirror for a second or two looking at my face. My makeup is understated, discreet, my hair nicely done. I look pretty.

All the same, I shiver when I see myself, lean forward and squint.

My face. So familiar. I can see my father's face in there. And Grandmother Klara, whom I've never met, only seen in many photographs.

And yet, it seems unfamiliar, too.

Who is that? Who am I? What am I doing here?

I stand there for one second. Two, three. Try to breathe.

Then the big door opens and Cathrine Monrad walks in. Her face is drawn, and she looks tired, but she's elegantly made up and coiffed, her hair coiled into a bun on top of her head. Her dress is pink.

I take the memory stick out of my little handbag.

"Here you go," I say, and hand it to her. It's white, anonymous, nothing like the shiny memory sticks with a logo from the ministry.

"Listen," she says, and puts her hand on my right shoulder. "How can I thank you?"

"Well," I say, and attempt a little smile. "By saying that you made the recording yourself?"

She laughs.

"Of course. But what I don't understand is . . . why are you doing this?"

I shrug.

"I was there, I heard what he said. It irritates me that Munch calls you a liar and denies everything. Are you supposed to slink off with your tail between your legs, stripped of all dignity, while he just continues with business as usual? No."

"As long as you understand that this could backfire on you," she says as she puts the tiny memory stick into her clutch. "If Munch goes down, you may go down, too. Quickly."

"If that's what it takes, I'll accept it."

I could have thanked her for not saying anything to Munch about Henrik, but I don't want to taint the meeting with even the hint of a quid pro quo transaction.

Immediately afterward we walk together up the broad staircase to the second floor. It's far too warm. The doors to the balcony are open, but we're not allowed to go out there; that's one of the things I was drilled on.

I gaze around me, trying not to appear as alone as I feel. Cabinet ministers, the prime minister, who I sense is inspecting me. Well-known actors, businessmen, guests from Iceland—everyone is standing together in the corridor outside the halls.

I rehearse silently, in my head. To the king and queen, one is supposed to say, "Good evening, Your Majesty."

To the crown prince, crown princess, and the king's sister, one is supposed to say, "Good evening, Your Royal Highness."

To all the other guests, one just says, "Good evening."

It's time for the procession. I grasp the arm of a stout, sweaty, bald man who is also alone. Together we stride toward the Royal Banquet Hall.

Photographers are lined up along the walls. These must be the pictures that end up in the tabloids.

Finally, we reach the royal family and it's time to greet them.

I curtsy and manage to remember who are majesties and who aren't. But when I raise my hand to greet the aging princess, the king's sister, my stout escort steps on the hem of my dress and I stumble toward her.

The old princess starts and looks at me in horror.

"He stepped on my train. Good evening, Your Royal Highness," I say, and to my surprise she laughs.

When we sit down at the table, I have a world-weary author on my left. On the other side of me is a man with blond bangs and a blue gaze. He's attractive, but has an odd, pretentious expression on his face, as if he were playing a part in a play. He doesn't introduce himself either. Clearly, he thinks I should know who he is.

I've seen him before. But I have no idea where.

Waiters dressed in livery begin serving us with military precision. The king stands up, welcomes us all, especially the Icelandic guest of honor, who then stands up and makes a speech to the host. Afterward, everyone stands up while we sing the national anthem.

The man I can't identify proves to be an easygoing dinner companion who talks a lot about himself and his doings.

"But why isn't Munch here?" he asks me. "Did he run away because of the Monrad situation?"

"No. He had a meeting in Brussels."

The king and queen get to their feet, upon which everyone else gets up, too; conversations fall silent and we remain standing until the royal family members have left the room. Now there will be coffee and cognac or liqueur. Protocol dictates that people cultivate their networks in the hall next door. If they have a network.

I walk toward the stairs. There I am stopped by one of the livery-clad men.

"Excuse me. Where are you headed?"

His smile is polite but stiff.

"Home?"

"I don't think that's such a good idea."

We stare at one another for a moment.

Then I turn around and walk back into the sea of people, resolving to become the new Clara. The one people want to take photographs of, who makes people think she likes to talk to them, who loves her new job. I dive into the buzzing, gossiping, jostling crowd, shake one hand after the next, say hello, smile, nod. Yes, I even kiss a few people on the cheek, even though it's the worst thing I can think of.

Then the prime minister approaches me.

"Clara, isn't it?" she says, and offers me her hand.

"Yes," I say, and almost curtsy, but stop myself in time.

"So, you're Munch's latest innovation?" she says. "Well, he surprised me there, I've never had the impression that Anton has understood that it's wise to hire women. But there's an exception to every rule, I guess."

"I guess there is," I say.

She studies me with a critical, inquisitive gaze.

A man is trying to get her attention; he has placed a hand on her upper arm. Probably an adviser.

She gives me a curt nod.

"It seems I have to go." She turns toward the man and leaves.

And so, finally, after about an hour, all the conversations die out again and silence fills the room while the royal family members parade out. In the cloakroom I'm invited to join the others for a nightcap at Lorry Bar.

I decline. "Must get home to my sitter," I say.

As I am walking through the Queen's Park on my way home, I realize who Mr. Pretentious is.

His name is Erik Heier and he's the host of a political talk show. I must work on my facial recognition skills.

What's worse is that Cathrine Monrad is right. A new cabinet minister will hardly be interested in retaining a recently converted, already compromised state secretary on his or her team. I thought I would have plenty of time to accomplish something, but now it might be over before it has begun, even though Henrik has been released.

But Dad's here. That helps.

CHAPTER 52

LEIF

She was too young. I knew that. But at the same time, she'd never really been young.

In the beginning I just told her how blue the sky was, how hot it was, how good everything smelled, that the coffee was divine, that people were friendly and beautiful.

But after a while I also told her about the shooting in Rachaya.

About the sound a projectile missile makes when it hits first one and then another body.

About the sound of a human being dropping to the ground.

About how it didn't feel like I was taking a human life, more like I was hitting a target and that my life depended on my taking it down.

Maybe I wanted to make her understand how close I had come to not returning at all. She didn't seem particularly pleased to have me back. But when I told her stories about Lebanon, it was as if she woke up. She sat closer to me and her eyes came to life.

I often fell asleep easily. But after a few hours I woke up.

In the mornings I was dead on my feet. I didn't always manage to get out of bed and sometimes I drank. I went to the barn, slept a bit on the couch, talked to the children, went back to the barn, kissed the children good night.

But it felt as if nothing would ever be easy or enjoyable again.

The doctor prescribed some sleeping pills, so I got some sleep, but the pills made me sick, too, and during the day I went around with a kind of hangover.

I didn't talk to Agnes. With Clara, I talked too much.

Then one day Magne, a colleague of Agnes's, appeared at our door. He was a guy who was full of himself and had a seat on the county council. I'd never liked him.

"Agnes is afraid of you, Leif," he said. "It worries me. She had a lot to deal with, having to manage all this by herself while you were away."

His voice was warm and compassionate, but his eyes were cold, mocking. As if someone were listening.

I glanced toward the door to the kitchen and could see Agnes behind it, like a ghost.

"Did Agnes ask you to come?" I asked, but I didn't receive an answer.

"You're too weak for this, Leif," he said instead. "You need help."

What I remember best is how my legs were shaking. How he shook his head at Agnes.

Poor bastard was what his body language was saying.

Next, she told me she wanted to move out. It was impossible to be here, *she* said to me, when I was the one who had put up with her during all those years when she just lay in bed and didn't help out, while I carried the children and lulled them to sleep and brushed their teeth and combed their hair, did the cooking and the laundry and scrubbed the toilet and God knows what else.

She wanted to take the children with her, she said. But Clara refused.

"You can go, I'm staying," she said to her mother.

"Clara, that won't do," her mother said halfheartedly, but deep down I suspected that she was relieved.

Agnes left and took Lars with her.

Clara howled and screamed and tried to prevent her brother from leaving.

CHAPTER 53

CLARA

As usual, I can hear my dad's voice as I'm buying my daily morning coffee—double latte with skim milk.

One caffe latte a day, in two years adds up to a car, Dad says. The man who mends his own shirts and sweaters and darns his socks. Who patches his old rain gear using materials from a bike-tire repair kit. Who reads the newspaper at the library once a week when he goes down to the village to do the shopping. Who buys the cheapest coffee and the cheapest eggs. Who pays the bills the minute they arrive, several weeks before they fall due, out of fear of being charged a penalty fee for late payment.

I try not to be wasteful, but I'm nowhere near the vicinity of his standards.

All these idiots who claim that money doesn't buy happiness.

At least it reduces existential anxiety. And strictly speaking, that's what life is about for many of us.

It's not about being able to buy everything you want. Or being able to hire someone to clean the house and wash the car and mow the lawn for you. But about being spared having to worry about how you will manage to pay the bills or hang on to your house.

That's a concept those who have always had money can't understand.

On my way from Youngstorget Square toward Akersgata Street, coffee in hand, I walk across the square where a young woman, an executive officer like I was, was killed when a bomb went off on July 22, 2011.

There, right there, at exactly 3:25 p.m. on a gray, rainy Friday in the middle of summer, her life ended. And my place of work, as I had known it, was obliterated.

I was at work, I survived, got down the stairs, made it through the demolished reception area and out onto the street. Without a scratch.

Several of my colleagues still have injuries from that day. A scar on a wrist, a missing leg, a disabled arm.

And then there were all the other injuries, the ones that don't show.

I walk through what used to be the lobby of The Highrise, the way I always do when I come from this direction. Many people will go to great lengths to avoid it, but for me it has become a ritual.

This was my workplace for several years. I punched in and out of this reception area hundreds of times.

I loved The Highrise, the combination of stone walls with 1960s teak furnishings and the tapestry by Hannah Ryggen, *We Are Living on a Star*, which always made me think of Astrup's painting.

All of this was mine. All of this was blown up. All of it is gone now.

Demolished, diminished to little more than smoke and dust. And then removed, cleared away.

Hannah Ryggen's tapestry had also been damaged in the explosion but has since been restored. The glass fragments and concrete dust were removed; it was painstakingly mended and is now on display somewhere else.

But the building has been left in this state for seven years. They have yet to decide on a new solution. The vestibule, which was formerly such a warm, vibrant place, is now just an empty, dismal shell.

Only the elegant water mirror between The Highrise and the government building R5, where our ministry was located, is the same.

Before, I would sometimes sit down and watch the water running silently and smoothly. I no longer have the time.

"*VG* wants to shadow Clara for a day," the head of communications says after going through the press clippings. "Preferably a day when there's a bit going on, good photo ops, good locations . . ."

"No," I say automatically. Both Munch, who is back from Brussels, and the head of communications look at me in astonishment.

"It's predominantly a matter of following you around during your workday. And there's a similar request, by the way. From Erik Heier at TV2. He wants to interview Clara."

"Heier? That old lecher?" Mona murmurs.

"TV2? Interview Clara?" the adviser says, and shakes his head, looking at Munch insistently. "But aren't *you* supposed to be the center of attention? Clara's feminine attributes notwithstanding?"

Mona clears her throat ominously.

"I'll manage, thank you. What do you say?" Munch asks, looking at the head of communications, who shrugs.

"Hard to get around it, I think. Then they'll just do a story about how she refused to be interviewed."

"Mona?" Munch says, looking at the secretary-general.

"No, I don't want to be involved in how you decide to work the press," she says, and sighs.

It's obvious that she's skeptical, but I believe she will warm up to me with time. I think she already appreciates that I am organized and quick to respond, have a no-nonsense approach, and don't overload her department with too many meaningless and resource-demanding requests.

"Both *VG* and TV2 have also expressed a wish to interview you in your house," the head of communications says. "They want to show the contrast between the career woman and the woman at home. How you juggle everything . . ."

"Why on earth is she getting all this attention? She's not a cabinet minister," the adviser sighs. Despite his young age, he has three children at home in Southern Norway. His wife takes care of the house, but he posts pictures of himself and his children on Instagram and Facebook when he's home on the weekends. But now, in fact, I'm inclined to agree with him.

"A beautiful woman, mysterious charisma, you know," the head of communications says. "That's all it takes. Besides the fact that she managed to come up with fifteen new firefighting helicopters overnight."

"They won't be coming to my home," I say.

On the way out of the meeting, the head of communications receives a call.

"Yes? What? I'll have to get back to you on that. I'll call you," he says, and hangs up.

"*Oh my God* . . . That was the *VG* news desk," he says to me, and glances around him. Munch is no longer in sight. "Guess what."

"I have no idea."

He sighs heavily.

"What a nightmare. Cathrine Monrad released an audio file proving that Munch in fact did say all the things he's denying having said and they're wondering if he wants to comment."

"Things such as?" Mona says, a wrinkle of concern forming between her eyebrows.

"Such as how it's not her job to be a media whore."

"Did he really say that?" Mona asks. "If so, he's been caught lying. That's one of the worst things that can happen. Do you remember how many people had to step down for trivialities because they were stupid enough to try and lie about it? And to threaten a subordinate director with censure if she doesn't keep her mouth shut—"

At that moment her phone rings.

"It's the office of the prime minister," she says after having glanced at the screen. She straightens her brooch of the day, which looks like a pelican. "No surprise there."

"What do they want?" the head of communications asks.

"The truth, the whole truth, and nothing but, of course. Immediately," Mona says, making a face and walking quickly toward her own office.

CHAPTER 54

———

LEIF

1982

In a way, things settled down after Agnes left.

I started breathing more easily, got more sleep at night, and spent less time sitting on the balcony with my shotgun in my lap. I talked to Clara, told her about the olive tree and the cave in the mountain, the goats and the crickets, about the grenades that shattered the enormous silence, and about the splinter I had pulled out of my hip and brought home with me.

"Where's the splinter now?" she asked. I went to get the matchbox out of my dresser drawer in the bedroom and showed it to her.

"Can I touch it?" she asked.

Then she sat there cradling it in her hand.

"It's my souvenir," I said. "One of them."

"Can we make it into a piece of jewelry?"

"Jewelry?" I said, astonished. "Yes, well maybe, if you like."

"Do you have anything else? Can I see?" she asked, and tilted her head to one side.

"Wait a minute," I said. I went back to the dresser drawer and took out the green beret with all the holes in it.

She spread it out on her lap and sat there turning it over and over.

"Did you take this off somebody's head?" she asked.

"No, it was lying on the ground."

"And did you make all the holes in it?"

"I don't know, but yes, probably. You know . . . the strangest thing is that in the midst of all that abomination I also felt more alive than ever before."

"Because you'd killed somebody?"

"No, not that in particular, not by any means."

"What was it, then?"

"It's hard to explain to someone who wasn't there. But everything felt so meaningful, in a way."

CHAPTER 55

CLARA

I'm sitting at the little café table in our garden, wearing a light-blue linen dress and holding an espresso cup in my hand while posing for a photographer from *VG*. After this I pose leaning against the pear tree in the garden. Kneeling beside a flower bed. Leaning out a window.

Like everyone else, I've made fun of how the cabinet minister travels all over the country to provide the press corps with good photo ops instead of staying in his office and doing his job. But here I am, ingratiating myself, smiling until it feels like my face is about to crack.

They brought along their own stylist or makeup artist or whatever it's called. I try to say that I don't like to wear all that much makeup, just some mascara and a little powder, but it's no use. They put bright-red lipstick on me and arrange my hair in the best Betty Draper style.

When they're finally ready to take the pictures, I receive thorough instructions. *Hold your hands like this. Look to the right and then at me, thank you. Lean a bit forward. Move back a bit. Thanks, thanks, thanks, click, click, click.*

And at all times our head of communications is standing in the background, cheering me on and giving me the thumbs-up, as if I were a show dog.

I told him before we started that he didn't need to be here, but he came anyway.

I have never really been fond of people. I find people stressful. All the noise they make, all the talking, it depletes me of my strength and concentration.

Being with Dad is fine. With my boys, up to a certain point. I used to like spending time with Henrik, at least in small doses. And Grandmother Edith. But otherwise? Not really. It's a waste of time.

I've always tried to seem as normal as possible. For a while I considered even changing my name, to Anne or Anita or Marie or something or other that was completely ordinary. Clara with a *C* was too eccentric in Norway, I thought.

I never did change my name. But I've made sure that nobody, not even Henrik, knows anything about me. That's how I want it to be. Live like an invisible bureaucrat, a conventional lady from the right side of the tracks. A foot soldier in disguise.

But now this. A horrific team has invaded my garden, preparing to put me on display for all the world to see. My colleagues at work, the neighbors, people at the store, the parents of my sons' classmates, everyone who doesn't really know anything about me will now come a step closer.

There's no turning back, I just have to smile and look into the camera.

Maybe my mother will see this article. Maybe Bodil or some other harpy at the home will bring her the newspaper, or the article, neatly cut out.

"Look, Agnes, it's Clara, your daughter, you know, in Oslo."

Had it been foolish of me to show up at Kleivhøgda?

I'd told myself that it was necessary, that after what happened at Ullevål that night, I needed to get a sense of how clearheaded my mother was, how much she remembered, how well she was able to express herself.

For all these years I've fooled myself into thinking that she doesn't exist. That she is really dead, the way I've told everyone she is.

But she is very much alive. And after meeting her I wasn't any wiser.

Most people had pretty much forgotten about Agnes Lofthus a long time ago. But everyone at the home, like Bodil, will be shocked when they read the sob story about my deceased mother in my interview. Then they will call *VG* to notify them that it was a lie.

"Seriously ill," I say now instead, to the journalist with long hair. "But I think you should just not mention her at all in the article. It's hard on the family."

"OK," the woman says, twisting a lock of hair around her index finger. "But you and your father are close, right?"

I sigh and bat away a wasp circling my iced tea with the same determined sense of purpose as this journalist, who is slowly closing in on me.

"I thought this wasn't going to be about private matters?"

The lady lifts her head, looks at me in surprise.

"This isn't private. Just a little personal. And it sort of has to be . . ."

"Does it?" I say.

"Yes," she says.

A silent power struggle. She smiles at me sweetly and demonstratively, and I decide to go with the truth.

"My father has been my rock," I say, and that is the truth. And at the same time, not. "All children deserve such stability in their lives. Many don't have it."

"No," she says distractedly, and chews on her pencil. I haven't seen anyone chew on a pencil with such concentration since I was in school. "Is it true, by the way, that you were in a car accident as a child?" she asks before I have the chance to continue.

Hell, she's not letting up. Clearly, she's an expert at probing, like a dog with a bone. And it's true, I've heard about this, and seen it in all the foolish in-depth interviews I've read. The journalist is always looking for some kind of painful, traumatic event to use as an angle for the article. An obstructed bowel as an infant, anything.

"Yes, but it's too traumatic, don't include that," I say, swiping at the wasp.

She nods again, even as I realize the list of things she can't include in the article is becoming exceedingly long.

This is the main reason why I don't like interviews.

"My commitment and passion stem from everything I've seen and read and heard. There are countless stories about children who've been subjected to serious violence and abuse at home. When they try to tell somebody about it at school, for example, nothing happens, except perhaps the parents may be notified, which only makes the situation worse. There are far too many people who know but don't do anything. Because it's simpler to do nothing. That's what we must change," I say.

"Thanks," the chick mumbles without any particular enthusiasm, and at exactly that moment, I finally succeed in swatting the wasp down. It lies beside my glass, cleaved almost in two, its body seizing in the grips of its final spasms.

The Susanne murder had knocked the legs out from under Munch's gang-killing theory, and he's really taking the heat for it now. He must appear on both the six o'clock and the seven o'clock news and on every other media channel as well and explain his actions with respect to both the Monrad case and the latest murder.

Has living in Oslo become life endangering? And why did he make such bombastic public statements about gang culture when it turns out that these murders haven't had anything whatsoever to do with gangs? Was it simply to stir things up so he came across as a man of action? Or was it a lame attempt to bolster his position in the debate about whether the police should start carrying firearms, of which he has been such a wholehearted advocate?

The media is speculating about domestic violence in relation to all three victims and has begun writing about children who are left in the custody of families even when there are suspicions of something being amiss. Why is this happening? Why doesn't the system prevent this?

He must answer for all of it.

And he doesn't do very well. He mumbles about a bill that is right around the corner, but otherwise has little to say.

A few days later *VG* runs a follow-up piece about how the Standing Committee on Scrutiny and Constitutional Affairs has asked Munch to explain the Monrad case. The Office of the Auditor General is also looking into the matter.

They run my interview in the newspaper's weekend supplement the following Saturday, under the headline "Rising Star in the Ministry of Justice."

At work, fires are being put out everywhere to try to save Munch, and the glorifying article about me is not particularly well received.

"Nice self-promotion there, Clara," the adviser says when he sticks his head through my doorway. We are both working late to try to get as much as possible out of the way before the summer break. "Good job! Just what the boss needed . . ."

"It wasn't my idea for them to interview me. *VG* contacted the communications department. You know that."

"That was the story we were told, yes," he says, and makes a face. "But maybe they received a tip? About the possibility of a story like this?"

"Well, believe whatever you want."

He becomes visibly uncertain.

"I see, so you admit—"

"I'm not admitting anything," I interrupt. "I just said you can believe what you want."

Then he just shakes his head and walks away with his clenched fists shoved deep into the pockets of his suit trousers, the fabric tightening around his buttocks.

He is seriously chubby, just like all of Munch's boys. Too much bad overtime food, too many chocolate bars from the vending machine in the hallway, too little sleep.

I must take care not to become like them.

When I get home today, I'm going to go for a long run in the forest, over tree roots and wet, boggy ground, and just run and breathe and sweat until the interview and Munch and the adviser and all manner of journalists are purged from my body.

Then it's summer vacation. And we're going home.

CHAPTER 56

LEIF

1986

I was supposed to have Lars every other weekend. It was not nearly enough, but that's how it is for other divorced parents, too. And it would certainly work out with time, I thought, as soon as Agnes descended into her darkness again and was unable to get out of bed in the morning.

Eventually, Agnes stopped answering the phone when I called. I turned up at the door to the cellar apartment she had rented. Nobody was home. The same thing the next day. Then I found Agnes up at the Lia farm, with Magne. She was standing out in the yard when I came driving up. There was no sign of Lars.

"I want to see my son," I said.

"And what if he doesn't want to see you?" she asked, and pulled the pink knitted mohair jacket more tightly around her, tilting her head at me. She drew her long blonde hair over one shoulder and peered at me inquisitively in a way I used to like. "I don't think it's good for Lars to be with you. Not Clara either. Not since Lebanon."

"But you, on the other hand . . ." I could hear my voice rising as I spoke. "You are the mother of the century . . ."

"Oh my God," she said, before retreating into the hallway and slamming the back door of the house.

I started picking him up at school then, which worked better. Lars seemed happy to see me, curling up in the crook of my arm in front of the television to watch *Sesame Street* while I studied his tiny nose, the downy fuzz on his face, and his crooked little smile. Lars was so fragile, almost weak, somehow more of a girl than Clara was. And quiet. He had his thumb in his mouth; he'd started sucking it again. He also started wetting his bed at night again, which he hadn't done for many years. I washed the sheets and his pajamas and the mattress cover.

Clara thought I should ask for custody. It was ridiculous for him to live with Mommy and Magne, it wasn't good for him, she said, look how jumpy he's become. That I hadn't been well after Lebanon was not something I should worry about. She would testify for me, she said, tell everyone that I was the best daddy in the world.

And I thought I would manage to do this, that I would fix it. I would take care of everything, I just had to rest a bit first, get my strength back, before I could stand up to Magne and Agnes.

Then finally I managed to bring Lars home one weekend.

That Saturday I gave him a bath in the expensive pink bathtub Agnes had forced me to install.

At first, he refused, but I insisted, he was dirty.

As I watched him undress, I had to swallow and look away.

No child hurts himself in that way. No child has bruises under their arms, on their hips, or on their tummy from natural causes.

"What happened?" I asked Lars.

"I hurt myself," he said, and sniffled a little.

I called Clara, got her to come and look.

After this I marched up to the desk of the woman at the municipal services office who was responsible for child welfare, among other things.

"So, you're saying you think that the boy's mother . . ."

"Or his stepfather," I said.

". . . hits the boy, because he's less talkative and has broken his arm."

"It's not just that," I sighed. "There are a lot of things. And bruises, like I said."

"Well, my children are also full of bruises and I don't hit them. These sound like some pretty vague suspicions to me," the social worker said, drumming her fingers on the desktop.

We had gone to school together, and I'd never liked her. I don't think she liked me either.

"We will of course look into it. But Magne Lia is a pretty solid fellow. And you've been having a bit of a hard time lately, haven't you?" she said, and looked at me defiantly. "Even if you don't like it that your wife has left you and you feel betrayed and disappointed, you *can't* go around making these kinds of accusations left and right, you understand that certainly . . ."

"Does that mean you don't believe me?" More than anything, I wanted to slap the woman across the face.

"I didn't say that," she replied.

Her eyes said the opposite.

When I left the office, I felt like I'd used up an entire life's worth of energy. I had no more fight left in me. I had left it all behind by the olive tree in Rachaya or up by Jeita Grotto.

I just sat there waiting for things to work themselves out, for Agnes to come to her senses and move back home or at least away from Magne, for someone to find out so they had to fix this, for a teacher to speak up and do something. Even better, I hoped that what Agnes said was true, that everything was fine. Because Magne and Agnes scared the living daylights out of me. I knew they would use Lebanon against me, say that I was an unfit father. Maybe everything would get even worse if I provoked them.

And then Agnes called and said that Lars didn't want to come and stay with me anymore.

"It wears him out," she said. "He needs peace and quiet. Stability."

She hung up. The blood ran cold in my veins. Now I would have to do something, complain, take action, whatever it took.

But first I needed to lie down and rest for a little while.

I could straighten things out later. Tomorrow. Not now.

CHAPTER 57

HENRIK

It's the day before our departure, after a series of delays. I have the day off. Clara had had a photo session at home, against my will, and then she went into the office.

There's a flower delivery guy on the front steps.

"Here you are," he says, and hands me a huge thing wrapped in brown paper.

"Thanks." I retreat inside and unpack the bouquet just as I did the others that have arrived. The flowers are mostly from organizations interested in building a relationship with the new state secretary, and they've already begun lobbying. Apparently, even more have arrived at the office.

This bouquet is traditional and ostentatious, white lilies and red roses and some bluish-lavender nonsense. All that's missing is the baby's breath. None of the four bouquets are the kind I would have bought. And tomorrow we're leaving for Western Norway. Nonetheless, I take out a vase, fill it with water, and place the newest bouquet in it without cutting the stems.

Then I glance at the card.

Congratulations on your wonderful new job. We are very proud of you, Clara. It was unbelievably kind of you to drop by! Hope you will come back the next time you're in Western Norway. Warm wishes from all of us at Kleivhøgda c/o Bodil.

Kleivhøgda? What is that? And who has sent such an effusive greeting? Clara has no contact with anyone at all in Western Norway, except for her father. We never visit anyone, never meet anyone—it's even rare to see her nod at someone in the store.

A quick Google search reveals that Kleivhøgda is a psychiatric hospital about twelve miles away from Clara's hometown. Without further ado I punch the telephone number into my iPhone and press the green button.

After three rings somebody answers.

"Hello, Kleivhøgda, Bodil speaking."

"Yes, hello, this is Henrik Fougner, Clara Lofthus's husband . . ."

"Oh, hello, yes . . ."

"I wanted to thank you for the flowers we just received. Clara isn't at home, but I unwrapped them and they're absolutely lovely."

"How nice," she says, sounding pleased. "Yes, we felt we ought to make a bit of a fuss over Clara . . . Are you often in these parts?"

"Actually, we're leaving for Western Norway tomorrow," I say, and summon my resolve. "Maybe we could stop by one day? If that's convenient?"

"Yes, please do," she says, and now her tongue has finally loosened. "I think it would be good for Agnes if they met again before too much time has passed. You know, she hadn't seen her daughter for thirty years, and then she suddenly appears, so of course she wants to see her again soon. And now that Agnes's health is finally improving, it's especially important to follow up."

"Of course," I say. "If Clara is busy, I might come alone, we'll have to see."

After a few farewell phrases we hang up. I remain seated, furrowing my brow, the phone between my hands, trying to think.

I was always told that Clara's mother, brother, and stepfather died in a car accident when Clara was only twelve years old. She had been in the car, too, and tried to save the others without success. Since then she'd never been able to talk about it, not until the one short conversation we had, the one I remember very well even after all these years.

We were lying in her narrow bed at Grandmother Edith's house, having just finished the evening meal. We were both on our sides, with our faces close together. I could feel her forehead against my own, my breath against hers, the kind of thing that's lovely at the beginning of a relationship, but later seems a bit over the top.

Her eyes were so close to mine that I was unable to focus on them. I couldn't see the blue irises, only a hazy blue, like the sky, like a meadow full of lavender.

Then she told me about her mother and Lars and Magne, breathed it out of her mouth and inside me.

I had to promise we would never speak of it again, ever.

I have kept that promise.

At the time, of course I thought we would have many such evenings, that this was just the beginning, that we would return to the subject again and again, become closer, talk more.

Little did I know that the intimacy of those days, that brief period, was the most we would ever share, the closest to her I would ever be.

I'd heard the children ask if they could come to see Grandmother's and Uncle Lars's graves, but she always changed the subject and it's been a long time since they've asked. I have never been there myself. Leif never wanted to talk about his ex-wife or his son. I know nothing about them, haven't even seen pictures of them.

It wasn't that strange. Many people react to trauma this way. I have even used it as an explanation for why Clara is such a closed person.

But my mother-in-law, who supposedly died thirty years ago, is alive.

What a demented lie Clara has told me.

PART 4

CHAPTER 58

CLARA

1987

Every single day Daddy said he would do something about it. Soon.

The days passed like that, until that Wednesday.

Just like every other day after school, I walked up all the steep hills from where the school bus stops down on the main road. I had just sat down at the kitchen table with my math homework and a glass of chocolate milk when the gray telephone on the table out in the hallway rang.

"Yes?" I said after lifting the receiver.

"Clara?" He spoke so softly I could barely hear him.

"Lars?"

"You have to come. I don't want to be here anymore."

"OK, we'll come get you. But what's going on?"

"I think they're going to give me a beating, a bad one, I . . . I have to hang up now. Sorry."

"Wait," I said. "Lars, wait . . ." But the only sound was a beep-beep-beep in my ear.

I pulled on my jacket and shoes. Ran out into the yard. Called for Daddy.

I ran into the shed. Into the barn. From room to room.

I ran back into the house. Daddy was nowhere to be found. He had to be up in the hills somewhere. I ran up to the orchard, calling as I ran, through the first and the second and the third apple orchard.

Daddy, Daddy, Daddy!

No Daddy anywhere.

When I got back to the yard, I sat down for a bit and waited.

It would take me a long time to ride my bike there, probably longer than waiting for Daddy to appear. But waiting like this was unbearable.

Finally, I jumped on my bicycle, new this very spring; I'd been saving and saving for many years. I rode my bike as fast as I could, down, down, down. I had to keep my balance, not tip over.

I sped down the road along the fjord for a mile or so, way out on the edge of the shoulder as the cars whizzed past, the slipstream from them making my bike wobble, until I reached the intersection where there was a turnoff leading up to Magne's farm. I rode up the hills standing on the pedals, pedaling as hard as I could, even after my muscles had reached their limit.

When I finally made it to the yard, I saw the ambulance parked there.

Magne's barking elkhound, the one that was always tied to the flagpole and yelped angrily whenever people came, wasn't there. No birds were singing in the trees in the yard.

Not a sound to be heard.

I walked up the steps to the front door, took hold of the door handle, and walked into the huge entryway. Lars was lying on the floor.

Two heavyset guys wearing jackets and trousers that were too tight were pressing his chest, over and over again, the way I'd done the time he almost drowned in the lake up at the summer farm.

Magne stood by watching, covering his mouth with one hand in that concerned teacher way of his. Mommy was nowhere in sight.

"Oh, Clara," Magne said when he saw me. "There you are."

I just looked at Lars.

His face didn't look the way it did that time at the lake in the mountains, when I squeezed his chest and breathed into him and finally the water came out of his mouth like the spray from a fountain.

It was completely different.

In the hospital I sat by Lars's bed. Mommy and Magne sat out in the hallway. For once they understood they had to stay away.

"Lars, Lars, wake up now," I said, again and again.

I sang "A Little Bluebird Flew Away" to him.

He lay there, as immobile as before.

Finally, Daddy came running down the hallway.

"Where are they? Where are my children?" he asked. Mommy and Magne stood up and tried to block the door to the room.

"Lars needs to rest now," Mommy said, as if there were anything in the world that could make a difference for Lars now.

"Yes, take a seat out here, Leif," Magne said, meekly for him.

"Oh no you don't," Daddy said, and plowed his way between them, through the door and into the room, over to the bed.

And then everything started over.

Because now Daddy would understand it, the way I'd understood it.

Lars lay there completely still with his two small hands on his tummy. His fingernails were short and jagged. He'd started biting his nails and picking at his fingers. I tried to tell him he mustn't do that, then he stopped for a little while, but soon he was at it again, pick, pick, pick. It had irritated me.

How could it have irritated me?

How could anything at all about Lars have irritated me?

Now he wasn't breathing and wasn't moving, and his skin was all blue and cold, and Daddy was crying, but I didn't cry.

It felt like I was just as cold and blue as the one who was lying there, as if I would never manage to breathe properly again.

I wanted to pick him up, carry him away, but I didn't. It was too late.

Everything was too late. And it was all my fault.

When Daddy hadn't been able to do anything, I should have done something. I could have gone to get Lars and run away with him, we could have lived in a cottage in the mountains, I could have saved him, but I didn't do it, and now I no longer deserved to live.

I didn't say any of this. I just bent down and kissed his cold forehead. Then I got up and went to stand beside Daddy, who had fallen to his knees and was lying on top of Lars and sobbing.

"Oh God, oh God, oh God," he said repeatedly. Lars's clothing got wet. I knew he wouldn't feel it, but all the same I didn't like it. I wanted to tell Daddy he wasn't allowed to do that, but I didn't say anything and stroked his back instead.

Lars was silent. And I was silent.

We were both dead, but I was dead in another way than he was.

I had to keep breathing, breathe in, breathe out. Again, and again.

I was certain that Magne would be punished.

But soon an explanation surfaced about possible epilepsy and some other mysterious diagnoses, which Daddy and I had never heard about, but which Mommy confirmed.

So did the doctor, who was also a good friend of Magne's.

It was the epilepsy that made Lars fall down the stairs the wrong way. This had caused a cerebral hemorrhage, Magne and Mommy said.

It was an awful tragedy, they said.

People swallowed it and spit it out again.

Daddy tried talking to the lady from the child welfare authorities. Apparently, she was dismissive and uninterested.

I didn't try talking to anyone. I understood it was pointless and had already started thinking along different lines. On the contrary, I made sure to speak nicely about Mommy and Magne to everyone.

Only Daddy and I and Auntie and her husband attended the funeral, along with the vicar, sexton, and parish clerk.

Two days before I had called my mother.

"You will not attend the funeral," I said. "Not you and not Magne. If you come, I'll kill you."

I'd insisted on being a pallbearer, even though Daddy said I wasn't old enough.

Even though Lars was small, and the coffin was small, it was still terribly heavy. But I decided to make sure the others couldn't tell and held it high with both hands.

The others cried. I still had no tears.

When we reached the grave, we placed the coffin on some boards. Then the boards were pulled away and we lowered the coffin into the grave. I heard a sound from down there, it must have been Lars sliding around inside. There was a horrible scraping sound made by a stone when the coffin hit the bottom and another horrible sound when the vicar threw dirt onto the coffin.

The only other sound was that of the rain hitting our jackets and the ground and the coffin.

In the dark, down there, was where Lars would remain, while worms and beetles crawled around in the blackness surrounding the coffin, until eventually they would dig their way inside to find him.

CHAPTER 59

Henrik

Leif and Clara's world begins where you turn off the highway and follow the curving, poorly maintained municipal road that winds through the valley. After passing a couple of abandoned farms, in the farthest depths of the valley, where the road stops, you come to Leif's farm.

"In the depths of the valley" sounds dark and oppressive, but the farm is situated on top of a steep hill, with a fabulous view.

I'd shown my parents pictures and they'd been enchanted. Western Norway is so majestic and the poems of Olav H. Hauge so beautiful, Mother said. They wanted to visit, but neither Leif nor Clara had invited them. Honestly, I think Leif would have a heart attack if he had to watch Mother wandering around the yard there, not to mention inside the house, with her hawklike gaze. It's been a long time since they've suggested a trip west. Mother just looks at me with a sorrowful and mildly accusatory gaze every time Western Norway is mentioned.

They would love the snow on the mountains and the grazing sheep and the green fjord and all that.

For a little while, Mother would find the limited selection at the consumer co-operative charming. But she *wouldn't* appreciate that there was often no water in the shower in the cramped stall. In the summertime we solve this by bathing in the river, no matter how cold it is. I'm pretty good at it, and I'm used to taking an early morning swim, regardless of the temperature, from the time I've spent at our cabin in

Kilsund. But I am way out of Clara's league; it's as if she never notices how cold the water is.

It's strange being here this time.

I've always liked the farm, despite the flies and other inconveniences. It felt like this was a secluded corner of the world, a peaceful green oasis from a bygone era. I liked seeing Clara transformed from a sleek, urban career woman into a hard-core milkmaid.

But this time everything is different.

The day before we left, after the conversation with Bodil at Kleivhøgda, I was determined to confront Clara the moment she came home, or at least when she was sitting there enjoying her evening joint.

The problem was finding the right moment and the right way to do it.

So, in the end, I chickened out and put it off.

We went on vacation.

And now there's an eerie sheen over everything, despite the idyllic surroundings.

The grounds around the farmhouse look relatively well maintained; the grass is a little long, but there are flowers and bushes everywhere. The barn is red and the house white, and the flagpole is still standing. Sheep are grazing on the hillsides.

The barn is full of all manner of junk accumulated over the course of several generations: old tires, bicycles, tractor wheels, containers for homemade wine, fertilizer, hay, sawdust, everything all topsy-turvy in a blissfully chaotic jumble, covered with a thick layer of dust. The dark cow barn, cramped with a low ceiling and filled with an intense odor of sheep urine and silage, must have been off the veterinary inspectorate's radar.

And then there's the house. Filled to the ceiling with clutter. An entire century's worth of books and magazines. Old clothes that must have belonged to Leif's parents. He must have simply given up. No wonder he never buys anything for himself; there's no room.

Thundering down between the summer farm and the main farm, where there's a difference in altitude of around a thousand feet, is the Huldrefossen Waterfall. Although the drop is short, the waterfall is a powerful natural force, particularly during rainy periods. From the farmyard the waterfall is just a distant, ongoing hum, but on the summer farm we can hear it rumble and roar, even though we can't see it.

Clara has invested a lot of energy in teaching us to stop calling the summer farmhouse "the cottage."

"It's a summer farm," she says. "The house we sleep in is the summer farmhouse."

The summer farm and farmhouse. Now the boys use the right names.

I still say "the cottage" when talking about it with Clara.

When we push the heavy door open now, I immediately spot the small, shriveled corpses of a mother mouse and seven baby mice in the green water bucket just inside the door. Presumably, the mother crawled up into it, gave birth, was unable to get out again and died with her litter.

"Oh shit," I say, and look away.

Clara stands inspecting the bottom of the bucket.

"Unpremeditated child neglect," she says, and picking up the bucket, she goes outside to dump the contents somewhere in the heather. Usually, I would think she was tough, but now her behavior feels like evidence of how callous she is.

In one corner there's an old stove with cooking coils for the pots hanging on the wall, burned black on the outside from many years of use, shiny on the inside.

There are beds in each of the three corners, which in Oslo we would have called built-in beds. They are so short that I always sleep on a mattress on the floor. The mattresses; a few wool, military-style blankets; and some old bedding are hanging over the ceiling beams.

The first time I came west with her it was in the fall, a few months after we met.

There was a beautiful sprinkling of white over the farm below. Up toward the summer farm, there were ten to fifteen inches of snow on the ground, the path was hidden, and we waded through snow that came almost up to our knees. When we arrived, we sat on the floor by the old stove and remained there, feeding it firewood for the rest of the evening. In that way we stayed warm on the one side of our bodies closest to the oven, while the other side was freezing.

After two hours, we heard a buzzing sound coming from the ceiling. A half-dead fly fell down, and then another. When I looked up, I could just make out a large, dark patch in the ceiling. All the flies in the village for the year must have congregated in the farmhouse roof, landing there to hibernate. As the heat ascended now and the temperature rose under their wings, they woke up and showered down upon us, onto the wine and cheese on the table, onto the lit candles where they lay waving their legs.

There were half-dead flies everywhere, lying on their backs or sides, helpless. It was like when the frogs rained down from the heavens in the film *Magnolia*.

I should have taken it as a sign.

The first morning at the summer farm I wake up, my decision made.

"I need to take care of something down in civilization," I say. "A few errands. Don't ask. I might have to sort out some work stuff, too."

"Can we come?" the boys ask in unison.

"No, not today."

I trot down the hill beside the waterfall, make it down in less than half an hour, walk right past the farm, get into the car, and drive down toward the highway, toward the fjord.

I turn in the direction of the neighboring village and plot Kleivhøgda into the GPS.

CHAPTER 60

CLARA

1988

I tried to comfort Daddy, tried sitting on the floor by his feet, resting my arms and chin on his knees and looking up at him.

Then he would start sobbing, so I stopped doing it.

"Dear Lord. I can't bear it," he said.

"It will get better, Little Papa," I said, the way they do in Swedish films.

Then he would always just cry even more, so I stopped calling him Little Papa, too, even though that's what he was.

I made coffee, set the table for breakfast, and laid his clothes out for him; I reminded him to shower when he started smelling sour and sweaty; I cooked dinner, did the laundry; I mucked out the barn and the cowshed, picked up the mail, took the bills out of their envelopes and spread them across the table, pointed at them, and said, Now we have to go to the bank and pay them. I reminded him to call my aunt back and the child welfare services, who were *now* checking up on me, to be sure that I was fine.

I just did sensible things, trying to steer clear of everything else.

Above all I did my best not to think about Lars.

He was gone and would never come back.

I no longer had a mother.

I just had Daddy; I had to get him back on his feet, keep him from falling apart.

Eventually, glimpses of light began to appear. Slowly, but surely. But then Daddy came and started talking about this dream of his.

"I keep having the same recurring dream. I'm driving beside the fjord. You're in the passenger seat. And then I lose control of the car and it flies off the edge of the road and into the water, and I just sit there, unable to lift a finger, while the car just sinks and sinks . . . I don't understand what it means. Am I going to lose you, too?"

We were sitting in front of the woodstove in the red armchairs Daddy inherited from his grandparents.

"Now, Daddy, I'm not going to drown."

"But why am I dreaming about it, then, as if it were an omen?"

"Because you lost Lars. And because you're afraid of losing me, too."

"But what if it happens?"

"Then I'll rescue myself, I promise."

Daddy had lost all faith in himself after what happened to Lars. I tried to remind him of all his victories, like Lebanon. But that was difficult, too; it was a little bit like walking across a quagmire or very thin ice.

"You did a good job in Rachaya, Daddy."

"Well," he said, and cleared his throat. "That was completely different."

"How so?"

"In situations like that you have only two options, fight or flight. You can never allow yourself to be paralyzed."

"Do you think I could do something like that? Become a soldier?"

I stirred the embers in the stove with a log and then laid it in the fire.

"Yes, I think so, you're good at everything you do, you can be whatever you want," he said, and smiled at me, but I could see that he didn't believe in me.

When Daddy finally started going out to work in the cowshed and showering again, Lars was all I could think about.

I started riding my bike through the cemetery on the way home from school. I would sit down there, lean against the rough, oval gravestone we'd found for him in our river.

The gravestone had two birds engraved in it, and those birds were more expensive than we could afford, but we had to have them anyway.

Sometimes I sang to him, there by the gravestone. But mostly I just sat there and talked to him.

"Hi, Lars," I said. "I think about you all the time."

At first there was no answer, but after a while I was able to hear him. He said just one thing, over and over again. It was a sentence he would never have used or understood the meaning of while he was alive.

Still, I could hear him, and his message was loud and clear.

Avenge me.

CHAPTER 61

Henrik

"So, you're Clara's husband," says the woman who greets me, introducing herself as Bodil. She looks me up and down.

"Yes, Henrik Fougner," I say, and offer her my hand.

"Goodness . . . Yes, I must say we didn't think that Clara would ever marry. She was never the type to be interested in boys and that kind of thing. Not in girls either, for that matter," she adds, and giggles a little. "She was just, like, different."

"She still is," I say.

"Yes, I just met her. And then I've seen her on television several times recently. So, you want to see Agnes? This is not really by the book, but I've decided to let it go."

"Thanks, that's kind of you."

"Yes, Clara hasn't been a part of Agnes's life for several decades. And now that Agnes has begun to come around, I think it's only right she should have the chance to get to know her family. If Clara doesn't want to come, it's good that you do. You're welcome to bring the boys sometime, if you like."

"I appreciate that."

"I never heard from Clara about the flowers I sent."

Good Lord, how many thank-you calls does a person need?

"Well, as you said yourself, she's something else," I say. "Don't let it bother you."

"I won't," she says, although her tone of voice suggests the opposite. "Ready for your mother-in-law? You're lucky, she's having a good day today. Some days she's like another person, but she's getting better all the time."

I am led through the building and the garden and into a house, up a stairway, and through a doorway.

There I see a woman sitting in a chair, staring at me.

She looks like Clara, except one eye is brown and the other is blue, which makes it hard to look her in the eyes.

"Agnes, this is Henrik," Bodil says. "Clara's husband. He's come to visit you. That's fine, isn't it?"

A slight nod.

The woman is surprisingly pretty and girl-like. Can she really be in her midsixties? She looks as if she's been preserved in brine for the past thirty years. Long hair, almost no wrinkles on her face, a trim figure, and dressed in clothing that looks like it was taken straight from the costume department of a film about the 1970s, a long skirt with a floral pattern and a tunic.

"Well, I'll be off, then. Enjoy yourselves," Bodil says, and disappears.

"Agnes," I say. "Do you know who I am?"

"You're the one who's married to Clara."

"Clara came to see you not long ago?"

A nod, nothing more. She is still sizing me up, I notice.

"It had been a long time since you saw her last, hadn't it?"

"More than thirty years."

"Why so long?"

She shrugs.

"Don't know . . . They want to forget about me."

"They?" I say.

"Clara. Leif," she says, in a voice that sounds like she has just put something dirty into her mouth.

"If I'm going to be honest, I always thought you were dead, that you died in the car accident along with Lars and Magne."

"The car accident along with Lars and Magne?"

A faint snort escapes from her mouth. Then she slowly shakes her head.

"Oh no, I'm alive, as you can see. In a way," she says, and looks at me scornfully. "I've been here for almost half my life now, without any contact with people. I see my only daughter on television, that's all. So . . . yes. But I am fed and have a roof over my head."

"And now you've started to remember more, haven't you? That's what Bodil said anyway . . ."

"Bodil, right. Stupid creature," Agnes says with contempt in her voice, and I have to smile.

This is without question Clara's mother. And now she seems extremely sharp.

"What do you want from me, anyway?"

"Um, I wanted to meet my mother-in-law, whom I've never met."

"OK," she says skeptically. "Now you have."

"Maybe you'd like to meet your grandchildren sometime?" I say, and know I'm on thin ice. I don't know if Clara will allow it. Or if I even want to bring the boys here to meet this woman. "And I would like to learn a little more . . ."

"More about what?" she asks, sulky again.

"First of all, about this accident. You didn't drown after all. What is it that happened?"

Again, she laughs the same brusque, mirthless laugh.

"Oh dear, you don't know a thing, now do you?" she says, and shakes her head. "Are you sure that you want to hear this?"

A part of me wants more than anything to say no, get to my feet, and leave. Never to return. But the other part of me needs to hear it. Now. Right away.

"Yes," I say. "I am."

"Well, they were inseparable those two, Clara and Leif, maybe they still are, for all I know . . . they were like that from the very beginning. From the time she was born, she was the only one who meant anything to him. And imagine how it was for me, stranded on such a deserted mountain ridge, he had no understanding of that. For Leif, the farm was the most beautiful place in the world, and I was supposed to thank my lucky stars for having been allowed to live there. If you ask him, he will probably tell you I was lazy. But he didn't know how it was to be inside my body."

"How was it, then?" I ask, after a moment of silence.

"Well, while I was pregnant it was as if I'd been poisoned. My arms, my legs, hands, feet—everything shriveled up, all my energy disappeared, like I was paralyzed. A mere trip to the bathroom took more energy than I had in me. The daylight drained me. Everything drained me. It was impossible to explain. If I tried to do something, it triggered these pains, like flashes of light everywhere in my body."

"I see," I say, even though I don't see at all.

What had happened to her?

Had she had chronic fatigue syndrome? One of the more crippling rheumatic disorders? Something else? Lyme disease? Or had it all been psychological? Postpartum depression?

"Now you're wondering whether I was ever diagnosed. I wasn't," Agnes says. "Truth be told, I don't remember what came first and last either. Just that everything was completely dark. As if I was already gone and nobody could see me. And Clara and Lars made me feel like nothing more than an empty shell. I didn't feel like a mother. It was as if they were another woman's children and just happened to be living in the same house as me. They made me angry. Leif made me angry. Everything about that damn farm made me angry."

"That must have been difficult," I say as benignly as I can manage, but I am shuddering.

"But in fact, the story starts a few years later," she says. "Are you sure you can bear to hear this? Some really horrible things happened back then . . ."

The nasty little smile of hers disturbs me.

"Go ahead," I say, even though I suspect I am going to regret it.

CHAPTER 62

CLARA

1988

My mother had many bad qualities. She was a cowardly, irresponsible, stupid cow. Sometimes she hit us. And it turned out that she was home at the time of the accident, she'd just stepped outside for a bit to hang the laundry out to dry, she claimed.

But she was his mother. She couldn't have pushed Lars down the stairs.

Besides, Lars changed completely almost immediately after they moved in with Magne. The happy, easygoing boy I knew was gone. Instead, I met a jumpy, quiet guy who had strange fits of rage, who kicked at the cat and no longer wanted to play.

All these things were typical signs, according to what I read later.

I knew that Magne had the day off on Wednesdays, because of the farm, which he leased out, of course, and because of all his commitments. And now Mommy was in the hospital for a few days for a minor procedure. She had called specifically to tell me, as if I cared. She wanted me to come and visit her. Out of the question, I said, and hung up. I hadn't seen her since we were at the hospital with Lars, and I didn't plan on going to see her now either.

But I made a note of the dates.

And now I was ready.

I walked up the long road leading to Magne's farm. Along the way I took a break, lying down on the grass between some birch trees, taking deep breaths.

When I reached the farm and the house, I stood before the front door, put my finger against the doorbell, and pressed it.

"School was let out earlier than usual, because the home economics teacher got sick," I said when he opened the door. "There weren't any classes afterward, so they let us go home."

"Is that right?" Magne said, and looked at me expectantly.

"So, I thought I'd come here," I said.

I knew that he usually sat home drinking on Wednesdays. Lars had told me. On Wednesdays, Lars was even more frightened than usual. He would stay in his bedroom and try to be as quiet as possible.

I could see that Magne had been drinking. His eyes were bleary and dull. That was good. Everything was going according to plan.

It was Dad's nightmare about my drowning while trapped in a sinking car that had given me the idea. I went to the library, read first aid books and driver's education books, took notes, drew copies of the illustrations.

The most important lesson was that when a car ends up underwater, people wait too long before responding. That's why they drown. You have to be quick. Just spring into action. Immediately. Almost nobody dies from hitting the water. They die from drowning, while they're stuck inside the car.

The night before I had also gone on a bike ride all the way to Magne's farm. As usual, the keys were hanging in the key cabinet in the hallway, the door was unlocked, and Magne was sound asleep.

"Oh yes," he said, furrowing his brow. "But Agnes isn't here. She's in the hospital."

"Yes, I know, I would like to go see her. Could you drive me there? Please?"

"Well, now's not really such a good time," he said, hesitating. I knew he would rather not admit he'd been drinking on a weekday.

"I wanted to talk with you about Dad, too," I said. "He's not feeling well these days . . . I'm a little worried."

And there, there I saw it flash in his eyes, a glimpse of the predator. Now I had him.

"OK. Just need to get my wallet," he said, and went inside.

From the door I could see that he went to the corner cupboard in the living room.

That was where he kept his liquor. I could hear the clinking sound made by somebody trying not to clink. Now all he had to do was manage to keep the car on the road.

The car was a relatively new, gleaming, and well-polished Opel; it was a strange yellow color. Inside it smelled clean, so the stink of alcohol from Magne was even more conspicuous amid all the sterile, chemical smells.

Magne couldn't stand messiness; Lars wasn't allowed to have his toys anywhere except in his room and eventually not there either. In the end Magne had thrown out all of Lars's toys, the LEGOs and the cars he was so fond of.

We drove down the narrow gravel road from the farm. Magne stared stiffly in front of him. He had to be even drunker than I thought. When he reached the main road, he turned on the blinker and made a right-hand turn. It was a twelve-mile drive to the hospital. The first six miles along the fjord were full of turns, narrow and treacherous. All along this stretch of road we risked meeting another car. Even now, early in the summer, German and Dutch cars could be seen all over the place, several of them pulling camper trailers. They often got stuck on the narrowest stretches and had to back up, unable to drive through, causing the people who live here to tear their hair out.

It was one of those sparkling, shimmering summer days with a bright-blue sky. The mountainside along the road was a peacock green, the way it was every year in the early summer. The fjord gleamed and sparkled under the warm, golden sun, but I knew the water had to be as cold as ice out there.

There was still snow cover on the mountaintops, and the streams meandered like fat, white worms down the mountainsides.

Meltwater. That was why the fjord was still an almost emerald green.

My heart started beating faster.

But I couldn't start doubting myself now. I had to go through with it.

We drove into a narrow, one-way section of the road and had to wait for an oncoming car. Magne backed up, cursing. Then it was our turn. We lurched through the narrow passage where there was barely four inches of clearance on either side. At least he drove slowly here.

Then we reached the only section with a broad stretch of road. Magne floored it.

Nine miles to the medium-sized city with a hospital where Mom was.

A mile to the place I had in mind.

Now we were getting closer.

Magne was driving too fast. That was good; that made it all easier.

On the way into the turn, the shoulder of the road was right beside my door. It was a sharp turn where there was neither a guardrail nor trees on the side of the road, just a vertical drop straight into the fjord. People who wanted to get rid of their cars to make an insurance claim often sent them over the bluff here late at night. The Public Roads Administration should install some kind of safety barrier along the turn before there was a serious accident, people said.

The bluff was on my side of the car.

I'd imagined it over and over, thought it through again and again. I knew I would get only one chance.

I took hold of the steering wheel with the hand closest to Magne and pulled the wheel toward me. Hard and fast.

We hurtled over the edge.

I held on tight to my door, bracing my feet against the floor in front of me, pinching my mouth shut. I wasn't going to howl and scream, that's for sure.

Again and again I had imagined how we would hit the water.

But what I hadn't anticipated was the enormous bang, the hollow jolt, the force of the collision of the flying vehicle against the water. The thunderous crash when we hit the water.

My head was thrown first backward and then forward, and then we started sinking into the fjord. Magne roared something or other, something with *fuck*, while I clung tightly to the door.

I had read all about this, I knew the water would quickly find many holes to seep through and the car would immediately begin to sink.

In such cases, almost everyone reacted by panicking and forgot to act rationally and sensibly. My big advantage was that I knew what would happen and had prepared myself for it. I had drilled it into my head that I had to stay calm, act quickly, and roll down the window while unfastening my seat belt.

Pretty soon, it would no longer be possible to open the window. Then you must try and smash the window with something in order to get out.

At any rate, it would be impossible to open the door due to the pressure from the water surrounding the car.

In the US, four hundred people die annually in sinking cars while waiting for some kind of miracle to take place, and the critical thirty to sixty seconds come and go.

People are really pretty stupid.

I rolled down the window with my right hand while undoing my seat belt with the left.

And exactly as I had read, the water gushed into the car much faster than you could imagine.

Blub, blub, blub, the water said. Panic started rising in me.

The car was about to sink to the bottom of a deep fjord with me inside it.

I glanced quickly over at Magne. He appeared to be completely paralyzed.

"Open your door, Magne," I said, before I kicked away from my seat and out the window.

Magne yanked desperately at his door, but opening it was impossible. If he decided to try to roll down the window, he would discover that it couldn't be opened.

I started swimming in toward shore.

When I turned to look, only the back end of the trunk of the yellow car was sticking up. And below me the bottom was nowhere in sight. There was only darkness.

It wasn't a beach that I came to, but there were stones you could climb over to get onto dry land. I had checked that when I rode my bike here yesterday.

I crawled up, sat down, leaned back against a rock, and looked out across the water.

He didn't come.

I had followed the plan and I had managed it.

Soon, I would have to start the next step, climb up the slope, get a car to stop, be panicky, crying, all of that, be driven to the medium-sized city, talk to the police. Leave out a thing or two, but otherwise explain it in a way that they would believe.

But first I would sit here a little bit, look out across the fjord, and catch my breath.

CHAPTER 63

LEIF

1988

When we drove slowly past the place where Magne and Clara had driven off the cliff earlier that day, where it was unusually and abruptly steep, where avalanches often slid over the road and down into the fjord in the winter, where there was no guardrail, I could see that Clara's eyes acquired a strange glassiness, like when she was a little girl and had a fever.

At that moment the policewoman who was driving glanced at us in the rearview mirror. She smiled tentatively, compassionately. Clara noticed her gaze, and I saw her make sad little-girl eyes.

I put my arm around her and rested my head against hers.

Just the two of us now. Just Clara and me, from now on.

But not long after we'd come home, there was a pounding on the door.

The sky had clouded over as I was on my way to the hospital, and on our way home, it started to rain.

Standing outside, with her hair plastered against her skull and her clothes soaking wet and clinging to her body, was Agnes. Her teeth were chattering, and she was shaking. I let her into the hallway, even though more than anything I wanted to slam the door in her face.

"You can't be here," I said, and stood with my back against the living room door. "Clara is resting."

"Something about that girl is not right," Agnes said, shaking her head. "Where is she? I have to talk to her."

"Oh no you don't," I said, and could hear the scornful sting in my voice. All the hate I had felt for Agnes during the past years, especially after Lars died, could now be released, like the waterfall behind the farm during the spring thaw.

"You are not to speak *with* Clara or *about* Clara. You are going to leave now and never come back. Do you hear? I will never forgive you for allowing Magne to come near my children."

My voice rose almost to a roar as I uttered the last sentence. She looked at me, her eyes wide, her face bluish white.

"It's not what you think, Leif," she said wearily. "Nothing is the way you think it is."

"Oh no? How is it, then? What? I have just one thing to say: stay away from my daughter."

"She's my daughter too . . ."

"Yes, but it sure as hell doesn't seem like it. The only time you had sole responsibility for the children was when I was in Lebanon. And when I came home, they were barely alive. You'd probably stayed in bed the whole time, furious and feeling sorry for yourself. And when you took Lars away, against my will, you managed to get him killed. How dare you show your face here? How dare you!"

I had moved closer, raising my forefinger ominously as I shouted into her face.

Agnes stood there, skinny and dripping wet. But now I was as tough as nails. Clara had given me courage.

"Leif, Clara isn't normal, she's dangerous . . . ," she began.

I spoke my response softly, but with extreme clarity.

"I'm going to say this one more time: I know what happened to Lars. Clara knows what happened to Lars. You know what happened to

Lars. And it's your damn fault that it happened. So stop these grotesque fairy tales of yours right now. Do you understand? Now I'm going to call the police and have them come and get you," I said.

"That won't be necessary," she sniffed. "I'll leave."

"Do that, right now," I said, ready to push her out the door.

"She won't bother us again," I said when she'd gone, and Clara came out from behind the stairs.

And that was in fact the last time we saw Agnes.

Three days later we received word that she had tried to commit suicide and had been admitted to a psychiatric hospital. The doctors claimed she was suffering from post-traumatic stress disorder or a personality disorder or something like that and wanted to see me.

I said that Agnes and I were not on speaking terms. That I didn't want to have anything to do with her or them. That they could do what they wanted. That as far as Clara and I were concerned, she was dead.

They called several times. I said the same thing.

They stopped calling.

I didn't visit her.

Clara didn't visit her.

A new kind of calm came over us now. I slept better at night. Clara went to school, came home, did her homework. Sometimes she went home with classmates, and occasionally some of them came home with her, but I never had the impression that this was important to her.

She went running up in the mountains. Sometimes she read aloud to me. Sometimes I read aloud to her. She accompanied me when I mucked out the cowshed, or when I went into the hills, into the forest. She was smart and hardworking, no male heir could have pleased me more.

Maybe I should have spoken to her about what had happened, but I couldn't bring myself to do it.

I milked the cows and took care of them, I mowed and plowed and sowed, made dinner and cleaned up, did the laundry, quizzed Clara on her English and German vocabulary words.

Sometimes I was awakened by my own screams, but it happened less frequently than before. And I stopped drinking.

Now and then we would drive to the cemetery together, often at times when nobody else would be there. In the fall we brought heather for his grave. In the winter, spruce branches and candles. In the summer, begonias and geraniums and lobelias.

When the weather was dry and sunny and we were alone, we would sit on either side of the grave, each of us with one arm over the stone as if we were embracing him.

CHAPTER 64

HENRIK

Clara has been busy clearing brush. She takes a short break, I see, and walks down to the little pebble beach where she likes to sit and meditate. She goes down there to sit all the time now.

Gone is the elegant, manicured state secretary with curls in her blonde hair, expensive suits, and high heels.

In her place is a farmer, a soldier, strong and resilient.

Clara the chameleon.

What an idiot I am. I don't know the first thing about the woman I married and had children with, and clearly never have.

What should I do? Should I try talking to her? Pretend nothing has changed? Try to forget the whole thing?

"How can you be so sure?" I'd asked Agnes. "How can you know for certain that's what happened?"

"Because Magne was a very good driver. Even when he'd been drinking—then he would be especially careful," she'd answered. "It's inconceivable that he would have driven the car off the cliff and into the fjord. He'd worked in the North Sea and was trained to handle such situations, so he would never have just sat still in the car underwater. He would have survived."

I nodded.

"And you know what? I just went around waiting for something terrible to happen. I could see it in Clara's eyes. That child was never normal. And after what happened to Lars, she was obsessed. After the accident, I would go to the farm, try talking to them. Leif wouldn't let me in the door. I understood I wouldn't be allowed to see Clara anymore. To be honest, I'm not sure it made any difference to me."

Agnes claimed that Clara has a dissociative identity disorder. It was presumably a diagnosis she'd come up with herself, or transferred from herself to her daughter, because Clara had never been diagnosed by anyone in the medical profession.

Once I found myself wondering who I would prefer to be, the victim or the murderer, I'd made the argument that we all have the capacity for both inside of us. And here's the proof.

I'm sitting on the back steps of the summer farmhouse and staring blankly into the thicket of ferns covering the slope at the rear of the farm. The ferns are tall, they come up to my chest, to the heads of the boys. I sit there until Andreas comes running because he's gouged himself on an ax or a saw. He's bleeding from a cut on his right index finger. It's difficult to get the details out of him. He's like Clara when he's in pain: completely mute.

"This is like when Daddy cut his finger at breakfast. I was fine afterward, remember?"

He nods.

"Can you try to bend your finger?"

He bends his finger.

"Great. You haven't cut the tendon. That's good. Now I'm going to get the first aid kit and we'll fix you right up. OK?"

He nods.

But the first aid kit isn't in my bag, and then I remember I took it out before we left. Damn it all.

We must have some Band-Aids here at the very least. Or gauze.

First, I look in my shaving kit. Nothing there.

Then I go to look in Clara's toiletry bag. Toothbrush, toothpaste, deodorant, shampoo, a range of skin-care products. No bandages. No gauze. I am just about to close her bag when I see it.

A scalpel. A scalpel with the Ullevål Hospital logo on it.

The kind of scalpel we have in our office.

The kind of scalpel we have lying around at home. In that sense, there's nothing remarkable about finding a scalpel from Ullevål Hospital in Clara's toiletry bag.

Not in and of itself.

But something compels me to take it out.

Last fall, Sabiya had stumbled in the forest and hit her head, which left a small gash in her temple. She hadn't thought it necessary to do anything about it, but I'd protested and in the end, I gave her stitches. A week later I'd taken the three stitches out, using a scalpel.

Afterward the scalpel was left lying in the nook in the corner between our desks, like a strange romantic keepsake.

Until the night of the murder, when suddenly it was gone.

The scalpel in the office had a clearly visible chip on the back of the handle, where there's no logo. Sabiya and I had joked about it. She claimed she'd chipped it so I couldn't steal it.

Now I take the scalpel out of Clara's bag, holding it up as if it were a dead rat. And there's no doubt.

There is a chip plain as day on the handle of this scalpel.

Clara must have been in my office. Recently. Without me.

And taken Sabiya's scalpel.

And then the pieces begin to fall into place. Click, click, click.

Clara was home the night Faisal Ahmad came in. The boys were fast asleep. It would have been completely possible for her to leave them alone for an hour or so.

I had told her about the abuse.

I gave her the description of Mukhtar Ahmad.

I told her he was headed for the prayer room.

I told her about the pistol in the drawer in my office.
I left the extra key card lying around at home.
I chose the same stupid code I use for everything.
I deposited both motive and opportunity straight into her lap.
And Clara had carried through.
But she made one mistake: she took Sabiya's scalpel.

CHAPTER 65

CLARA

I sit on the tiny beach, thinking.

After the day I avenged Lars's death, it was as if I could see everything more sharply and clearly than before. I felt different from everyone else, exalted. And everything shone in a different way.

I understood that from now on, nothing would ever be the same.

Nothing ever was.

But as the years passed, the sun inside me also burned less brightly. The joy I had felt over having rid the world of a scumbag like Magne began to fade.

It had been such a long time ago.

Since then, many others just like him had moved into circulation. Maybe by now Magne would have died of natural causes anyway. All of this diminished my achievement.

The compulsion to feel once again that I had done something concrete, something that really helped, that saved someone, grew stronger and stronger with every passing day.

But for thirty years, from Magne to Mukhtar, I sat calmly observing everything that happened, memorizing legislation and writing white papers for presentation in Parliament.

For thirty years I didn't really do anything, the way Daddy and I had done nothing.

For thirty years I did not allow myself to think about Lars, refrained from thinking about how old he would have been, how he might have looked, what his interests might have been, what he would have talked about. But when Andreas and Nikolai began to approach the age he'd been at the time of his death, it was all stirred up again.

I observed their gestures and their shenanigans, listened to all their questions about numbers and the alphabet, heard the strange things they said and realized they were exactly the things Lars might have said. I noticed the sway in their backs and their skinny legs and hands that still had something baby-like about them.

The hands are often the last part of the body to mature from being a baby's to those of a child.

And then suddenly, my boys were older than he'd been. They started outgrowing him, reminding me of everything he'd never become.

Maybe Lars would have lived at the farm with a sweet, little wife and a new tractor and three snotty-nosed children. They could have moved into the old house and built a retirement cottage for Daddy, kept goats or a pig or three, along with the sheep. Chickens, a dog. A yard full of life and activity, brightly colored toy tractors, a trampoline, a jungle gym. A new era, a new generation on the farm.

Most likely it wouldn't have turned out like this. Maybe Lars would have lived in the city and had a job in the oil industry and been too rich in the way of money and too poor in the way of values, with thinning hair and a bulge around his midriff, coming home to sleep in his old bedroom a couple of times a year and otherwise vacationing in Dubai or Bangkok or God knows where when he had time off from work.

Maybe he would have been gay, happy with some partner named Erling or Raymond, Marius, Bjørn-Fredrik, or Hans-Petter. Or spent his evenings unhappily surfing gay dating sites, searching for someone or something.

Maybe he wouldn't have been Lars any longer, maybe he would have become Line or Lena or Lone, someone who didn't dare to return to his hometown, and if she did, would have to stay on the farm the whole time. Or, the opposite, tall and proud, parading down the roadside wearing lots of makeup, her hair long, the person everyone talked about in the pub.

Maybe he would have sat watching soccer matches at a sports bar in the evenings and on the weekends, consuming plates of french fries covered with melted cheese and red, peppery spices and playing a game of pool from time to time.

But no matter what or who he would have been, it wouldn't have mattered. Because he would have been my brother. And such a huge vacuum wouldn't have been left behind in his wake.

More and more often I can feel the wind blowing through my body, or I can hear his voice.

I am closest to him here on the beach, where once upon a time I blew the life back into him. Blew and pressed, blew and pressed. That's why it's so important that the beach and the meadow around the summer farm remain the same, that nothing here changes.

Only in that way can he still be alive.

I remember the feeling of his chest beneath my hands, that I was afraid of pressing down too hard, of breaking something, but still I kept going, again and again.

I remember I blew my breath into his mouth, again and again and again.

I remember his eyes when he opened them, how his body jerked when he finally coughed, the water that spurted up in my face.

I remember he gazed around him in confusion.

I remember I didn't care that our useless mother came running, as usual too late to be of any help.

I laughed, feeling invincible. I thought that now nothing bad could touch us.

"You understand I have to do it, don't you?" I say to Lars. He's sitting beside me. "That I have no choice? Almost like back then?"

Earlier in the day, Bodil from Kleivhøgda had called to tell me that she'd allowed Henrik to visit Agnes without asking me first.

Afterward, because of his behavior, she realized I didn't know about it, and felt guilty, so she called me to confess her sins.

"That's fine. Really. Don't give it another thought," I said.

That was where he had gone, then. I'd found it strange he'd been gone for such a long time. He'd been sitting at a café doing some work, he'd said, but that wasn't like him. And when he came back, he was different.

"I don't know," Lars says finally. "I don't always understand you, Clara. Sorry."

"You just did it again. Don't apologize," I say, and smile. "I never do."

"Goodbye, Clara," he says. Then he's gone. I get to my feet and walk up to join the others.

CHAPTER 66

HENRIK

"Listen," Clara says. "I promised Dad some time with the boys, without us. Would you mind taking them down to him and then coming back up? Then we can have a night or two without them, maybe go walking in the mountains?"

"Sure," I say.

Leif usually has the boys for one night during our vacation, and we go hiking without them.

On the other side of the pond, there is a wild, magical mountain landscape where almost nobody walks, not even the sheep, but where the scenery is more beautiful than anywhere else.

If you make it up to the top of Trollskavlen Peak, there is a view of purple mountains on the horizon as far as the eye can see.

I must play along, not give her any reason to suspect I've been to see Agnes.

Clara is the Ministry of Justice's biggest star. A person who emanates confidence and seriousness. And the smartest person I know.

She's not one to leave behind any evidence.

I have lied to the police myself, been a suspect, even been incarcerated.

I can't just show up with a scalpel I've found in Clara's toiletry bag and start going on about some random chip in the handle. We have numerous such scalpels at home. Nobody would believe me, and I won't manage to stop her. It's more likely that I will basically be digging my own grave and end up behind bars again. Or put my own life at risk.

She also has an alibi: she was home with the children. Maybe it's not airtight, but good enough. Who leaves their children alone at home to go out and commit murder?

The last time Leif had been there. Of course he will vouch for her if need be. He probably knows all about it, would never turn in his daughter anyway. The loyalty between them seems boundless.

Besides, it is the legacy of sin I've seen running through all the cases I've studied. Abused children often become bad parents themselves.

Clara wasn't an abused child. But she was a neglected child, neglected by her useless mother, by her father who went to Lebanon, neglected during the time she lived alone with him after he came home.

And she has questionable genetic material in her veins.

By all appearances, everything had gone well.

Clara was an underprivileged girl who'd had a difficult homelife and triumphed against all odds.

I'd always viewed her as a wholly adequate mother, although she was absentminded and distant. But what will it do to the boys to grow up with her? What could she decide to use them for? What will she teach them to be?

"Yay! Hooray!" is the boys' response when I ask them if they want to go spend some time with Grandfather. There they'll be allowed to watch as much television as they want and stay up late, and he'll give them all the ice cream they can eat.

They run ahead of me down the path, hopping and dancing. They know they must be careful, where they must stop.

Before we arrived, there had been a massive rainstorm that lasted for several days. The waterfall is thundering ominously, but after a while I don't notice it any longer.

"How are you doing up there?" Leif asks when we're seated at the stone table having a cup of coffee before I head up to the summer farm again. He has even put out some sweet custard buns that he must have bought at the grocery store earlier that day and cut them into four pieces, the way Clara usually does. She doesn't like sweet custard buns but buys them all the time for the boys and her father.

"Just fine," I say, and place my hand on the stone table. "Clara is at war with the birch forest."

"Good," Leif says. "See, the mist reaches all the way out onto the fjord, Henrik. Or the sea fog, as they say on the weather report."

"Too bad," I say. Because as I've learned from Leif, we don't want mist or sea fog, it just ruins things. "Let's hope it stays away from Trollskavlen Peak tomorrow, then."

Twice, once a couple of years ago and once before the boys were born, Clara and I had been unexpectedly caught in the mist on the way up Trollskavlen Peak and had to turn around, navigating our way down using a compass and unable to see more than a few feet in front of us.

"OK, goodbye now, boys," I say twenty minutes later, as I hug first Nikolai and then Andreas. "Be good for Grandpa now."

"Don't go, Daddy," Andreas says, and looks at me gravely. He hasn't been fully himself since the arrest.

"Now, Andreas," I say, embarrassed because Leif is standing there listening. I don't want him to think they don't want to be alone with him.

"Don't go," Andreas says again and looks terrified, but I ruffle his hair.

"Enjoy yourselves," Leif says, and slaps me on the shoulder, man-to-man.

CHAPTER 67

LEIF

"Come on, boys," I say. "Let's go inside and see if there are any cherries. Then we can see if there's ice cream in the freezer."

They hop and dance away in front of me, while Henrik walks up toward the waterfall.

Tomorrow he and Clara are going to hike up Trollskavlen Peak.

Lately I've seen my daughter on television. On both the six o'clock and seven o'clock news. She is elegantly dressed. Earrings and impeccably groomed hair smoothed away from her face. Beautiful, in fact. That's what they say, the guys in the café downtown, if I walk by. That they've seen my Clara on television and isn't she a pretty one, my daughter. I can see it, too. The bright-blue eyes. The confidence-inspiring gaze. Cool and clear, like water tapped from the lake on the summer farm.

She has this kind of calm, Clara. This face that reveals nothing. A soft, slightly hoarse voice.

But there's been something else there lately. Something that has caused me to lean forward in my chair with the remote in my hand. Of course, I press the red record button. I do that every time she appears on the screen.

She really *is* beautiful. Elegant.

But there's a feverish flush on her cheeks that cannot come from any rouge and makes me shudder.

I've seen it before, the glassiness in her eyes, the unnaturally red cheeks.

Clara has become a good foot soldier with all the qualities I must have had once upon a time.

But she also has a courage and brutality that I've never been anywhere close to possessing.

CHAPTER 68

HENRIK

Clara is different tonight.

She serves a casserole she made at home and warmed up here. She also brings out an expensive wine. After dinner we light a fire on the big rock between the farmhouse and the water, the way we sometimes do, usually to roast hot dogs. We lie on our backs, she with her joint, each of us balancing a glass of wine on our chest, as we stare up at the clouds racing past in the sky above us.

Oddly enough I feel close to her, maybe since I finally know who she really is, maybe because this will probably be the last time we'll be alone.

She sits up, picks up a log, stirs the embers, and looks toward the edge of the rock that ends with the waterfall, where the sun has just set.

"The mosquitoes are eating me alive," she says. "Shall we go inside?"

Inside we drink the rest of the red wine, play three rounds of crazy eights. Clara wins two, I win one.

And then we have sex for the first time in ages.

It's completely incomprehensible that she takes the initiative. Here. Now.

But it's better than I remember it being. It is in fact very good, intimate and intense. Maybe it's been so long since the last time that it feels like the first time. Maybe it's because I know I'm having sex with a crazy lady. Or maybe it's just because I'm feeling blue.

Through the tiny window I can see the mountains on the other side of the valley. They look grayish black in the evening light. But just above the mountains the sky has a bright golden hue and farther up darkens into midnight blue.

"It's all overgrown up here for sure, even worse than on the farm," Clara says as we walk up the mountain the next day. There are small, gnarled birches and dry juniper trees everywhere. As the saplings thin out, they are replaced by thistles and tall grass.

"Nobody walks here anymore," I say.

I pull myself up the slope by grasping a stunted little birch tree. Here the path forms a kind of stairway running along the outside of a rock. The birch saplings and the small juniper bushes growing on the inside of the path have made the steps narrower, so it's barely possible to put one foot in front of the other.

To the left the mountainside is steep, with a 160-foot drop.

Nobody would survive such a fall.

And people do fall off the sides of mountains in Norway. It happens every summer, mostly foreign tourists, but also locals. A farmer from the village perished on the mountain on the other side of the valley last year. I have to concentrate to make sure I don't stumble or slip.

The problem is that *she* is walking behind me.

"Can't you take the lead?" she'd said when we started walking.

Clara always goes first when we're walking in the mountains, knows where the path goes, and likes to lead the way.

It doesn't add up.

I don't know if I have it in me, the way she clearly has it in *her*. But I know that I must, for my own sake and for the children's sake.

After two hours we reach the foot of Trollskavlen Peak, which is actually a gigantic, sloping scree, shaped like a dome.

It is at the base of this dome that we've been forced to turn back on several occasions because of the sea fog. But there's no mist now. The sky is an intense blue color, and there's not even the hint of a breeze. Today we will reach the top. And on the way up we will have to climb over big stones to reach the glacier you must cross first, and finally, the cairn at the very top.

There are ravines between the big stones, and in some places you can't even see where they end.

Only yesterday we talked about Trollskavlen Peak and the sea fog, and Leif reminded me how dangerous this climb is.

This is where it must happen. This is where I must push her.

"I have to pee, go ahead," I say, and try to get her to walk ahead of me.

She nods, walks past me, keeps going.

I turn to one side, press out a few drops, and wait a bit, fumbling with the fly of my pants. When I turn around, she is about twenty yards farther up the path. Ten yards in front of where she is standing, there's a huge ravine. It's perfect.

I hurry to catch up with her. Finally, I am just five yards behind her.

Three.

Two.

Still she hasn't turned around and looked at me.

The ravine beside us is black and bottomless. I feel my stomach plummet; I mustn't stumble and fall into it myself.

I've come so close that I can touch her, push her out into it.

I must remember that she's the one who got us into this situation.

It's either her or me. And I know that she knows it.

Again I count to three in my head.

When I have reached three, she turns around, puts her arms around my neck, and pulls me close, the way she used to do sometimes in the old days. It startles me, I almost stumble.

She is sweaty. But her skin is cool.

"Look there, Henrik," she says, and points toward the fjord, barely visible down below, far off in the distance. We can even see a tiny dot moving across it. The ferry. "Isn't it ludicrous, how beautiful it is?"

She says it in the happy, childish voice she only has up here. A place-specific naivete I've always liked.

"Yes," I say, cursing silently. "It's ludicrous how beautiful it is."

"The weather's supposed to be good tomorrow as well," she says as we fight our way down through the underbrush above the summer farm. "Maybe we can hike up to Witch Mountain before we go down to the farm again?"

Some annoying, tiny green insects land on my arms and T-shirt and in my ears and on my neck and everywhere. They don't sting but are damn irritating.

I look up at Witch Mountain. The front of it looks like the scarred, furrowed face of an old witch with a long pointy nose. The children love that she has a wart on her nose.

The hike up Witch Mountain is much shorter than up Trollskavlen Peak. We always walk out onto the nose. Of course, Clara loves to stand there looking down—she walks out to the far end of the outermost ledge at the top of every single mountain we climb. Andreas usually follows her. Nikolai, who is a little afraid of heights, refuses.

"Sure," I say. Why not?

A fall from Witch Mountain, that's somehow fitting.

Tomorrow I *must* succeed, not allow myself to be duped or tricked, consciously or unconsciously.

"But how about an early morning swim first?" Clara says.

A thought occurs to me.

OK, she knows this lake.

But I am a man, after all. And stronger than she is.

Then I won't have to push her off a cliff with my bare hands.

"Fine, an early morning swim," I say. "Why not?"

CHAPTER 69

CLARA

The river descends from the mountain into one end of the lake. The water is ice cold and green, regardless of the time of year or the air temperature.

At the other end of the lake, the water pools, becoming glassy and smooth, before vanishing over the edge in a huge, white inferno.

In between is a classic mountain lake. And on the hillside along the one long side of the lake is our summer farm.

The morning light is fresh and soft. The air, cool and clear. And Henrik and I are standing side by side on the beach like two competing swimmers, each in their respective lane preparing for battle. Earlier this morning I stayed in bed for a long time after I woke up, doing my breathing exercises while Henrik slept. Today I really must be on my game.

"Skeptical?" I ask.

"Very," he says, and is clearly freezing. His skin is covered with goose bumps, and he hugs his body with his arms.

Still, he looks like he's on the offensive, in a way.

It's him or me now. He sealed his fate when he went to speak with Agnes.

On the walk up the mountain I made sure to walk behind him, watching my back. It worked. I will be able to continue doing so.

He came here with me, didn't turn me in, hasn't even said anything to me. But things can't stay this way for long. He will either turn me in or kill me, and my money is on the latter.

This is the only way I can save myself, the only way I can continue with my project, fulfill my calling.

I walk over to him, stand on tiptoe, kiss him, and see a confused, fearful joy in his eyes about the kiss, a continuation of the intimacy we'd shared two nights ago.

Earlier, after we had both put our phones in the farmhouse and I had gone up to the house to put my watch there, I sent a text I'd written to Sabiya Rana from his telephone.

I buried our animal in the forest as agreed. But it may start to stink. Should perhaps be moved? Summer greetings from Western Norway.

They were the ones who started calling the Glock "the animal."

Now I raise my hand, stroke his cheek. "Ready?"

"As ready as I'll ever be."

It's shallow near the shore here. Henrik has never been farther out than up to his knees, at least not that I can remember, but he walks out with determination.

I wade out until the water reaches my midthighs. The reflection of the sun against the water, the pale sand on the bottom, and the tiny ripples moving across the water surface make everything look like glittering gold.

Then I start swimming.

The water against my body is freezing. But as always, after a few seconds, the cold against my skin grows warm. It burns, purifies.

"Come on," I say, and turn to face Henrik.

"I'm going a little farther to the right," he says. He wants me closer to the waterfall.

Because the current is stronger there.

"We should stay here, in the middle," I say. "It's safer."

Behind me I can hear Henrik gasp, probably in response to the cold water.

I swim quickly, keeping to the left, away from the waterfall.

When the time comes to move into the section where the currents are the strongest, there's an abrupt drop-off.

"Clara? You know what you're doing, right?" he says. "Are you sure it's not safer farther to the right?"

I turn around, he's right behind me. He has a strange expression on his face.

"Which one of us knows the lake best? Come on now," I say, and force myself to smile.

I am the better swimmer of the two of us, I know this lake, this is my home turf. Still, I don't feel safe.

He's a man. He's in good shape. And he's stronger than I am.

I haven't been this far out since I rescued Lars here. The water was warmer then; there was less meltwater, less of a current.

This spring the weather had been dry for just as long as in Eastern Norway, but during the past few weeks the rain has poured down here in the west. The rivers and lakes have risen at a record rate, and the water level is higher than ever before.

There's no guarantee that I will succeed.

Worst-case scenario, the boys will be orphaned.

We're approaching the middle. So far he's stayed to the right, while I have kept to the left. But now he starts swimming closer to me. Is he planning to pull me under? Drag me toward the falls?

It makes no difference, because I've managed to lead him to the spot where I want him. The middle of the lake, where it appears calm and harmless.

I turn around, notice the look of concentration on his face, how hard and closed it is.

It has to happen now. This is the moment.

I count to three while I take a deep breath, do a little somersault on the surface, and dive under.

Down, down, down, down.

Toward the bottom.

Then I am far below the surface. But even here I'm being pulled to the right. The current is stronger than I remember.

Shit. I'm not in control.

I have to swim even deeper. At last I can feel the bed of the lake beneath me, against my elbows, the tips of my toes. There's less of an undertow from the falls down here.

But I need air. I have to surface, my body feels completely stiff, unable to move.

Up now. For the boys. Upward, forward, breathe, breathe.

I'm up. And there's the shore. But where's Henrik?

I roll over onto my back, see that Henrik is still out there. He is farther out than he was when I went down. Hanging on for dear life.

"Clara," he shouts. "Clara! What are you doing? Come here!"

For a second or two I consider swimming out to him, trying to help him back to shore.

But I can't. Now it's impossible, in every way.

Still I have to pretend not to notice he is trapped in a kind of spiral without entrance or exit, a whirlpool that spins him slowly but surely toward the thundering, white inferno.

He grows smaller, drifting closer and closer to the place where everything pours over the edge.

People often got caught in the falls in the old days, if you believe the tales that people tell. Wood nymphs. Cattle. I don't know if any of it is true. Henrik will at any rate be the first person in modern times.

I hope they will find his body.

That would be nice for the boys, to have a grave to visit.

An image of him on our first trip here flashes through my mind, how amazed he was when he came here. This was different from the cottages he grew up with in Ustaoset and Kilsund.

And then an image of his face when he held the boys for the first time, cradling them in his arms. Tired, bloated, happy. His face when he plays with them, rolling around on the trampoline, tickling them, pretending he's going to eat them. They still think this is fun.

They never retrieved Magne's body. I told the police how I tried to save him, the way I will explain how I tried to save Henrik.

They will believe me. People always believe me. It's one of my strengths.

"Farewell," I whisper as I watch Henrik disappear into the falls.

When I've made my way back to where the water is only a foot and a half deep, I squat down, digging my fingers into the pale, almost desert-colored mountain sand around my feet. I lift my hands, let the sand run out, repeat the movement.

Dig my way into the sand, into him.

All around me the clear water glitters and gleams and ripples beneath the rays of sunlight teasing their way out from between big, dark-gray clouds.

And then, unusual for this time of day, the oppressive mugginess erupts in an intense clap of thunder in the distance, up behind Witch Mountain, toward Trollskavlen Peak.

A sudden rain shower begins pouring down.

The drops, almost like hail, hit the water surface around me, creating little circles.

They also hit my skin like the lashes of a tiny whip.

For the second time in my adult life, I start to cry, and now there's no stopping it.

PART 5

CHAPTER 70

SABIYA

Thank you, I write to my husband, in response to his offer to pick up the children and make dinner so I won't have to rush home.

As the message goes out, an intuition causes me to check my news feed, even though I usually never surf the internet at work.

The lead story makes my head spin.

Henrik is dead. He drowned in a tragic accident in the mountains.

The story contains a dramatic photograph of a white waterfall and a yellow emergency rescue helicopter, a blue sky and clouds in the background, in a photo montage that includes a picture of him, which I recognize from the hospital website.

The photograph is a few years old. He is wearing his white doctor's coat, his face is tan, his hair long. He looks confident and happy. And handsome.

Now I can smell his hair, feel his face between my hands.

"No," I whisper, tears filling my eyes. "It's not true."

I don't want to read anymore. But I do. Am unable to stop myself.

According to the article, his name has been released with the permission of his next of kin:

> Pediatrician Henrik Fougner (43 years of age) from Oslo had been in the mountains at the home of his wife, Clara Lofthus (43 years of age), state secretary at

the Ministry of Justice, in Western Norway when the tragic accident occurred.

The cause of death has not been confirmed, but sources claim there was a drowning accident in a cold mountain lake where the current is strong.

The man's wife was with him. She tried to rescue him without success. She sustained no physical injuries but is in shock.

Then there's a link to several news items about Clara, about her state secretary appointment, about initiatives she has fronted and an in-depth interview from a few weeks back. I'd read the interview, marveled over the amount of column space they dedicated to her, a mere state secretary. But she has a kind of aura, I could see that. Beautiful, elegant, smart. Cool and tough. And with an indefinable X factor. It was easy to understand why Henrik had fallen for her way back when.

I shudder as I scroll down through the article.

How can he be gone? Is it really true?

Will I never again see him turn around to share a laugh with me?

Never again will he flick small chunks of eraser or folded Post-its at me, console me when I'm upset about something, put his arms around me, pull me to him, kiss me on my neck, my forehead, all over.

"Hey, Sabiya," Roger says. He walks down the corridor in my direction, stops, and places his hands on my shoulders. These days he is the person I confide in the most.

"How are you?" he asks, and looks at me with concern.

I shake my head.

"Henrik," I say, but then I stop talking. I feel like I'm being strangled.

"What about Henrik, Sabiya?"

"He's dead."

"My God, what are you saying?"

I can't bring myself to meet his shocked gaze and look over his shoulder instead. Bente comes around the corner, cheerful and energetic, and pulls up short when she sees us.

"Sorry," I say. "I have to go. I just have to go."

And then I run.

CHAPTER 71

ROGER

She doesn't look back.

"What was that all about?" Bente says. "Did you offend her?"

"No, far from it . . ."

I am completely dumbfounded and unable to speak another word.

"What was it, then?" Bente asks impatiently.

"Well, she was just standing there staring at her phone, and she looked upset. And when I asked what was wrong, she said that Henrik is dead and that she had to run . . ."

"Henrik is *dead*?" Bente says. She loosens her ponytail, gathers her hair again, and tugs it back into the rubber band, something she does when she gets stressed. "That can't be right. Henrik's on vacation, he's in Western Norway."

Her cocksure tone irritates me.

"I don't know anything more than you do. A car accident, maybe? Horrible, anyway. Poor Sabiya . . ."

"What do you mean?" Bente asks, and wrinkles her brow. "It's just as bad for all of us, if it's true, isn't it? We all worked closely with him, we nurses too . . ."

"Good Lord, haven't you understood a thing?" I sigh. Women's intuition is really overrated.

Afterward I walk around performing my job duties on autopilot while pressure mounts behind my eyes. We hadn't been close, Henrik and I, but this is shocking.

Here I was looking forward to this evening, to seeing my new boyfriend again. Lovely, trusting, handsome Mohammed, who appeared out of nowhere and has brightened my days in a way I thought I would never experience. A man who loves going to fine restaurants and sharing a meal and a good bottle of white wine with me but is also just as happy lounging in front of the television in sweatpants and watching an HBO series. The man with whom I can talk about everything.

Sabiya's the only one who knows about him. The two of us have developed such a good connection this summer. She is happy for me. But she, more than anyone, understands how complicated this is, that we must proceed with caution.

I'm still looking forward to seeing him. But a shadow has been cast over all of it.

Henrik. Dead.

Now I regret telling the police that I'd seen him and Sabiya. But I just told the truth.

I couldn't bring myself to tell them that I thought I'd smelled the special perfume Henrik's wife wears, the state secretary lady, in the stairway leading down to the swimming pool at Lysebu.

The scent caught my attention on the one occasion when she stopped by the unit. I remember odors. And I haven't noticed anyone else who wears that perfume.

But I could tell the police were starting to tire of me, they weren't all that interested in listening to me any longer and who can blame them.

I decided I must have imagined it. I've always had an overly active imagination.

CHAPTER 72

SABIYA

Thoughts are racing through my head on my way home.

During the past year there had been moments when I felt I loved Henrik, even though that's a word I've never understood.

But then the murders happened, and he behaved oddly, as if he suspected *me* in a way, or was trying to throw suspicion on me.

Either way, it drove a wedge between us.

I never really managed to take an interest in his list of abusive parents either. Obviously, his notes wouldn't have any practical consequences; it was all just talk and maybe a bit of attention seeking.

And then the murders started happening. People from the list. The murders were still unsolved. The police were stumbling around in the dark.

The day after Ahmad's murder I checked to see whether the Glock was still in my drawer.

It wasn't. And I hadn't moved it.

I had slammed the drawer shut, as if I'd burned myself. Tried to forget all about it. It was impossible. And after the second murder, I'd told the police about the Glock, told them that Henrik and I were the only ones who knew about it.

I felt I had to say it, afraid that keeping my mouth shut would get me into even more trouble. I have a past, after all, and I'm Pakistani.

It seemed unlikely that Henrik, of all people, would murder these individuals. But he *had* been behaving strangely. Like when he came rushing toward me in the corridor at Lysebu—it seemed like he wanted to knock me down, his eyes aflame with anger.

They'd arrested him. I never believed it was him, not really, and soon they released him. But then the innocence between us was gone. It all shriveled up and died. It was a relief to let the affair wind down, an excuse to straighten out my life.

The last few times Henrik tried to contact me I hadn't replied. And lately he'd been silent. But yesterday morning, out of the blue, he sent me a text, even though that was something we'd agreed not to do. I'd panicked, sat down on the couch at home, and deleted the message immediately, without even reading it. Now I regret it. He must have sent it right before he died.

Oh God. That I'm thinking about all this right now.

I walk slowly downhill. It's a nice, warm day, the air is already shimmering with the heat of midsummer, but the shock is still in my body.

I walk home from the subway station, and when I reach our door and look up, I see them. A police car is parked right in front of the mailboxes. And their faces, far too familiar.

"Sabiya," says the female officer whose name I can never remember. "We have to ask you to come with us."

In the interrogation room at the police station, they tell me about the message I received yesterday, which they claimed was an encrypted message, about how Henrik had buried my pistol at our special place in the forest.

The Glock, which they dug up, was used for all three murders. It is a key piece of evidence.

There are testimonies from witnesses who observed me in the vicinity for the murders of both Mukhtar Ahmad and Melika Omid Carter.

Beyond this, there is DNA evidence linking me to the victims. My fingerprints are all over the pistol.

Nothing strange about that.

What I really don't understand is that strands of my hair with hair follicles containing my DNA were found on the last victim, Susanne Stenersen. I've never been anywhere near her.

How is that possible? Who has done this to me? I can't breathe, there's a weight on my aching chest, as if I'm having a heart attack. But I know it's psychological, that it's a panic attack having its way with me and I just have to let it run its course, until at some point it will finally subside.

CHAPTER 73

CLARA

I'm sitting at home under a blanket on our cozy, mustard-colored couch. There is a vase of orchids behind me. My legs are crossed, and I am dressed for the office in a dark-blue silk blouse and black trousers. A coffee cup bearing the words *World's Best Mom* rests on my knee. I'm wearing a little powder and mascara, but no lipstick, no blush. My hair is nicely done in stylish waves, the way Henrik liked it; he said with the curls I reminded him of Betty Draper in *Mad Men*. It could be that it made him feel like the unfaithful Don Draper, too.

My earrings are discreet, as are my wedding ring and my watch.

Project grief, calm, dignity.

Now I am a widow and will never remarry, but I don't say that. I will never be in another relationship, but I don't say that either.

I say that Henrik was the love of my life, the person I thought I would grow old with. That I'm pleased with the dialogue I've had with the police after the accident, how they've shown such concern for my well-being. That I don't believe I will ever recover from this, but I must give it time, concentrate on taking care of the children.

All the children, I say with a little smile, building a bridge that will allow me to smoothly transition to saying something about my work, about the issue that is my passion.

I agreed to do the interview strictly on the condition that I would have the opportunity to say something about this issue and that they must quote me. They accepted without batting an eye. My market value has increased further, I've understood. So the interview isn't just going to be about the tragic accident and my recent widow status, but also about my passionate commitment to helping all the children suffering in Norway.

"And there are many," I say. "An enormous number of unreported cases."

"Was your husband also passionate about this issue?" Erik Heier asks. He has been given this exclusive interview with me. He has the same irritating television-face, the same facial twitches and expressions he had when I met him at the Royal Palace dinner.

"Henrik shared my concerns, yes," I say, and change my position. "He saw many awful things through his job. It affected him."

"Wasn't it true that at one point Henrik was a suspect in the so-called child abuser case?"

"Where did you hear that?" I ask, and grip the cup more tightly.

"Reliable sources," Heier says.

"Let's take a break," I say. Heier nods at the cameraman. One of my conditions was that the interview be taped. And that I would have the final say on the footage, be free to edit it as I saw fit.

"Yes," I say when the cameraman has turned off the camera. "But the suspicion was proved groundless. The police have apologized. The correct person has been arrested. Now I hope for the sake of my children that we can refrain from dredging this up again. Otherwise, this interview is over."

"That's fine," Heier says, even though I can tell he doesn't like it. He nods to the cameraman again. The camera starts rolling. "So, you have the strength to work in spite of everything you've just been through?"

"Yes, my work has always been important to me and is a huge source of comfort now."

The rest of the interview goes smoothly.

The next day, when we are texting back and forth a bit, Heier invites me out to dinner later in the month. I accept. Maybe I can find out more about what he knows, even though I have no desire to go. Or time.

The days fly by even more quickly than before.

Work, work, work, take care of the boys after school, be there for my in-laws, who fell apart after losing their only son. I have to talk to them several times a week, spend time with them at least every weekend, preferably even more often. Luckily, Christian and Axel also stop by frequently.

And then there's Daddy. We try to visit him as often as we can.

I haven't been to see Agnes again and have no plans to do so. Bodil calls me from time to time, leaves messages on my voice mail, asks me to call her back. My mother wants to tell me something, she says. Something important.

Maybe I should go, try to make friends with her so I'll have better control over her. But I can't bring myself to do it.

Henrik is the only one of my murder victims I'd cared about, the only one who wasn't eliminated out of consideration for his children. I've done the right thing, what I had to do. But it came at a price.

I spend most of my free time doing what I can to help the boys get back on their feet.

Both of them were shattered by Henrik's death. One of them shows it more than the other, one of them cries himself to sleep at night, the other is awakened by nightmares. But both are grieving, and I must to the best of my abilities try to make up for their loss.

I comfort myself with the thought that children can cope with losing their parents. Eventually. Losing a child, that's something people never recover from. Then they are destroyed forever.

CHAPTER 74

LEIF

I'm sitting at the kitchen table, up against the window, where I've eaten breakfast almost every day of my life.

Far off in the distance I can see the mountainsides. They are still black and still bare, but one morning soon they will be covered with the first sprinkling of white powder snow.

I've started lighting the stove already; otherwise, the air inside the house gets too raw. There's a lot of work involved in hauling and chopping all the firewood I need to keep the living room warm in the winter, but I like it, like that I can still manage it.

Henrik had suggested installing a heat pump.

I won't do that unless it's absolutely necessary.

But now I think about heat pumps all the time, because I'm thinking about Henrik.

It bothers me, what happened.

Right outside the window I can see the leaves in the yard, red and yellow, like a blazing fire. Eva Cassidy is singing "Fields of Gold" on the radio. Before her it was Kari Bremnes. A beautiful, elegant lady, even though those strange eyes of hers make me think of Agnes and her two-colored gaze.

In the evenings I have to take a sleeping pill to get to sleep. I've managed without for years, but last summer I started taking them again.

But I just take one, no more. I mustn't lose it, must think about something else besides Henrik and Clara and the boys and Agnes.

This Bodil person calls me all the time from Kleivhøgda and says I must come and talk to Agnes, that it's important, that there's something she wants to tell me. I haven't done anything about it.

Bella rubs against my feet. I get up, walk with her over to the refrigerator, take down the box of cat food, lean over, and pour the red, green, and yellow pellets into her bowl. She crouches over it and purrs contentedly, making the usual crunching sound when she starts chewing.

I go back to the table, sit down to eat my toast with jam, and take a sip of coffee. I open the newspaper, which comes three times a week. Clara gave me a subscription as a gift.

Today there's a story that dominates almost the entire front page.

The headline reads "Divers Find Car at 600-Foot Depth."

It's as if I can feel my blood pressure rising. I have that claustrophobic feeling I often get when the doctor or nurse tightens the sleeve around my arm and pumps it up. I close my eyes, try to breathe, open my eyes again, and drink a sip of water.

After five minutes I manage to read the entire article.

Some US divers, among the best in the world and using state-of-the-art equipment, have been diving in the region for several weeks. They're here to document the animal and plant life at the head of the fjord. They have ties to Greenpeace and are fighting against the idiots who want to fill the fjord with mining sludge and other waste. New reports are being released all the time about rare plankton and porpoises. The newspaper has printed several articles about them.

But now this. A car wreck. At a depth of six hundred feet, close to the spot where there are always avalanches in the wintertime.

The registration number discloses that this is the same car that has been missing since the dramatic accident at Storagjelet in 1988. A car drove over the cliff and sank to the bottom of the fjord with a man trapped inside. A young girl managed to escape from the car. The car and the man were never found. Nobody had been able to dive deep enough.

Not before now.

The police were looking into the possibilities for retrieving the wreck. An exciting and particularly surprising discovery, the sheriff said.

I close the newspaper and push my plate away, feeling dizzy and unwell.

CHAPTER 75

CLARA

Then one day, when the air is starting to grow cool and I wade through yellow leaves on my way to work, Vigdis appears at my office door.

"They called from the Office of the Prime Minister," she says, unable to restrain the excitement in her voice. "Do you have time to stop by there for a chat with the prime minister?"

"Um . . . yes, OK," I say. "When? And together with Munch?"

"In an hour. And no, just you. God knows what that means."

It isn't every day a state secretary is summoned to the prime minister's office. For a meeting with the rest of the staff? Yes. For a private audience with the prime minister? No.

While I exchange a few words with Vigdis, two men arrive carrying an enormous something or other wrapped in plastic.

"Is that . . . ?" I ask.

"Sure is. Oddbjørn. Fully cleaned, vermin-free, and ready for duty."

At that moment Mona comes out of her office.

"So, you're going in for questioning about the Monrad case?" she says, and shakes her head. "That's really too much. You shouldn't have to make excuses for your own cabinet minister, after all. But you don't really have any choice, I guess."

"No," I say, and glance at my watch.

"I'll whisper a few words into the ear of the secretary to the government about this when the opportunity presents itself. But good luck!"

"Thank you," I say, and leave.

The Monrad case has been a source of strain for the entire government, and the way it was handled only made matters worse. Munch made a poor impression when he was called in to explain his actions to the internal control committee.

He's been frozen out now; you can tell from the way his fellow party members and government colleagues talk about him. They behave the way women do when speaking about a lover they have dumped and can no longer bear the thought of or even the sight of his name.

And I am his creation, a legal professional from the civil service staff who has been transformed into a state secretary and attracted more attention than most cabinet ministers. That is unfortunate.

In a way it would be liberating to step down now, to be relieved of the task of trying to be a politician and have the chance to concentrate on other things.

Maybe the boys and I can move to Western Norway, get a fresh start. At least we don't have any immediate financial problems to contend with, thanks to the inheritance and the life insurance and all of it free and clear.

An hour later I sit down in one of the visitors' chairs in the prime minister's office. I look her straight in the eyes, feeling calm.

"Well, Clara," the prime minister says, and folds her hands.

Everything reminds me of the set of the prime minister's New Year's Eve speech; only the coffee cups between us disrupt the scene. Her suit is blue. Her blouse white. Her hair is blonde and nicely done. The air between us is heavy with the scent of starch and hair spray. "So we finally have the chance to talk. It's been a turbulent time for you. My condolences."

"Thank you."

"I'm sorry I have to bother you with this now. But Munch has put himself in an embarrassing position on several occasions. The episode with Cathrine Monrad? What do you think about that?"

"That wasn't good, no . . ."

"I can't even bring myself to talk about it . . . Men like him who strut around like peacocks never seem to work out. And I don't like it that there's a crowd of unscrupulous cynics just waiting for the chance to knock me off my game either. It's all every bit as violent as in Shakespeare's day. People are primarily concerned about not getting caught with blood on their hands."

I laugh a little. It seems like the best reaction.

"It's nice being number two, the way you are now. Being number one is something else altogether. Then there is nowhere to hide. A cabinet minister must sleep with one eye open and fight constantly to handle the pressure from the inbox on the one hand and the media on the other, without losing all sense of direction. It's almost impossible. Most people become afflicted with hubris from the unrelenting pursuit of attention, power, position."

Now it's her turn to laugh, a weary laughter.

"And then they feel alone fighting with the Ministry of Finance, the prime minister's office, and they develop a fear of heights, become paralyzed. All of that. They should all have a sign on their desks with the words *memento mori* on it. Because one day they will be out again. And now it's Munch's turn. I would like to ask you what it is you think a new minister of Justice ought to focus on, if you were to mention one or two things? More firefighting helicopters, perhaps?"

I smile a little, clear my throat.

"Well, I dislike that we put people into security cells when they are not a danger to themselves or to others. None of our neighboring nations have a similar practice. I would want to do something about that. I would also have a better legal aid system created for the most disadvantaged. Yes, and then I would carry into effect the bill I have been working on. Immediately."

"All right, then," the prime minister says, and smiles. "That all sounds promising. So, Clara, what do you say? Would you like to take over as the minister of Justice?"

ACKNOWLEDGMENTS

First and foremost, my family deserves thanks for putting up with a frequently distracted author.

In addition, I've had the support of subject-matter experts from a variety of fields, readers who have helped me greatly. They all deserve a big thank-you: nurses, physicians, politicians, lawyers, and many others.

I would also like to thank both professional readers and good friends who have provided constructive criticism and positive feedback along the way.

Finally, I want to extend a particularly large thank-you to my editor, Aslak Nore. This book might never have been written had it not been for his initiative, enthusiasm, and faith in me as an author. His knowledge and understanding of and love for the genre have been of immeasurable importance throughout the writing process.

Ruth Lillegraven, August 2018

ACKNOWLEDGEMENTS

ABOUT THE AUTHOR

Photo © Ann Sissel Holthe | www.fatmonkey.no

Ruth Lillegraven was born in 1978 in Hardanger, Norway, where she grew up on a small farm. She debuted as an author with a poetry collection in 2005. Since then she has written sixteen books, including children's books, several poetry collections, a novel, and two plays. Her work has been translated into Dutch, English, French, German, and Spanish. Among other prizes, she has won both the Brage Prize and the Nynorsk Literature Prize (for the poetry collections *Urd* and *Sickle*). Her first crime novel is the prize-winning *Everything Is Mine*, which has become an international bestseller.

ABOUT THE TRANSLATOR

Photo © 2020 Nuria Pizarro Sabadell

Diane Oatley is a writer, independent scholar, and translator. She began her undergraduate studies of English literature at the University of Maine and went on to complete an MA in comparative literature at the University of Oslo. Her poetry has been published in anthologies and journals in England, Norway, Spain, and India, and she is the author of three poetry chapbooks. In 2014 Diane received NORLA's annual Translator's Award for nonfiction, and two of her literary translations have been long-listed for the International Dublin Literary Award. She is a member of the Norwegian Non-Fiction Writers and Translators Association and the Norwegian chapter of PEN International.